Praise for These Dangerous Fates

"A wickedly sexy ride. These Dangerous Fates starts off with a bang, and takes on speed from there. It's a wild ride, with plenty of twists and turns. Add in three very sweet, but also very deadly paranormal paramours and you've got the perfect recipe for a story that'll keep you turning the pages."

-Lou William
Author of The Hex Next Door

"This book is the equivalent to chips... Sensual, wicked, chips... You dip into the book and before you know it you devoured it all!"

-Elle Beaumont
Author of Seeds of Sorrow

THESE DANGEROUS FATES

FATES

BOOK ONE

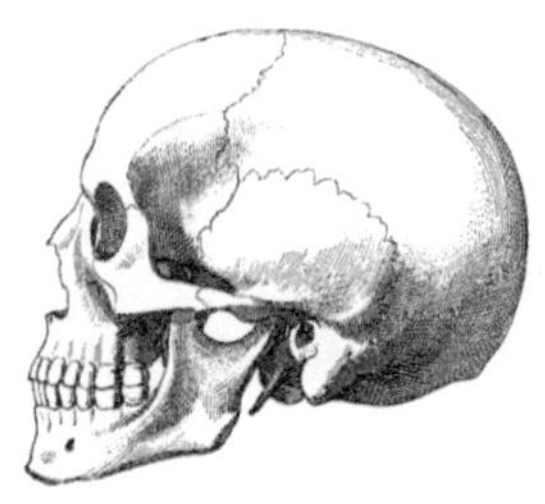

WHITNEY L. SPRADLING

Midnight Tide
PUBLISHING

To My Family...

If you are in any way related to me, please put the book down. I beg you, do not make our next family gathering awkward.

I appreciate the support, but DO NOT READ THIS BOOK!

Thank you.

CONTENT WARNING

This book contains adult themes that may not be appropriate for all audiences. These themes include: on page sexual assault, on page non-consenual sexual encounters, graphic sex, drugs/alcohol, violence, language, and blood play.

This is a why choose romance, meaning the main character will end up with at least three guys by the end of the series. If you enjoy tattooed bad guys who'd do anything for their girl, MM relationships, and plenty of heat, then join the fates in These Dangerous Fates.

National Domestic Violence Hotline

If you or someone you know needs help, please call the National Domestic Violence Hotline at 800-799-7233. You are not alone. Help is available.

To the girls who have been told they aren't good enough.
You are.

To the girls who have been told they aren't worth it.
You are.

To the girls who don't think they are strong enough.
You are.

You are beautiful, strong, brave, and powerful. I hope you find your inner fire.

PROLOGUE

ELLIS

How did I get here? I ask myself that question over and over as I watch the water in the sink run from red to pink. I've used almost an entire bottle of soap trying to get my hands clean. There is blood on my hands. Literal blood. It's caked in the crevasses and stuck under my nails. I scrub and dig and scrape.

It won't come off.

A sob works up my throat, but I swallow it down. There is no use for tears now. My reflection in the mirror above the sink calls to me, trying to get my attention. I avoid it. I know what I'll see when I look at it. Bruises. Cuts. Blood.

But it's the eyes that are the worst to look at. The amber eyes I see in the mirror every day. The ones that have steadily gone from bright and shining to dull and dim. Eyes that once shone with happiness now only look sad, defeated, and scared.

My phone rings in my bedroom, and I jump at the sudden noise. With my heart now pounding in my chest, my gaze catches the mirror and I cringe. *This is the worst yet.* Already, my right eye is swelling so that I can hardly see out of it. I gently prod the dark purple-blue skin and wince. A cut on my right eyebrow is dripping blood, and I softly swipe it away with a wet washcloth.

I press my lips together to keep another sob from escaping, and the motion splits my bottom lip further. It burns as blood wells, and I wipe that away, too. My medical supply stash is well-stocked for this very reason. I apply ointment to the cuts and shut off the water.

The sink no longer looks pink. My hands are no longer covered in blood—at least physically. In the mirror, I see that the reddish-brown staining my sunny yellow dress is drying, the fabric turning stiff and scratchy. I'm pretty sure it's not my blood. With a sudden need to rid myself of him—the one who did this—I yank the dress over my head and cry out.

The movement steals my breath as sharp pain, like lightning, radiates out from my ribs. Another glance in the mirror, and my eyes fill with tears. Black and blue splotches cover my right side. The knife-like pain when I inhale tells me at least one rib is broken.

My phone rings again, and this time I exit the bathroom, leaving the bloody washcloth and dress on the floor. I know who it is before I answer. My bestie has a sixth sense for things like this. She always knows when something's happened.

And things happen a lot.

Fuck. He deserved everything I gave him.

ONE WEEK EARLIER

ELLIS

"FUCK, ELLIS! YOU DON'T HAVE TO HIT SO HARD."

I grin evilly at my bestie and bounce back and forth on the balls of my feet. Allie takes her gloves off and rubs her now red cheek. I keep my guard up, though. She tricked me once with a move like that, and I'll never fall for it again.

"I'm done," she says. "I have to get home and shower before work."

She packs her gloves in her gym bag, her blond ponytail swaying with the movement. Grabbing two bottles of water, she tosses me one, but it falls to the floor as I fumble it with my gloves still on. I sigh and take them off before bending down to pick up the bottle. A catcall whistles across the gym, and I scowl as I straighten. Irritation and anger flood me.

"Ignore it," Allie says quietly.

"Ugh! I'm so sick of that shit." I shove my gloves in my bag and shoulder it.

"I know. I am, too. But there isn't much we can do about it. It's safer to just let it go."

Unfortunately, she's right.

We live in Lustros—a magical world filled with magical beings. Vampires, shifters, mages, witches, and fae being the most common. It's a beautiful world, full of glistening cities, picturesque landscapes, and power.

At least it's beautiful for the magicals.

I, however, am not magical. I am merely human. Somehow— and no one, apparently, knows how—I was born without any powers, despite both my parents being mages.

For us measly humans, Lustros is a dangerous place to live. Without magic running through our veins, we are subjugated to prejudices. We are treated as inferior beings who are often used and abused. It's a system I am more than fed up with.

As Allie and I weave our way through the gym to the exit, I continue to lament my lot in life. Not only do I have to deal with society and what they think of humans, I also have to deal with my dad. A powerful mage who has a powerless daughter? Yeah, suffice it to say, he makes my life more of a living hell than anyone else.

Well, almost anyone.

I'm brought out of my musings by a rough hand around my wrist. The man who grabs me is a shifter, I can see it in his eyes and the way they shine, almost animalistically. He spins me around and shoves me against the wall, all while keeping his hand wrapped tightly around my wrist.

A mixture of fear and irritation spreads through me. I could break his hold. A throat punch would drop him to the ground. A knee to the balls would incapacitate him. I do nothing, though. Instead, I swallow my pride and anger and let him pin me to the wall, ignoring the disgust that makes my gut churn threateningly. I've learned it's best to just let it happen. Fighting back only brings more pain.

"What do we have here?" The shifter's gaze slides over my body and a slow, cold smile spreads across his face. "Aren't you a pretty little thing?"

Before he can do anything, a muscular body pushes the shifter away. "Back off," Connor, the mage who owns the gym, growls. He stands between us, arms crossed, his face a mask of fury. "You don't touch them. If I see you near either of these women again, I'll revoke your membership. Got it?"

The shifter glares and mutters something under his breath before stalking away.

Connor turns to me and gently grabs my wrist. "Are you okay, Ellis?" His kind blue eyes scan me for injury.

"I'm fine." I pull out of his grasp and rub the aching skin. "Thanks for that." I can't quite meet his eyes. He knows as well as I do that I could have taken that shifter.

He studies me for a moment more, irritation making a muscle tick in his jaw, before turning to Allie. He smiles at her and says, "Are you okay?"

"Yeah. Thanks for the help." She smiles shyly back.

Connor and Allie have been crushing on each other for years. It was ultimately what got us a free membership to his gym. It was also the reason he began teaching us how to box. He'd intervened when Allie got assaulted behind the gym, and he decided he wanted to help us protect ourselves.

"Anytime," he responds. "You know, I trained you girls for a reason. I hate seeing you pushed around like that. Why didn't you fight back?"

"I've told you before. It's no use," I mumble as I move around him and head for the door again. "It only makes things worse."

He stops me with a hand on my shoulder. "Then why do you keep practicing? Why keep up the skill if you're never going to use it?"

I shrug off his hand and ignore the way it makes my skin crawl. "One day it will be fight-or-be-killed. Until that day, it's best to just let it happen."

Before he can respond, Allie and I exit the air-conditioned gym into the stifling heat of the city. More sweat immediately breaks out over my skin, and I desperately wish a breeze could get past the skyscrapers climbing to the sky, but they block any wind from cooling the overheated air.

As soon as we round the corner, Allie stops and grabs my arm.

"You sure you're okay?" She gently prods my reddened skin and moves my wrist around, checking for injury.

"Yes, Nurse Allie," I joke. "I really am fine. I've had worse."

Her blue eyes darken at my words. She knows I've had worse. Over the past two years, she's been the one to tend to my many cuts and bruises. As an emergency room nurse for the only human hospital in Altair, she is more than capable of doing so. She also knows better than to say anything to me about my situation.

Releasing my wrist, Allie stares at me for a moment before shaking her head, a small frown tugging down the corners of her mouth. "Hey, let's do lunch tomorrow," she suggests instead of what I know she wants to say.

"River's Edge?" I ask, fanning myself rather uselessly.

"Perfect! I'll meet you at noon. I should go now, though. I don't want to be late again."

"Yeah, I should, too." I give her a quick hug. "Be careful tonight."

"Always!" She grins at me, then sobers. "You be careful, too."

I walk away instead of reassuring her with words she knows aren't true. We've had this conversation many times, but we both know there is nothing I can do about it.

I keep my eyes open, constantly scanning my surroundings as I make my way home. The city of Altair is the perfect example of what living in Lustros is like. During the day, Altair is beautiful. Elegant glass and steel skyscrapers line the streets and reach toward the clouds. The River Altair winds between the buildings, its blue-green waters contrasting with the gray and white of the cityscape. Bridges of twisting steel span the river, almost more artwork than useful structure. Shops and cafes line the streets, and pedestrians move about the city with few concerns.

At night, however, when darkness descends, the monsters come out to play. The bustling city of business and shopping transforms into a playground of depravity. In the shadows and darkened alleys, crime comes to life. The quaint shops and cafes close up. Bars and clubs on every corner open their doors and provide every kind of vice you can dream of. If you're not a top predator, you do not want to be caught alone on the dark streets of Altair at night.

Already, the sun sinks to the horizon. Shadows are getting longer. The alleys darkening ominously. I hurry my steps through the city, heart pounding and unease slithering through me until I reach the outskirts. The sleepy neighborhoods surrounding Altair contrast sharply to downtown. They almost seem to not belong. Tree-lined streets with old-fashioned lamp posts that provide a soft romantic glow. Two- and three-story houses, oozing charm and character, sit on grassy yards that, during the day, are filled with laughing children.

My house is at the end of one of those streets. The richest street in Altair, to be exact. The farther down the street you go, the bigger the houses become. Eventually, the large Victorian-style homes make way for opulent mansions. My house is the largest. A grand palace that screams elegance and wealth.

Standing on the sidewalk, I grasp the ornate metal gate with one hand. From the outside, one would think the people living in the house behind the gate would have every happiness they could ever ask for. Inside the walls, it's another story entirely. Memories haunt the marble halls. Memories that are more akin to nightmares, filled with death and bloodshed.

I make my way through the gate and up the winding path lined with colorful flowers. The pale colors and bright landscaping draw me in and feed me lies. The ornate wooden front door mocks me. This house is one giant illusion. Its sole purpose is to hide the truth behind pretty facades and welcoming accents.

I know the truth, though. No amount of paint and colorful flowers could hide the reality that's hidden behind the front door.

This house is haunted.

It's not the typical ghosts and ghouls, spiderwebs and dust that dwell behind those walls. There is no darkness, nothing that goes bump in the night. It's the memories that sit just inside the door that haunt this house. They lie in wait for you to let your guard down. As soon as that happens, the trap springs shut.

The graveyard of your memories slams the gate closed and you can do nothing as the clang of iron echoes through your head. Trapped. Captured. Beholden as the vision shifts. The bright and lovely memories melt away, smearing the windows on the way down. Stuck in the darkness as the screams emerge. The violence. The bloodshed. Terror and despair seep into your skin and bones, sinking deep with claws that refuse to let go. They hold you captive. Prey on your weaknesses. Destroy you slowly from the inside out.

I forcefully push away the memories that assault me the moment I step through the front door. It's impossible to walk these halls without being ambushed by the nightmare of that night ten years ago. Even after my dad had the entire house gutted and remodeled, I sometimes get sucked into the past. Thrown into the darkness of my mind, unable to escape.

And it's not just the past that haunts this house. It's the present as well. It's my dad and his hedonistic views on society and magic. It's the way he sees me as less because I'm not magical. It's the way he blames me for every bad thing in his life. For a while, I went to therapy. I was taught breathing techniques and ways to ground myself in the present. I was taught meditation and mindfulness. It's hard to find peace, though, when your whole life has been filled with horrors.

My room is the only one on the top floor. It used to be two separate rooms, mine and my sister's, but after that night, my dad had the entire house remodeled. The wall separating the rooms was knocked down. I turned her half into a small library. Comfy reading spots, shelves of books, and potted plants all fill the space now. I think she would have approved the new use of her room. Unfortunately, I don't get much joy from it anymore. I don't get much joy from anything anymore.

When I get to my room, I drop my gym bag on the floor and

strip out of my sweaty clothes in the attached bathroom. As I let the shower heat, I grab a towel and hang it next to the shower, avoiding the mirror. Always avoiding the mirror. Before I step in, I tie my wild curls into a bun at the top of my head and shove the whole mess into a shower cap. I'm not going to fix my hair for him. He doesn't deserve it.

I shower quickly, and, standing in front of the mirror, I take a deep breath before raising my eyes to look at my reflection. It has become a job, something I have to force myself to do, because I don't like what I see staring back at me anymore. It's not the same person from two years ago. Hell, it's not even the same person from ten years ago.

It's not the first time I've wondered how I got to this point in my life. And I'm sure it won't be the last. There is no use dwelling on it, though. Sighing, I push those thoughts away, forcing them deep inside where I can ignore them, along with everything else in my life. I need to make sure I look presentable. I can't disappoint him. Not again.

ELLIS

Nerves flutter in my belly as I get ready for the night, and they aren't the good kind of nerves. I miss the kind of butterflies you get before a first date. The ones that flicker in your stomach and make you all tingly inside with feather soft wings. I had those for a time. Now, they've morphed into strange creatures with razor tipped wings that cut and gouge as they fly about inside me.

The doorbell chimes and echoes through the house. My stomach drops so fast it leaves me reeling. Before I make my way to the stairs, I have to fortify myself. With a deep breath, I take that first step. By the time I reach the second floor, I see the butler has already let him in.

Forcing a smile to my face, I greet my fiancé. "Hi, Sam." Hopefully he doesn't notice the slight tremor in my voice.

"Is that the best you can do? It's like you're not even trying." His laugh is carefree, but the green shimmer of his magic glinting in his brown eyes promises pain later.

He steps past me with a patronizing pat on the ass and continues toward the fourth floor while I stand on the stairs to gather my courage—I need every ounce in his presence. In my room, Sam is already sprawled on my bed with his hands behind his head. The sight sends bitter sadness washing through me. I can't help but miss what we once had. Or at least what I thought we had.

"Why that look, doll?" He reaches up with his hand to brush a blond curl from his forehead.

"I miss you," I whisper, before I can stop myself with a click of my teeth.

Gods, I really miss him.

I miss the gentle kisses and the late nights spent talking about nothing and everything. I miss the smiles he would give me, blinding in their brightness and adoration. I miss the connection we had and having someone to always rely on.

"I'm right here, Ellis." He spreads his arms wide, like he is inviting me to come lay with him.

And damn if I don't want to. This isn't the Sam I fell in love with, though. The one who made me feel cherished and loved. That's all gone now.

Tears blur my vision, but I blink furiously until they no longer threaten to fall. I won't cry in front of him. Shaking my head, I whisper, "I miss what we had. I miss the Sam I used to have. Before."

"Before what? Nothing has changed." Even his voice is a punch to the gut. The tone, so similar to the gentle way he used to talk, but tinged with anger and judgment.

"Are you serious, Sam?" A harsh laugh escapes me. "Everything has changed! I thought you were dating me because you wanted to, not because my dad basically bribed you." It's impossible to keep the bitterness from my voice.

His eyes flash with unchecked anger. "He didn't bribe me," he growls. "We've been over this, and I don't appreciate you accusing me of shit that isn't true."

I swallow and wrap my arms around my middle. "You mean you didn't date me because my dad asked you to? You didn't date me so you could inherit the estate and my dad's company when you marry me?"

A muscle ticks in Sam's jaw as he grinds his teeth together. "I may have started dating you for those reasons, but I fell in love with you." He shakes his head, his blond curls falling into his eyes. Shifting his powerful body, he sits on the edge of the bed and pierces me with his brown eyes. "You're the one that's changed, Ellis. Not me. You're the one who wanted to break up. Not me."

I stare at him, disbelief stealing my words. Of course I wanted to break up. He lied to me. He made me believe he was someone he wasn't, and when I told him I wanted to break it off, the switch flipped. The real Sam came out. The monster that he truly is.

Sam stands and crosses the room. He towers over me, his presence shifting from calming to threatening. I can't help but flinch when he raises his hand, and he smiles at my reaction, eyes glittering with amusement. Instead of the bite of pain I expect, his warm palm on my face is gentle. The tenderness throws me off guard, exactly what he wanted to happen. His thumb rubs back and forth across my cheek, and my eyes close as I lean into his touch without thinking.

"I've been here this whole time," he whispers. His breath fans across my mouth and I realize he's leaned in. "Nothing has changed, doll."

His kiss is gentle, just a soft brush of his lips against mine. It hurts almost more than his fists, because it reminds me of everything I've lost, everything I thought I had. With a surprising amount of courage, I push him away.

"No. Don't do that." My voice wobbles, and I swallow, drawing on every ounce of strength I possess. "Don't act like that. I can't handle it."

His smile turns cruel, and he steps closer to me, pushing me against the door, and I know I'm in the exact position he wants me in. Helpless and at his mercy.

"Is this what you want?" he whispers in my ear as his hand encircles my throat, squeezing painfully. "You like the pain?"

No. I hate the pain, but it's better than the false sense of love that threatens to tear down the walls I've built around my heart.

This I can endure. I know I'll survive his violence. I'm strong enough for that. For now, at least.

His fingers loosen enough for me to gulp down a breath of air before he tightens them again. He kicks my feet apart with his foot and shoves his thigh between my legs. A whimper tries to climb up my throat, but I bite it back. Giving him any reaction will only make it worse. The doorknob digs painfully into my back as Sam presses his body tight against mine.

I get in another breath before his mouth crashes against mine. It's rough and bruising. The iron tang of blood blooms on my tongue as his teeth scrape my lip, before he shoves his tongue into my mouth. I fight the urge to gag and instead kiss him back, because I don't know what else to do, and if I don't, he'll make it hurt even more.

With his hand still around my throat, he drags me to my bed and shoves me down. My stomach swoops as I land on the mattress, both from the movement and the fear of what I know is coming. In rough, jerky movements, he removes my clothes, tossing them to the floor carelessly. And once I'm completely bare to him, he steps back to admire me. Nausea roils in my stomach, the threat of vomiting very near the surface as his eyes travel over my naked body. Those eyes are now almost black with power and lust, the green of his magic barely visible. Every instinct in me screams to cover myself, but if I do, he'll hurt me.

He unbuttons his shirt, slowly shrugging it off his muscular shoulders. "Hands above your head. Legs spread. Eyes closed," he commands, his voice thick with eagerness and desire. Hesitating at his belt, he waits for me to comply with his orders.

My arms tremble as I lift them over my head, squeezing my eyes shut at the same time. Knowing what comes next, my breath stutters and catches painfully in my chest when I shakily spread my legs for him. Heat burns my cheeks, embarrassment making me flush. The biting pain of his magic wraps around my wrists and ankles, holding me in place. If I open my eyes, I know I'll see green bands shimmering over my skin. It would be beautiful if it wasn't so awful.

Fabric rustles as Sam removes his shoes and pants, then the bed dips at my feet. He crawls toward me, the heat of his body hovering over mine makes my skin crawl, but he doesn't touch me yet. The anticipation of where his touch will fall is torture. My muscles are tense to the point of aching, and my breath is rapid and uneven. His fingers finally brush my skin as he grips my thighs and spreads my legs further apart, baring me completely. I'm unable to hold back the whimper that escapes my throat, and shame burns through every part of my body.

The bed dips more as he places his hands on either side of my head. He holds himself still for what feels like hours. My heart races with the fear of the unknown, and a fine sweat coats my skin. I can sense his gaze on my breasts as my chest heaves, gulping in air.

Despair washes through me. I just want this torture to end. I want him to get it over with. Of course, he knows that, so he takes his time. He lets the anticipation build and my anxiety grows with each second I have to wait. The jittery, nauseous sensation in my gut intensifies, and I have to replay my mantra in my head. *I can do this. I am strong. It will be over soon.*

Finally, the mattress shifts again, and this time the drawer next to the bed opens and closes. The pop of a cap echoes through the silence, then the wet slide of lube being applied. That's all the warning I get before Sam forces his cock inside me with quick, rough thrusts.

My attempt at keeping the scream inside fails. The Sam I had once known and loved is gone, replaced by a violent, possessive monster. The monster that beats and rapes me. Tears leak from the corners of my eyes, somehow making their way past my tightly shut lids.

Each thrust of his cock is like fire burning through me. I feel dirty and used. His fingers on my hips are like a brand, like he is claiming me as his. Bile burns the back of my throat and I fight the urge to vomit. My body is being shoved toward the head of the bed with each hard thrust. Soon my fingertips graze the headboard.

Sam's rough breathing surrounds me. Sandalwood mixed with male sweat, shoves up my nose. I'll never be able to smell sandalwood again without the memories of him forcing himself on me.

Just when I think I can't take anymore, he pulls out. I get a brief moment of relief as he removes his magic from my legs and flips me over roughly. He lifts my hips and forces his cock inside again. The blankets muffle my screams and I bunch them in my fists as his hips pound faster and harder. The sound of flesh against flesh is loud while my tears are silent as they soak the pillow and I pray for it to end. I pray for all of it to end.

Sam's body stiffens, his fingers somehow tighten even more on my hips, and he grunts his release. He stays like that, his cock softening inside me, before he pulls out and flops on his back. Sweating and panting, his face is a mask of male arrogance. It makes me sick. His magic disappears from my wrists and I curl up in my bed, as far from Sam as possible. Aching and throbbing, my tears stain my pillowcase as I wait for him to fall asleep.

When his breathing slows and deepens, I climb out of my bed and head to the bathroom, locking the door behind me. With the shower on and heating, I stare at myself in the mirror. This reflection is one I have come to recognize all too well. Puffy amber eyes, red from crying. A handprint marks the column of my neck, and fingerprints are already turning purple on my hips.

Steam from the shower soon wafts through the room and fogs over my reflection, erasing the image I couldn't bring myself to look away from. Stepping into the shower, I hiss as the water scalds my skin, even as I welcome it. If I could make it hotter, I would.

This is the only time and place I let myself fall apart. With my knees drawn to my chest, I sit on the floor of the shower and cry. I let all my hurt, anger, shame, and fear run through me and down the drain. I let the sobs wrack my battered body, wishing I could just shake into a million pieces to be washed away. The heaviness in my chest suffocates me. I don't remember the last time I was able to take a full breath.

Somehow, I've endured this for the past two years, but I'm starting to fall apart at the seams. I'm not sure how much longer I can do this. The fog I surround myself in isn't enough anymore. It gets worse each time, harder to detach myself from what's happening to me. A small piece of my soul gets chipped away with each fist that lands on my skin and each thrust of his hips against mine. How much longer until there is nothing left? What will I be when he has completely destroyed every piece of who I am?

Once the crying stops, I stand and wash. I wash my body three times, but it's never enough. I'm still dirty. I can still feel Sam's hands on me, his cock inside me. By the time I'm done scrubbing, my skin is raw and pink. Only then do I get out and dry off, wrapping my towel around me like a cloak of resolve. Inhaling a deep breath, I fortify my strength and courage before walking back to my bed, and the monster sleeping in it.

Allie eyes my neck with a frown. The handprints from Sam are barely noticeable under the layer of makeup I caked on, but her eagle eye spied them immediately. Thankfully, she says nothing, but her look is enough to send shame coursing through my body. My shoulders curl inward and I pull my hair over my shoulders, hoping to hide the marks better.

I'm spared further embarrassment when a server appears and leads us to a table at The River's Edge, an upscale cafe along the river Altair. A cobblestone patio decked out with wrought iron seating arrangements and potted fruit trees runs right up to the edge of the river. The gentle burble of the water over the rocky shore sets the backdrop, with hidden speakers softly piping in the latest hit songs.

"So," Allie says once we've taken our seats. "Connor called me last night."

My head snaps up from my menu. "He did?"

She nods her head and brushes her blond hair over her shoulder. "He did."

I stare at her. "And ..."

"And he asked me to go to dinner with him tonight."

I squeal loudly enough to draw the attention of the other people eating lunch.

Allie's face turns bright red, and she makes a shushing motion with her hands. "Quiet," she hisses. "I didn't give him an answer."

"What? Why not?" I rear back in my seat, brows furrowed in confusion. "You've been waiting for this for, like, forever."

"I know, but why ask now?" She sighs and runs her fingers through her hair. "He's had plenty of opportunities to ask before. Why ask after an incident in the gym?"

"Who cares why? Allie, come on," I shake my head at her. "He clearly likes you. You guys make goo-goo eyes at each other all the time. He's constantly finding excuses to correct your already perfect form. I'm sure he has a reason for waiting. Go to dinner with him, and maybe you'll find out."

She looks at her menu, but I can tell she isn't really seeing it. Her eyes are glazed over and staring at one spot, unmoving.

"Allie," I say quietly, grabbing her hand. "What's up? Why the sudden fear of going on a date with him? It's all you've talked about since we started training there."

She takes a breath and looks at me, a mixture of fear and shame swimming in her eyes. "Because he's a mage."

"And?"

"And I'm a human," she says, like it's the most obvious thing in the world.

"I'm failing to see the problem here." When she doesn't respond, I reach across the table to grab her other hand. "Why don't you go to dinner with him tonight? Talk to him. Let him know your concerns. He obviously doesn't care about you being human if he asked you in the first place, right?"

She nods reluctantly, but the tiniest sliver of hope lights her eyes.

"Okay. So it's decided." I grin at her, and I see her fighting her own smile.

"Fine. I'll text him," she huffs and pulls her hands away from mine.

After we place our orders, we both scroll social media while we wait for our food. I enjoy the quiet chatter of the other patrons, the burbling of the river, and the sun warming my back. For a little while, I can pretend my life is normal. I can pretend I won't have to go home to an abusive fiancé and a dad who doesn't care. I can pretend that one day Allie and I will have a conversation about me going on a date with someone. Someone who isn't Sam. It always makes it harder to return home after pretending, but if I don't, I think I'll drown in my despair.

"Oh. My. Gods!" Allie squeals. "Have you seen the newest picture of Malakai?"

I chuckle and reach my hand over the table, wiggling my fingers for her phone. "No. Let me see." I glance at the screen and my mouth goes dry. "Holy sexy vampire," I mutter.

My eyes can't move over the picture fast enough. Malakai Thorne is a Lustros celebrity, along with his two best friends, Sterling and Cade. And in this picture, the vampire is positively edible. My fingers itch to trace the grooves of his abdomen proudly on display under an open leather jacket. With his tousled black hair and bedroom smirk, he looks as if he's just been debauched. Allie snorts when I attempt to tilt the phone like I'm trying to get a better look inside his unbuttoned pants.

Grinning, I toss her phone back to her. "He'll make some girl very happy one day."

She blanches. "If he doesn't eat her first."

We're still giggling when our food arrives at our table, and I'm halfway through my meal when a commotion draws my attention to the sidewalk outside of the cafe.

"Allie," I kick her under the table, and motion with my head to the cause of the ruckus.

Sterling Harrison. One of Malakai's best friends, a wolf shifter, is striding down the street. His rugged looks, tight jeans, and flowing silver hair gain plenty of attention from the ladies. And that scar cutting through his right eye, gives him a dangerous air. As he passes the cafe, his gaze snaps to mine, landing on me without err. For a second, I'm sucked into those icy blues and everything around me disappears. It's like a fog has surrounded the cafe, and only Sterling and I exist. The sounds of the cafe are muffled, like I'm sitting under water. And my heart pounds erratically, the force of it echoing all the way to my fingertips. There is nothing I can do to pull my gaze away from his.

When he looks away, reality crashes into me. Sound returns, seeming louder than it had been before. I sag in my seat and suck in a lungful of air, as sweat drips down my back and between my breasts. No one around me seems to have noticed what just happened, and I tuck my hair behind my ear with a shaky hand.

"Now, *that one* I would gladly go home with," Allie whispers dramatically.

I smile, but it's forced. What the hell just happened?

MALAKAI

Screams, blood splattering, and the thump of bodies hitting the floor are nothing new to me. I'm used to the copper scent of blood and the foul stench of shit as bowels let go in fear and death. What isn't normal is the amount of rage coursing through my system after completing one of my father's missions. It rides me so hard my arms tremble and my hands ache from how tightly I'm clenching them.

My whole life I have trained for two roles: assassin and prince.

As the son of the Vampire King, I've long ago learned to comply with my father's wishes and never question him. For a hundred years, I have done just that, as far as he's aware. But tonight, I struggled to keep my cool. I had to bite my tongue to prevent myself from telling my father to fuck off. Even now, I want to march to his office and tell him he can take the next missions and shove them up his ass.

Red tinges my vision as I make my way through the estate, and it's not because I need to feed. Never, in my hundred years of existence, have I ever been so pissed off. Even with my abilities filtering all the emotions from everyone around me, I've never been this out of control. My body vibrates with it. My fangs have elongated—something that happens when I lose control of my emotions. The tide of anger rises higher and higher, and before I know what I'm doing, I throw out my arm and my fist connects with the wall.

The marble splinters under my fist. Fissures spiderweb outward and a few small pieces of stone fall to the floor. I pull my hand back and grimace at the damage—not only to the wall, but my fingers as well. Pretty sure I broke a few knuckles. The dull ache of broken bones doesn't help ease the anger like I hoped it would.

Sighing, I reign in my emotions and head to my bedroom. I need to shower. I'm covered in blood that isn't mine, and the scent is making me nauseous. Before I even open my bedroom door, the thump of a familiar heartbeat meets my ears. I recognize it immediately.

"Why am I not surprised to find you here?" I drawl as I push open the door.

Cade Campbell gives me a lazy grin from the window seat and raises his glass of bourbon in salute. "You would think after all these years, you would stop asking us to leave you alone after your solitary missions. We're not going to listen."

A grunt is my only reply as I head straight for the bar in the corner of my room and pour myself a generous glass of blood bourbon. Whoever the hell invented this shit is my hero. Blood and alcohol mixed perfectly together. The only way to get a vampire drunk.

"What's wrong?" Cade's violet eyes narrow as he studies me, and his smile disappears. "And what happened to your hand?"

"I punched a wall," I say flatly, looking at my broken knuckles.

He studies me some more before understanding dawns. "You're angry."

Of course he could read me. Only two people in all of Lustros know me well enough to do that. The fact that Cade is surprised by my anger only pisses me off more. I'm always the cool one of the group, the one who jokes and takes nothing seriously. I have to be. With my powers, even the slightest bit of emotion can drive me to insanity. For once, I just want to feel what I feel and not repress it.

I down the blood bourbon in one gulp, barely registering the burn as it slides down my throat, and throw the glass against the wall. It shatters, glass flying everywhere. Of course, it doesn't take the edge off. Neither did hitting the wall. I try to flex my fingers and wince. Thanks to my fast healing as a vampire, they'll heal on their own in a couple of hours, but it will hurt like a bitch while they do.

Cade stands from the window seat and sets his glass on the bar. Purple light flares as he grabs my wrist and runs his fingers over my knuckles. A squeezing sensation, like a blood pressure cuff, envelops my hand, and the itch of healing settles under my skin. One blink is all it takes and I'm good as new again.

"You didn't have to do that," I mumble, flexing my now healed fingers.

He shrugs. "You know I don't mind." Pausing, he looks into my eyes. "Do you need an outlet for your anger?"

I clench my jaw and look away. The friend that he is, he will offer himself up everyday if needed, even knowing how much I hate using him. I'm not sure what I did to earn a friendship like his.

"I'll repeat myself," Cade says darkly. "You know I don't mind."

He steps closer and his cologne hits me—a woodsy floral scent that is all him, like cedar and lilac. His heart beats in his chest, slightly elevated but steady. And those violet eyes stare into my own as if he can see into my soul.

"I need to shower first," I ground out.

Before I can walk away, he stops me with a hand on my chest. "I don't mind the blood." His voice has lowered, a gravelly, husky sound that shivers over my skin.

"Fuck," I growl, losing the little control I have over my body, and shoving him against the wall.

My mouth crashes against his, and it's fast and violent as our teeth and tongues collide. I grab the brown strands of his hair and tighten my fist, making him moan into my mouth. This is exactly the kind of outlet I needed.

Cade's hands fumble with my belt and I push them aside as I shove him to his knees. He looks up at me with his wide, violet eyes and I almost lose my shit right there. This man is the perfect friend, willing to do anything for the people he cares about.

I get my belt and pants undone and pull out my cock. It's hard as a fucking rock, and I want nothing more than to shove it down Cade's throat. I restrain myself, though, as he opens his mouth. His tongue slides up the underside, trailing over the piercings there, making my knees tremble. A teasing smirk pulls up one corner of his lips. He knows exactly what he's doing to me. I growl and he sucks the head of my cock inside his mouth, his tongue tracing the slit.

All I can see is the top of Cade's head as he slowly continues to tease me. He ramps me up with slow, steady movements until I can't take it anymore. It's euphoria. The suction and warmth, his violet eyes. A flutter in my chest almost pulls me out of the moment. It's weird and unsettling, and I have no fucking clue what it means.

Needing to push that sensation to the back of my mind, I grab Cade's head and slam my cock to the back of his throat. I hold him there for a second while he chokes before I release him, only to repeat that again and again. He meets my gaze through lowered lids, and I piston my hips faster, harder, fucking his mouth with everything I've got, trying to ignore that damn fluttering.

It's not enough, though. Even as unsettled as I am, the anger still courses through my blood. The white hot rage burrows deep, trying to splinter my bones from the inside out. With an animalistic growl, I pull out of Cade's mouth and haul him to his feet, bending him over the window seat. I have his pants unbuttoned and around his ankles in record time.

Cade looks back at me over his shoulder, violet eyes glittering dangerously, as I grab the bottle of lube off the bar. "Do your worst, Prince." He smirks and kicks off his shoes and pants.

The words incite me, just as he intended them to. I press on the back of his neck and shove his head down. Anticipation swirls through me as I kick his legs wider and run a finger down his crack to his hole. Cade tenses as I press my finger inside, quickly followed by another. A breath rushes out of him and he hangs his head down, relaxing into my touch.

I fist my cock and roughly jerk my hand up and down while I prepare Cade. The pressure is building, my heart is pounding, and I need release. Desperately. When I can't wait any longer, I remove my fingers and grasp his hips tightly, guiding my cock to his ass and slowly pushing inside. We both moan as he takes me in. The tight ring of muscle squeezes me deliciously, and I tighten my hold on his hips.

I try to start slow, to give him time to adjust, but I can't prevent my hips from bucking faster and faster. Our skin slaps together and sweat soon coats both of our bodies. Our breathing is heavy, punctured by moans and grunts. Cade fists his dick and I lower over him to cover his hand with mine.

"Fuck, Kai. I'm—" He cuts off and stiffens under me as he comes, a thick stream that splatters the window seat.

It's enough for me, and my balls draw up as I follow him over the edge, grunting my release into his ass, pumping my hips until every last drop has been milked from my cock.

The fluttering didn't stop. If anything it seems to have intensified. Leaning against the window seat we catch our breath as the sweat cools on our bodies. When I pull away, Cade turns around to study me closely. He says nothing about what he sees, but his brow furrows and he pulls his bottom lip between his teeth before he grabs his clothes from the floor.

"Go shower," he says. "We'll talk when you're done."

I groan and tuck my now limp cock into my pants. Talking about feelings is not my favorite thing to do, but I know he won't let it go. I pour myself another glass of blood bourbon and swallow it in one gulp before heading for the bathroom.

I'm slightly more centered when I emerge from the bathroom in a cloud of steam with a towel wrapped around my hips. The fluttering in my chest has subsided. Either that, or I pushed it far enough to the back of my mind, I'm able to ignore it. Cade's put on his pants, but he's still shirtless, and I can't keep my gaze from trailing over his sculpted chest and abs, and the galaxy tattoo on his arm. That damn violet gaze is too all-seeing and all-knowing, and I shift uncomfortably as he reads me.

"It's been awhile since we've done that. Not that I'm complaining," he says with a smirk from the window seat. "But, what's up?"

Flopping on my bed, I shake my head and try to decide what to say. "My dad ordered me to kill the Parkers."

His brows raise to his hairline. "All of them?"

I nod.

"Don't they have twin six-year-olds?"

I nod again.

His chest inflates on a breath. "Well, this isn't the first time your dad has ordered you to murder children. What's different about this one?"

"I don't know," I sigh heavily and let my head thump on the mattress so I'm staring at the ceiling. "I was already in a pissy mood after he dropped the bomb that he arranged for me to marry the Valentino girl."

"The Valentino girl? You mean Carlo Valentino's heir, Guilia?"

"The one and only."

"Shit, man. That seriosly blows."

I appreciate he doesn't placate me or ask if there is a way out of it. He knows better. "I mean, I always knew this day was coming." I shrug, like it's no big deal, even though we both know that's a lie. "It's all I've heard about since I was old enough to marry. I guess I pushed it to the recesses of my mind since my dad never seemed in any hurry. But, Guilia?"

Cade snorts. "Yeah, he certainly picked a winner. She's pretty enough, but that personality is definitely lacking."

"Understatement of the century," I deadpan.

"When does all this go down?"

"This winter."

He whistles through his teeth. "Wow, not a lot of time."

Instead of answering, I get up and make myself another drink.

"Alright," Cade says as he stands from the window seat. "Get dressed, we're going out."

I don't ask. I have no fight left in me, so I shower and prepare for a night of debauchery with the boys.

———

At night, the streets of Altair transform into the devil's playground. Monsters roam the darkness, looking for their next hit or victim. My friends and I are the top predators in the city. The rumors about us are mostly true. Yes, I am a prince and trained assassin. Yes, I can stalk your nightmares. Yes, I enjoy the taste of blood. But there is more to us than most people assume, although we're content to let them paint the picture of us as the evil derelicts of Lustros.

I park my Ducati Diavel next to Cade's shiny red Corvette in the parking lot off the main strip of downtown Altair. Before I even take my helmet off, people are staring. Cade's Corvette and my bike are well known in the city, as is Sterling's Land Rover.

"How long before someone posts to social media where we are?" Cade asks as we make our way down the sidewalk.

I snort and adjust my leather jacket on my shoulders. "It's probably already happened." I'm more relaxed than I have been in a while. The ride to the city on my bike and getting back to the constant attention from the public has re-centered me. And the sex with Cade.

We ignore the whispers and the cells pointed at us, and make our way to our favorite bar. The crowd parts for us, our names whispered ahead of our arrival, so we don't have to contend with throngs of people on the street. The three of us—Cade, Sterling, and I—are the three most eligible bachelors of Lustros. We can't go anywhere without the attention of the women, something all three of us greatly enjoy. I try not to think about my upcoming arranged marriage and the idea of being tied to one woman. I don't want to ruin my somewhat good mood with those dark thoughts. The very idea is suffocating and makes my skin crawl.

Cade and I shoulder our way past the crowd of people waiting to get into the bar. Being one of the Triad, as the public likes to call us, has its perks. One glance from the bouncer and we're through the front door and into the seediest nightclub in Altair.

With the dingy lighting, the edges of the main room of The Black Crow are shadowed. At any given moment, you can find at least three couples hooking up in the darkness. The farthest corner—the darkest corner—is the reason we frequent this joint. Our drug of choice flows freely in The Black Crow.

The heat from the multitude of bodies presses down on me as soon as I step inside, making sweat instantly break out over my skin. Magicals, as well as the bravest of the humans, pack the bar. The thumping bass blaring from the speakers vibrates my bones, and people pack the dance floor, grinding on each other in a dance that might as well be one giant orgy. I crinkle my nose at the scent of cigarettes and sweaty bodies that permeate the space. Emotions hit me in the face as soon as I walk in, and I tighten my mental shields, shutting them down.

To the left of the bar, a door leads to the back hallway where you can find rooms dedicated to sex, gambling, and hard drugs. On the right side of the dance floor, tables and booths hide in the shadows, and it is in that direction Cade and I head.

Sterling sits in the booth farthest from the door in the darkest section of the bar. His long silver-blond hair is a beacon that draws us forward, and his icy blue eyes shine like an animal's in the darkness.

"It's about time you assholes showed up," he says gruffly as he sets his beer on the table.

"Sorry to keep you waiting, princess," Cade drawls, settling next to me in the booth.

Another perk of our fame is the waitress bringing out drinks without us having to order them. The three of us relax and fall into the typical rhythm of a night out in Altair. We bicker, tease, argue, laugh, and, of course, flirt with the ladies who approach our table. No talk of my mission tonight or the bomb my dad dropped about marriage.

Molly and alcohol flow freely, although for me and Sterling, the buzz is minimal and wears off quickly. Our vampire and shifter natures quickly burn off the effects before we get to fully enjoy them. Cade, with his mage blood, doesn't have that problem, and soon, he is higher than a kite and enjoying the attention of a curvy blond.

After Sterling wanders to a back room with two brunettes I'm pretty sure are twins, I settle into the booth and wait. It's only a matter of time before I spot a woman approaching with a determined glint in her eyes. My hands settle on her hips as she sits on my lap and nips at my earlobe. Excitement burns in my veins at the prospect of what's to come, and I bury my face in her neck. The shock that shoots through me almost throws me off my game as the scent of her human blood hits my nose. This one is brave.

We trade a few flirtatious words, but we both know where this is heading and quickly cut to the chase. As she leads me to a darkened corner of the bar, I smile eagerly. Getting my dick wet twice in one night. This is exactly what I needed.

ELLIS

Days pass without another visit from Sam. I'm both relieved and anxious. He rarely goes so long without stopping by. I'm sure it has to do with him needing to remind me of the threat constantly looming over my head if I were to try to break it off with him again. Usually, when I don't see him for a while, the next visit is torture. Literally.

Allie's worry about me only continues to grow. Every time we hangout, she eyes my fading bruises with concern. Only once since his last visit has she broached the subject of me leaving him. I shut her down hard enough she hasn't mentioned it again.

My dad has been busy with work, so I've barely seen him this past week. But he knows what is going on. He's seen the bruises and cuts after every visit from Sam. It's impossible he hasn't heard the screams coming from my bedroom when Sam is here. He won't do anything, though. He has a plan, and that plan includes me, married and out of his life, with a son-in-law he can show off and be proud of. It doesn't matter if that son-in-law abuses his only surviving daughter.

Every day my depression grows. The constant weight sitting on my chest gets heavier. The cold emptiness inside me spreads further. None of the coping techniques I learned in therapy work anymore. My life has been in a downward spiral since that night ten years ago, and Sam's betrayal only quickened that decline. Reading no longer brings me joy. The peace I used to find while playing piano is gone, and I don't know where to find it again. My energy is almost non-existent, and I have to force myself to go to the gym because I know Allie will tear me a new one if I don't.

Most of my time is spent in bed lamenting my life, and wishing I could find a way out of this horrible situation. Thinking about the future, about the rest of my life tied to that abusive asshole, is too much to bear. I'm not sure how I'll survive this life. Something has to change.

Allie has noticed my weight loss, but I have no appetite, and everything I manage to swallow threatens to come back up anyway. I don't want to deal with her concern though, so I force myself to eat. Making a salad, I keep my thoughts solely focused on what I'm doing—tearing lettuce and chopping veggies—because numbing myself is better than all the emotions that threaten to overcome me. The rhythmic chopping as the knife hits the cutting board is oddly soothing. It's predictable. I know when it will happen, and it's in my control. Unlike so many things in my life.

I'm so focused on keeping my mind blank, I don't hear him approach until his arms wrap around my middle. It's like ice water poured into my veins. My heart ceases beating for a second, and I squeeze my eyes shut. I want to crawl out of my skin as his warm breath fans across the back of my neck.

"I love when you wear your hair like this," he whispers and grabs a handful of my messy bun. He painfully yanks my head to the side and licks up the side of my neck.

Shivers erupt over my skin, and not the good kind of shivers. "I wasn't expecting you." Even I can hear the bleakness of my tone. It seems I can't even muster enough fear anymore.

He chuckles darkly. "I thought I would surprise you."

I don't comment because he doesn't really want me to. My scalps stings as he grips my hair tighter and uses it to pull me around. Dragging me across the kitchen, he leans against the door, blocking anyone from coming in. Not that anyone ever does—I've accepted the fact that no is going to save me. He shoves me to my knees and the pain barely registers as I plunge down deep into the numbing fog that I try to surround myself in whenever Sam touches me.

"One of these days, you will learn to appreciate the things I do for you." Sam releases my hair long enough to undo his belt and pants, shoving them down his thighs.

A glittering green light swirls in the air and sends my heart racing. I wait for the pain as he fists my hair again, tugging the strands roughly. The magic wraps around my wrist, binding them together in front of me. It burns. I always think I'll see blackened flesh curling from my bones, but it never leaves a mark. The green light slithers up my arms and chest to wrap around my neck and jaw, bringing tears to my eyes as it forces my mouth open in a fiery vice.

Sam's eyes glow with twisted desire and madness. He rubs his thumb along my lower lip before slipping it inside, pressing down on my tongue. The taste of salt from his skin makes saliva pool in my mouth. At eye level, I have nothing impeding my view of his free hand fisting his cock and moving up and down as he pleasures himself. A bead of precum forms on the tip, and just the sight of it makes bile crawl up my throat, the burn of it matching the band of magic wrapped around my wrists and jaw.

He thrusts his hips forward without warning and shoves his cock into my mouth. It hits the back of my throat, making me gag. Tears spring to my eyes as my stomach heaves. He holds it there until the tears run down my cheeks and stars flash in my vision. I try to breathe through my nose but I can smell him. Sandalwood and soap. It makes me gag even more.

"That's it," he grunts. "Take it like the little slut you are."

He pulls back and I suck in a breath before he slams his hips forward again. His hold on my hair prevents me from moving and each thrust tugs at the strands, the pain minimal in comparison to the rest of it. All I can do is close my eyes and ride this out. Saliva, snot, and tears run down my face as he pounds in again and again. His grunts and groans disgust me, as does the musty taste of his precum as it leaks from the tip of his cock. So much assault against my senses—his scent, his taste, his sounds, his cock in the back of my throat. I'm seconds from vomiting up what little is in my stomach.

Sam is so lost in what he's doing, the presence of his magic diminishes slightly without him realizing. But I do. The burn against my skin is less, and I'm able to move the slightest bit more. With the bonds around my jaw loosened, I don't hesitate. Without a single thought of the consequences, I bite down as hard as I can against the little restraint holding my mouth open.

Sam roars. He pushes me away and bends forward, grabbing himself protectively. He pushes me hard enough that I slide across the marble kitchen floor. Stars burst in my vision as my head slams into the island and pain flares over my skull. I lay dizzily on the floor for a moment and try to get my bearings. The second I bit down, Sam's magic disappeared entirely, so my jaw and hands are free. I tentatively prod my head and wince. There is no blood, but it hurts, and a bump is already forming.

My vision clears and I see Sam approaching, slightly bent, with his hand still grabbing himself. His steps are measured and slow, and each one sends a jolt of fear through my veins, chilling me to the core. The look on his face is one I've never seen before. His eyes are pure thunderclouds and shadowed under his lowered brows. His lips are pressed into a thin line, and his jaw is clenched so tightly I can see the strain in his neck muscles.

Instinct kicks in, and I know I have to stand up. I grab the counter for support but I'm shaking so bad I miss, knocking off the bowl of salad instead. The bowl shatters on the ground, shards of porcelain skittering across the floor and mixing with the lettuce and veggies, as well as the knife I'd been using.

Before I can get to my feet, he bends down and grabs my ankle, yanking me toward him. I catch myself before my head hits the ground again, but the pieces of the broken salad bowl slice into my palms. The sting barely registers through my fear as Sam crouches over me and glares. My heart is pounding so fast I'm positive it's going to beat right out of my chest.

"That was the wrong thing to do, princess," he growls. "You know I'm going to have to punish you for that, and I hate punishing you."

His mock sympathy brings a hysterical laugh up my throat. The scowl on his handsome face deepens, and he rubs his chin as he decides what to do with me. My thoughts are racing as I try to think of how to get out of this. A glimmer catches my eye, and I notice the knife on the floor. Hope bubbles in my chest. If I can get to the knife, I can protect myself.

His foot connecting with my ribs punches all the air out of my lungs and pops the bubble of hope instantly. I can't even cry out as I curl into a ball. It takes a second for the pain to register, and when it does, it steals what little breath I had left in my lungs. He kicks me a second time, and a third. The pain is like fire so hot it's cold as it spreads through my torso. I try to protect myself as much as I can, but it's no use. Sam is too strong and too fast.

"Is that what you wanted me to do?" He crouches in front of me, chest heaving and eyes wild, and he grabs my chin in a bruising grasp. "Did you want me to punish you?"

I am so fucking sick of his treatment and gaslighting. I am so fucking tired of being the one blamed for his actions. In a burst of anger and despair, I spit on him, and it lands on his cheek. "Fuck you, Sam," I rasp through my wet and labored breathing.

His eyes flash, and I know I've gone too far. The world slows down, and for the first time, I'm truly afraid. The fear crashes into me at the same time Sam does. His fists land on my face repeatedly. The burst of pain with each blow makes my vision blacken, and it doesn't take long before I'm wavering on the cusp of consciousness. I almost hope I'll pass out. Anything to relieve me of the pain. But he stops and stands. The brief pause of assault on my body doesn't last long as he draws his foot back then kicks.

The snap of bone is drowned out by my screams. Agony tears through my middle like a knife slicing into me.

Knife. My gaze slides to the one on the floor glinting in the kitchen lights. Desperation burning through me, I suck in the largest breath I can manage with my broken ribs and battered body, and reach for the utensil. The blood and cuts on my palm make it difficult to grasp, and Sam just keeps kicking. It's with fierce determination, and a throat searing scream, that I keep my hold on the handle, sit up, and swing the blade.

It connects with his abdomen, a gash opening and spilling blood that covers me with warm stickiness. Shock almost paralyzes me, but I squeeze the knife harder. Sam freezes in disbelief, mouth slack and wide eyes staring at his open stomach. Using his moment of surprise, I slam the knife into his belly again. This time I hit deep and yank the blade to the right, gritting my teeth as my arm strains to tear through intestine and muscle.

When Sam curses and slumps to the floor on his knees, I drag myself to my feet, groaning and whimpering as pain washes over me. Hunched over, and arms wrapped around my middle, I avoid Sams's last attempt to grab me. His cursing fades as I stumble my way to my room. The blood coating my arms and hands brings bile to the back of my throat. It's sticky and thick, starting to itch in the places it's drying and crusting over.

I lock my bedroom door and head to the bathroom, legs shaking so badly I can barely stand. The breath in my chest saws in and out, and the pain from each one sends tears streaming down my face, burning as they encounter the cuts left by Sam's fists.

What have I done?

PRESENT DAY

ELLIS

ALLIE'S NAME IS DISPLAYED ON MY PHONE SCREEN, AND it takes three attempts to swipe to answer the call with my shaking fingers.

"Allie," I whisper, voice hoarse.

"Are you okay?" Her ability to sense when bad things happen always amazes me. I assume she had a seer in her family at one point. Allie is as human as they come, she just gets these feelings sometimes, and they have never steered her wrong.

"I think I did something horrible." The edge of the bed dips as I sit down. There is no comfortable position. No matter how I try to sit, some part of my body throbs painfully.

"Talk to me, Ellis," Allie's voice is laced with worry. "You're freaking me out."

"I ... I ..." Unable to put into words what I'd just done, I stammer as tears slide down my face.

"Ellis, what is going on? You have to give me something or I'm coming over."

That gets my attention. I never let Allie come over. The risk of her ending up in the crosshairs of either my dad or Sam isn't worth it. I don't think they would do anything to her, but it's not worth the risk.

"I stabbed Sam." My whispered words tremble as they fall from my numb lips. The longer that thought sits with me, the more the fear grows. Shaking overtakes my entire body, the movements jarring my bruises and broken bones, sending fire through me.

Silence greets my statement, then Allie explodes. "What the fuck? Is he dead? Do you need me? Are you hurt?"

"I'll be okay, I think," I wince, not entirely sure that's the truth, but not wanting to freak her out either. "And I don't think he's dead. He'll be able to heal himself enough to get to a hospital."

"Okay, okay." I hear Allie pacing through the phone. "That's good. He'll be okay, then. And you're sure you're okay?"

"Good?" I exclaim. "Allie, that is the worst possible thing that could happen. I should have made sure he was dead. Can you imagine what he is going to do to me now?" My voice cracks as the reality of my situation sets in. I have royally fucked up.

"Shit," she mutters. "What do you need me to do?"

"I need some place to hide. I can't stay here. I have to get away."

"Come over here. You can stay here for the night and we'll figure something out tomorrow. I'll get you out of there, Ellis. I'm not leaving you to him anymore."

Despite my fear, warmth blooms in my chest. At least I have one person in my corner. My wild heart rate calms a little at the realization.

My bedroom door slams open, cutting off my reply. Wood splinters and flies everywhere. I jump, pain radiating from every part of my body. Dread curls in my gut when I see my dad standing in the now open doorway.

My dad is positively livid. His neck is suffused with blood and I can see it steadily creeping up to his cheeks. "In my office. Now," he snaps. His fists clench and unclench as he turns around and heads toward the stairs.

"Ellis?" Allie asks over the phone.

"I have to go," I whisper.

"Ellis, wait …"

I hang up before she can say anything. There is nothing either of us can do at this point. I quickly, but gingerly, put on a pair of shorts and tank top and pad down the stairs to my dad's office. My ribs are killing me, and a tiny construction worker has taken up residence in my brain, drilling holes in my skull. My right eye is completely swollen shut now, and my rapidly quickening pulse throbs in each bruise and cut on my body.

Outside of my dad's office, I pause and take the deepest breath I can manage. It's not much, and it does nothing to calm my racing heart. I clutch my phone tightly in hand, like it can protect me from what's coming. Distantly, I notice my fingers shaking as I turn the knob and push open the door.

I was expecting to see Sam, bloodied and angry, sitting in the office. He isn't, thank the gods. My dad is alone, sitting behind his massive mahogany desk, framed on either side by bookshelves filled with thick tomes and ancient scrolls.

Thomas Kennedy has aged since his wife and daughter's murder ten years ago. His black hair is graying at the temples and fine wrinkles surround his eyes and mouth. His mind is still sharp, though. Maybe even sharper than it was ten years ago. His brown eyes drill into me, and only the pain in my body keeps me from shifting back and forth on my feet.

He crosses his arms over his chest and leans back in his chair. A cursory glance at my injuries is all he does to acknowledge what just happened to me in his house.

"What the hell were you thinking?" he barks.

"Oh, I don't know," I snap at him. "Maybe I was trying to stay alive?" Sarcasm laces my words. I know my dad won't hurt me physically, so it's safe enough to push the boundaries with him.

"Sam wouldn't kill you," he snorts. A vein has popped on his temple, and it pulses with each beat of his heart.

"No, he would just beat and rape me to within an inch of my

life." The disgust is plain in my voice, and my dad's eyes darken in anger.

"Lose your tone with me, girl. I won't put up with your shit anymore," he growls. "You cost me a lot with your little stunt today."

"Gee, I'm sorry Sam almost beat me to death." If I didn't hurt so bad, I'd roll my eyes and shake my head. As it is, I can barely draw in a breath without crying.

He slams his hand down on the desk making me jump then groan in pain. "Enough! I have done everything in my power to make sure you have a nice life. You have a house to live in, food to eat, clothes to wear. I made sure you would be comfortable when you move out by arranging a marriage with someone who would provide for you like I have. And this is how you repay me? How you repay Sam?"

"You can't be serious?" I breathe. "You expect me to lay down and quietly take everything Sam does to me?" The disbelief quickly turns to anger, igniting in my veins like a wildfire. "You know what happens behind my bedroom door. There is no way you can deny it!" I gesture to my body, bruised and broken. "Look at me! Is this what you want for your daughter? To live a life of torture and abuse?" Tears prick my eyes, but I'm so angry, so bewildered, they don't fall.

He ignores everything I said. "If you think someone else will treat you any better, you're sorely mistaken. The daughter of a prominent mage born with no powers has no place in this world. I am going to make sure you fall in line. You don't want to marry Sam? Fine. You want to play games? Even better." His lips pull into a malicious grin and my heart stops in my chest. "Let's play."

MALAKAI

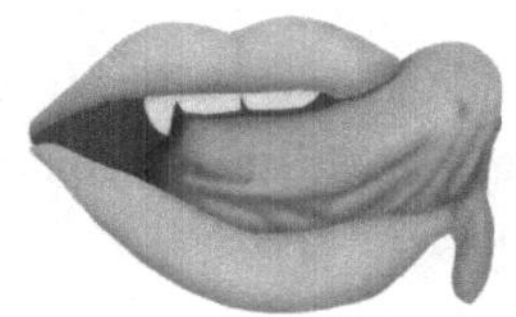

I GRUNT AS MY SHOT GOES WIDE. I'VE BEEN OFF MY game lately. Rarely does Cade beat me at pool, but the past few days he's whooped my ass. Cade chuckles darkly and approaches the table with a calculating eye.

This is the one place I can let my guard down, the library-turned-man-cave in my dad's estate. Hell, it's the one place Cade and Sterling can let their guards down as well. I glance around at the shelves full of books that have been shoved to one side of the large room. There is still plenty of space to walk between them and browse the titles, but now there's room for more entertaining stuff. Stuff like the pool table, a small bar, black leather couches, a giant flat screen TV complete with gaming systems, and workout equipment.

The genius mage currently lining up his shot laid down a bunch of wards around the room to block anyone from overhearing our conversations, and to alert us when someone approaches. Those wards are the reason this place has become our sanctuary. We can be ourselves, enjoy ourselves, and not worry about a single thing knowing we'll be alerted to any hint of danger.

Knowing Cade will likely hustle the table for a while, I sit next to Sterling in the window seat as he scrolls through his phone. I watch Cade, his dark hair falling into his eyes is more distracting than I'd like to admit. My fingertips tingle with the urge to run my hands through the silky strands, which serves to remind me of the other night and what we did. It wasn't the first time, and it certainly won't be the last time we fuck, but there was something different the other night. Like something in my chest moved places, replacing one feeling for another. It was as unsettling then as it is now. Rubbing my chest to ease the squeezing sensation, I force my thoughts to something else.

Sterling snorts next to me, providing me with something to focus on other than Cade. I glance at him from the corner of my eye. His long silver-blond hair is tied back in a bun, wayward strands escaping and framing his face. The scar that starts above his right eyebrow and slices down to his cheek is a chick magnet, and I kind of wish I had one.

"Nice picture, bro." He grins at me as he looks up from his phone, his icy blue eyes shining with amusement.

I peer over his shoulder and laugh. The picture is of me from a few weeks ago, wearing a leather jacket and no shirt, pants unbuttoned, and a satisfied smirk on my lips. I'd probably just finished fucking some random chick at The Crow.

"You're just jealous," I tease. "I mean, look at those abs!"

"Right. Like I want those scrawny arms and tiny dick," Sterling mumbles."Why don't you just walk around naked? Half the time you're almost there, anyway."

I grin at him, flashing my fangs. "Well, that wouldn't be fair to anyone else. I have to make sure you guys stand a chance, too."

Cade laughs, causing his shot to go wide. "Dammit, Kai!"

Before I can stand and take my place at the pool table, Sterling looks up at us. "This is interesting," he says, brows furrowed. "Apparently, Thomas Kennedy announced a contest earlier today."

Cade perks up at the mention of his boss's name. I lean back in the window seat and wait for Sterling to read the article.

"A contest will begin in three days," Sterling reads. "A series of challenges to overcome in order to win my daughter's hand in marriage. Whoever applies for the contest will compete in three tasks set to weed out the strongest potential suitor for my heir. The tasks will be dangerous, and I cannot guarantee the safety of any involved. To apply please go to ..."

As Sterling rattles off the web address, I quickly pull my phone from my pocket and type it into the browser.

"Do you know anything about this?" Sterling asks Cade.

"No." Cade shakes his head with a frown. "I'm not privy to Thomas Kennedy's inner workings. I've seen his daughter before at functions, though. She's pretty."

"Ellis, right? Isn't she human?" I ask distractedly as I scan the webpage and read the details regarding the contest.

"Yeah. I've always wondered how that happened." Cade shrugs. "Both her parents were mages, but she's human. So was her sister."

"Her mom and sister are dead, aren't they?" Sterling asks, still perusing the article, although a muscle jumps in his jaw.

"Yep. About ten years ago, I think." Cade leans his hip against the pool table. "They were murdered in their house. Somehow Ellis survived."

I nod and type my name into the field for contestants. "I'm doing it."

Both Sterling and Cade look at me with their mouths agape like I've lost my mind. Perhaps I have.

"Doing what?" Sterling asks incredulously.

Instead of answering, I keep filling out the form, excitement already starting to bubble inside of me.

"Is that a good idea?" Cade asks. "You're engaged, remember?"

"How could I forget?" I grouse. "It sounds fun. I could use some fun right now. I don't have to actually win, but competing against others in dangerous challenges? Sign me up. We could look at it as a training exercise."

"We?" Sterling's eyes are wide as he looks over my shoulder just as I hit submit on the form.

"Yeah, we. I'm not doing it alone. You don't have to sign up, but you can be my unofficial teammates." I grin at my friends and my fangs descend slightly at the anticipation of bloodshed.

Cade stares at me with a gaze that sees all too clearly my reasons for doing this. Eventually, he sighs and grins back. "Alright, let's do it."

Sterling whips his head in Cade's direction, mouth falling open. "You can't be serious?"

Cade shrugs his muscled shoulders. "Why not? Like Kai said, we might as well use it as a training exercise."

Sterling crosses his arms over his chest and transfers his glare to me. Of course he's the last one on board. Always the serious one, he takes his role as alpha of our group to another level. Our safety is always his top priority. Sighing heavily, he reluctantly nods. "Fine. What can we expect?"

I scan the confirmation email I already received and relay the information provided. "To begin the contest, we will have to break into the Kennedy mansion and essentially kidnap Ellis from her bedroom. Once we have her secure, we text the provided number and let her dad know. He will then release the information for the first challenge to all contestants." I silently read a few more details before announcing, "the person who has possession of Ellis at the end of the contest, wins."

"Break into their mansion? Is he an idiot?" Sterling snorts. "This will only give people insight into their security and how to get around it in the future."

"Thomas Kennedy isn't the smartest when it comes to that kind of thing," Cade says as he sets his pool cue on the rack. "He has people for that, whom I'm sure are shitting their pants right now thinking of all the implications."

"What can you tell us about their security?" Sterling asks Cade. He grabs his iPad to begin making notes, already in planning mode.

"Absolutely nothing," Cade replies with a shrug. "But I can hack into their system and get everything we need."

I grin and rub my hands together. "Perfect. Get started on that. We only have three days to plan."

Cade grumbles, but grabs his own iPad from his bag and settles onto the couch to begin his work.

"Why would he do this?" Sterling muses. "I thought she was engaged to one of his cronies."

"You know how the rich and powerful are," I say darkly. "They do whatever the hell they want. Take my dad for example." I walk to the bar and make Cade a drink. He doesn't even look up when I hand it to him, just grunts a thanks and continues on his quest.

"What do you think we'll need for this challenge?" Sterling asks. "He said he can't guarantee anybody's safety. We should have weapons and magic ready."

"Agreed." I list off some weapons and Sterling jots them down on his iPad. "Oh, and I'd like Cade to make some more of that enchanted jewelry. Something for protection would be helpful."

"Enchanted? I'm not a fairy," Cade mumbles, keeping his eyes on his iPad. "It's spelled jewelry, and I can do that. Also, I'm sending you guys the floor plan now."

My phone and Sterling's iPad buzz as Cade shares the blueprints for the Kennedy mansion. Sterling and I quietly go over ideas, writing down the best possible scenarios and scratching those that aren't feasible. Hours pass and before we know it, Cade announces he has the security plans and can hack into the system of the Kennedy mansion. He tests his ability to do so by quickly hacking in to find Ellis's room.

With Cade's information, we scratch a few ideas we know won't work and eventually settle on the one we think will. Without knowing how many contestants we'll be up against and what abilities they'll have, it's difficult to nail down a solid plan. We keep a few extras as backup, just in case. You never go in with only one plan.

I will be the one doing the actual breaking and entering, although Sterling will follow me through. As I make my way to Ellis's room, Sterling will help keep others off my trail and provide distraction. Cade will remain outside, monitoring the cameras he hacks into to keep us both appraised of our opponents' movements. He'll wait below Ellis's window and use his magic to lower her to the ground once I get to her room.

Once we have Ellis in our possession, we'll make a break for the cliffs that border the Kennedy property. Using satellites, Cade found a cave we'll hide in during the day before we make our way down the cliffs and to the coast, where we will have conveniently left a small boat. We'll use the boat to circle around the coast to the delta where the River Altair meets the ocean. Taking the river up to the city, we'll ditch the boat and sneak our way here, to my father's house on the outskirts of Altair, where we'll hide out and wait for our first challenge.

"Okay, first question," Cade says after we settle on a plan. "Is it smart to bring her to your place with your dad around? You are engaged, after all. I don't think he will be too pleased with you taking part in this."

I shrug. "He'll never know. We can keep her here, in the library. Your wards will keep her protected and undetected."

He nods and hums in the back of his throat. "Second question, and probably the most important. Ellis knows about this, right? We aren't just going to be busting down her door and scaring the poor girl to death, are we?"

Silence meets his question. I hadn't thought about that. How fucked up would that be? To not know your dad planned this contest with your life and future being the prize? To be relaxing in your room only to have some random crazy person break in and steal you away? The excitement that had been building in me during this process dims slightly.

"She has to know," Sterling says. "First of all, what kind of person would do this and not tell their daughter about it? Second of all, it's all over social media. There's no way she doesn't know."

His first point doesn't ease my concern. This is exactly the kind of thing powerful people do. I could easily see my dad doing something like this. However, Sterling's second point is right. If it's on social media, she has to know. I wonder what she thinks of it?

ELLIS

TONIGHT IS THE NIGHT. THE NIGHT MY DAD DECIDED I would be abducted from my home and stolen away. I guess all things considered, this punishment could be a lot worse. I mean, I did almost kill one of my dad's favorite employees—my so-called fiancé. This punishment could be way worse.

At least I'll get out of the house for a bit and away from Sam. Unless he competes. Fuck. What if he competes? What if someone just as awful as him is competing? Maybe this isn't the safest thing after all.

I sit on the edge of my bed, leg bouncing uncontrollably. My bag is packed and sitting by the bedroom door. I packed everything I could think of possibly needing: extra clothes, shoes, toiletries, chargers, and of course, a couple of knives. The inside of my cheek is a raw, mangled mess from the constant chewing—a nervous habit I've had for ten years.

When my dad told me what he planned, I didn't even bother to yell at him. His mind was set and there was no way I was going to change it. It hurt, though. Like a gaping wound that continued to bleed, leaving me feeling less and less human. The words he spoke that night had stuck with me. *The daughter of a prominent mage born without powers has no place in this world.* I'm not sure

I'll ever be able to forget them. What did I do to deserve this kind of treatment? You would think after losing one daughter and his wife to murder, he'd hold on tighter to his remaining daughter. Love her stronger. Protect her harder. But my reality couldn't be more opposite.

Not for the first time, I run through all the ways he could have punished me. At first, this contest didn't seem like such a horrible idea, despite how drastic it is. The longer I wait for my kidnapper and the more I'm able to think about it, I can't help but question my original thinking.

Some random guy I don't know is going to break into my house and abduct me.

Fuck.

My nerves racket up a notch higher, firing through me like lightning. Unable to sit still any longer, I stand from my bed, wincing as knife-like pain radiates outward from my ribs, and pace the length of my room. I glance at the clock at the same time something crashes on a lower level. It sounded like splintering wood. Good. I hope they destroy this house.

Distant shouts and curses reach my ear and I know people must be getting closer if I can hear them with my subpar human hearing. Silence follows and I strain to catch any sound, any hint of what might be coming my way. The silence stretches and my heart pounds faster in my chest, a cold sweat breaking out over my skin.

The door to my room bursts open, and I jump, the throbbing from Sam's beating pushed to the back of my mind, my fear taking over. My heart tries to eject from my body through my throat and I barely contain a scream, clapping my hand over my mouth. When my gaze lands on the man standing in my doorway, bloodied and grinning like a maniac, I think I might actually faint from fear as the room wobbles and my vision blurs.

Fucking hell. Those dark gray eyes set in that pale, classically handsome face. Unruly black hair, styled into messy perfection, longer on top than the sides. Broad shoulders and long, lean muscles shifting under leather armor. I don't need an introduction to know who's here to abduct me. There is only one vampire as terrifying and sexy as the one standing before me.

Malakai Thorne. Prince of Darkness. Ruler of Nightmares.

Holy. Shit. The crown prince of the vampires is kidnapping me. Malakai takes two steps toward me and his steps falter for the barest second, his nostrils flaring. He recovers quickly, and his fangs glint as his smile grows wider. My breaths are coming rapidly, each one sends stabbing pain through my torso, and I think I'm on the verge of hyperventilating. I take an involuntary step backward, my eyes never leave those fangs, as dread curls in my gut.

Even as every instinct in my body screams at me to run, there's something inside me that wants me to move closer instead. It's like a magnetic pull that is fighting the urge to get as far away as possible. The polarizing sensations make my stomach tumble uncomfortably, and I fist my hands against my belly.

"Malakai Thorne, at your service." He bows dramatically with a feral smile, the hand on his chest holding a bloody knife dripping crimson drops onto my pristine white carpet.

My eyes widen, glued to the blade and the blood staining the surface. It's like there's a boa wrapping around my chest, squeezing me until I'll pop, constricting my lungs and forcing the oxygen from my body. I've completely forgotten how to breathe, and even if I remembered, I don't think I'd be able to. My lungs burn with the need for oxygen and my vision wavers, blackness creeping in to slowly claim me.

"Shit," he mutters under his breath, the smile slipping from his face. Malakai steps toward me, the gray of his irises taking on an eerie glow. "Breathe," he says, staring into my eyes, his voice low and melodic with an undercurrent of command ringing through my room.

I gasp, oxygen flooding my system, and I suck in mouthfuls of the air my body needs.

He looks at me, his eyes no longer glowing. "You good?" One pierced brow raises questioningly.

Panting, I stare at him. "Good? Good?" My voice has taken on a hint of hysteria. "No, I'm not fucking good! Malakai fucking Thorne just broke into my room, brandishing a bloody dagger, ready to abduct me. Why the fuck would I be good?"

"Malakai fucking Thorne?" His mouth pulls down in a frown. "I think I like that," he mumbles.

Oh, shit. I just yelled at a vampire. And not just any vampire, but the Prince of Darkness himself. A small sound escapes me as I step back. "I ... I'm sorry. I didn't mean that. It was the lack of oxygen. I'm good now. It's good. We're good." I clamp my mouth shut to stop any more words from spewing forth.

He hums in the back of his throat and looks around my room. "Well, isn't this cozy?" He spots my bag by the door and snatches it up. "I assume you want to bring this?"

I make a sound he must take for consent, because he throws my bag over his shoulder and heads for the window.

"You know," he says casually as he opens the window, "I never thought I'd play the role of Prince Charming rescuing the princess from her tower, but here we are. Guess there's a first time for everything, huh?"

I'd laugh at his joke if I wasn't scared shitless. I certainly feel like a princess locked in her tower waiting for Prince Charming. Prince of the vampires isn't who I would have chosen, though. He's sexy and all, but absolutely terrifying.

"Come along, now," he says in a fake formal accent. "Time is of the essence." He gestures to the open window and leans out.

I stare at him. He can't be serious. Climbing out the window? It's four stories high. I'll surely die on my way down. He turns to look at me over his shoulder with one brow raised in question as I'm frozen in place.

"I can't climb out the window," I gasp. "I'm only human."

His brows lower over his gray eyes, darkening them ominously. I almost apologize for disappointing him, although

I'm a little surprised he doesn't know. I thought everyone knew how worthless I am.

He stalks toward me with slow, steady steps. "What do you mean—" A quiet growl works its way up Malakai's chest and stops whatever he was going to say. His gaze roams over my face and my attempt to cover the bruises with makeup.

He raises his hand as if to stroke my cheek, and I flinch. Something flashes in his eyes that I can't read, and instead of touching my face, he grasps my upper arm in a surprisingly gentle grip, pulling me to the window. Right. He won't be so patient with me as I break down in utter terror.

"Cade, we're ready," Malakai says, pressing on something tucked into his ear I hadn't noticed before.

When he turns to face me again, he smiles, although it doesn't reach his eyes. The tips of his fangs are still visible, and I can't repress the shiver that races down my spine at the sight of them. "Cade is down there, waiting. He'll use his magic to lower you to the ground."

Cade Campbell? It has to be. Where one of the Triad goes, the others go as well.

Despite having been raised by parents who were mages and experiencing magic frequently, something about trusting a stranger to lower me to the ground safely doesn't sit well with me. Not to mention all my recent experiences with magic have been less than desirable.

A crash sounds behind us, followed by a growl and someone screaming. Malakai sighs and slides one arm around my back and the other behind my legs. Stabbing pain flares in my torso from Sam's brutal beating as he effortlessly picks me up. I barely contain my wince as I reflexively wrap shaking arms around his neck and cling to him like a spider monkey when he leans out the window. Nothing but his arms are preventing me from falling to my death.

"Ready, Cade."

I flinch again as purple bands of magic surround me. Waiting for the bite of pain that always came with Sam's, I barely notice as Malakai pries my arms away and he leans back inside, leaving me to the fate of Cade's magic. There is no pain, though, only a soft warmth and gentle buzz of electricity that zips across my skin. Still, I whimper and squeeze my eyes shut tight as I'm lowered to the ground.

I keep my eyes closed until I feel arms around me again—the touch causing my breath to catch—and the magic dissipates. Even with my feet on solid ground, I can't stop the trembling running through my body. It's only when I look up into the stunning violet eyes of Cade Campbell that the shaking stops, something calming crawling under my skin and easing my fears. I could happily get lost in those swirling purple irises.

The soft thump of Malakai landing next to me pulls my gaze from Cade's, and I turn my head to see the vampire stand smoothly from a crouch. He tosses me a black hoodie. "Put this on. That white shirt is too noticeable in the dark." He slaps his thigh and snaps his fingers. "And your phone. We need to leave it here so you can't be tracked."

Leave my phone? Fear trickles through me. I will be completely at their mercy. But truthfully, who would come save me, anyway? Taking a deep breath, I pull my phone out of the pocket of my leggings and hand it to Malakai, watching it quickly disappear as he tosses it into the bushes. I stare at the bushes for a second longer, heart beating an erratic rhythm as I try to wrap my mind around what's happening. My only lifeline, tossed away like it was nothing.

Malakai motions to the hoodie I'm holding in my numb fingers, and I pull it over my white shirt and push down the fear. Instantly, I get a whiff of spice and cherries that make my heart flutter in my chest, calming the pounding just slightly. The hoodie is huge and falls almost to my knees. The sleeves end well past my hands and I have to quickly roll them up. Malakai's gaze roams over my body and I'm glad I wore olive green leggings. I'm not about to strip out of my pants for these guys. I must pass his inspection, because he grabs my hand and drags me through the backyard.

"We're out," Malakai says, pressing on his earpiece with his free hand.

I glance at Cade and see him keeping pace with my bag thrown over his shoulder. We're halfway to the back fence when a silver wolf charges past like a streak of moonlight through the darkness. I screech, and if it weren't for Malakai tugging me along with him, I'd surely have frozen in place.

"Shh," Malakai hisses, slapping his hand over my mouth. "It's just Sterling. He's scouting ahead."

Of course, if Malakai and Cade are here, Sterling Harrison would be as well. I wrack my brain of everything I can think of regarding the Triad as they drag me through the darkness to an unknown location. Of the three, I know Malakai is the most dangerous. He is known to have murdered people and, of course, gotten away with it because of who he is. And as a vampire, he has special abilities, such as speed, strength, and compulsion. However, he also has a few extra abilities, which is rare for a vampire—empath and dream manipulation, being his strongest two.

Cade is a mage, and I know he works for my dad in some capacity. He is rumored to be one of the strongest mages of his time, with a rare violet magic. Sterling is the one I know the least about. A wolf shifter who doesn't have a pack. Not a lot of info to use against these three as they abduct me. With my mind focused on everything else, I completely lose track of my surroundings and I stumble over a branch. I curse, free arm pinwheeling as I try to regain my balance.

"Careful," Malakai mutters, as he steadies me with an arm around my waist. "Cade, make sure we didn't leave any sort of trail."

Our pace slows as we approach the massive stone wall surrounding the property. Cade stops and turns to face the way we came, raising his hands and letting a blast of purple light fan forth, erasing all tracks and scents.

"Up and over," Malakai indicates with a nod toward the gray stone wall.

Before I can remind him of my lack of supernatural abilities, violet magic wraps around me again and lifts me up. I swear I hear Cade's breath catch and feel the pressure around my middle loosen slightly, but that could just be my imagination. My memory conjures up pictures of green bands burning my skin. Nausea climbs up my throat and I have to physically hold back my whimper, even though these bands don't hurt. In my fear, I barely notice Sterling jumping, massive paws landing on the top of the wall. He propels himself forward in one smooth motion and lands effortlessly on the ground on the other side.

Malakai follows in a single jump, clearing the top and landing in a crouch next to Sterling, who quickly takes off at a loping run through the forest behind the property. I'm lowered into Malakai's arms and Cade follows, his magic lifting and lowering him just like it did me. My hand is sweaty in Malakai's and it's only partially due to the heat. Nerves are wreaking havoc on me, making me nauseous, jittery, and dizzy.

The night is hot. Even with the sun down, the temperature is scorching. I'm sweating under the hoodie Malakai gave me, and I'm grateful I wrangled my hair into a bun on top of my head. Still, random escaped curls are plastered to my forehead and neck. The crescent moon provides little light, and with my human eyes, I can barely see where we're going in the darkness. Trees pop up out of nowhere and I stumble and trip frequently, making me rely on Malakai to keep from falling.

The guys set a punishing pace, and it doesn't take long before we clear the forest. The cliffs ahead of us with the panoramic ocean view is one I know well. My sister and I used to come here when we were kids trying to hide from our parents. I haven't been here since my sister died ten years ago. My heart stutters in my chest and I feel the telltale sign of tears stinging my lashes, but I blink them away. These guys don't need the waterworks.

We approach the edge of the cliffs and the sound of waves crashing far below echoes in my memories. If I close my eyes, I can almost picture Gracie here with me, brown curls a tangled mess around her face. The wind blows warmly, only slightly cooling my overheated skin, and whipping my own curls on my head.

"Where is the path, Sterling?" Malakai walks along the edge, peering over.

I stumble to a stop. He can't be serious. We're going to climb down the face of the cliffs? Are they trying to kill me?

Sterling whines a little ahead of us, and we make our way to him. The giant wolf takes a step off the edge and I gasp. He doesn't fall, though. Instead, he takes another and another until he disappears from sight. Leaning over the edge, I see him picking his way carefully along a small path worn into the edge. One wrong step and he'll tumble to his death.

I'm already shaking when Malakai tugs me to the narrow path and takes a step down. I reluctantly follow, instantly turning to face the wall when he releases my hand to plaster myself against the rough stone in front of me with my fingers grasping for any kind of purchase. My heart thunders in my chest as I inch my way along, following Malakai who is facing away from the wall with a crazed smile on his face. Of course, he has nothing to fear. Unless a rock shard pierces his heart or skull, he'd survive the fall. I, on the hand, would splatter like a cracked egg as I bounced my way down the cliffside. The image is all too realistic and I freeze, unable to move one more inch. If I shake any harder, I'll slip and fall.

This is it. This is how I die.

A warm pressure settles across my back. I turn my head to see Cade carefully shuffling along the ledge behind me. He gives me a small, encouraging smile. The warm pressure on my back is his magic gently pressing against me to keep me from falling. For the moment, I forget my fear of his magic. I'm just grateful for the extra safety net. I pry my tongue from the roof of my mouth and take a deep breath to relax my muscles. Turning forward again, I keep inching along, the safety of Cade's magic calming me. Rocks and pebbles slide loose from under our feet, endlessly bounding down the cliffside, and I have to force myself to tune them out or I'll freeze up again.

The path switchbacks multiple times along the way. My calves and hamstrings are burning by the time it opens up onto a larger ledge. I gracelessly sink to the ground and rest my forehead against the dirt to catch my breath.

"Come on," Malakai says, as he pulls me to my feet. "We need to stay hidden."

I glance up and see a cave before me. The dark mouth opening to pitch black nothingness. Sterling lopes ahead, and his silvery pelt is quickly swallowed in the gloom. I balk, but Malakai pushes me forward.

"Once we are far enough in, we can get out the flashlights." His voice echoes all around us.

Flashlights? None of them have any bags. Where are these flashlights coming from? I don't ask, content to keep silent, and follow Sterling and Malakai blindly. Literally. Malakai's hand around mine is the only thing I know of the vast, empty darkness. Sounds echo strangely, and my imagination conjures cave monsters into existence, waiting to devour us whole. I think I hear Sterling shuffling ahead of us, but I can't be sure. Maybe it's one of those monsters. The air is marginally cooler, but I'm still dying to take off this hoodie.

When Malakai comes to a stop some time later, I'm momentarily blinded as a bright light pierces the darkness. I squeeze my eyes shut and wait until they adjust to slowly crack them open again. Lined up along the wall are three bags, one of which Malakai is digging through and pulling out supplies. Flashlights, water bottles, protein bars. Cade joins him and pulls blankets from another bag. Sterling sniffs the air then turns around and heads back to the mouth of the cave, disappearing outside.

Cade spreads the blankets on the ground and sinks gracefully onto one. The light from the flashlights cast harsh shadows on his face, and his violet eyes almost seem to glow. He glances at me and his smile is sweet and tugs at my heart. I sit next to him and accept a bottle of water and protein bar.

"We'll hang out here for the day, since Mr. Sensitive over there doesn't like the sun," Cade jokes and nods toward Malakai. "When the sun sets again, we'll make our way to the beach. We have a boat waiting for us. I placed wards along the path and at the entrance to the cave. We'll know if anyone approaches."

I nod and take off the hoodie, sighing at the bit of relief the cooler air gives me as it hits my skin. "Then what?" I ask timidly. Normally, I'm not a timid person, but this situation has me thrown off my game and all kinds of confused. Also, I'm scared another verbal tirade will come spilling out of my mouth if I let myself speak.

"We'll head to my place," Malakai answers as he sits on a blanket across the cave. "We'll hang out there until your dad announces the first challenge."

I glance down at the bottle in my lap and pick at the label. I want to ask why they're participating. The whole reason for this stupid contest is to win my hand in marriage. Which one of them wants to marry me? And why?

"Did you know about this contest?" Cade gently asks me.

Everything about this man seems gentle. A contrast to Malakai's constant edge of violence, and Sterling's aloofness. I find myself inching closer to him.

"Yeah." My answer is barely audible, even in the quiet of the cave.

"You didn't want to do it?" Malakai's brows furrowed over his gray eyes. Thankfully, his fangs are not visible at the moment.

"Who would want to willingly take part in something like this?" I shake my head, my bun sliding slightly to the side with the movement. "I didn't have a choice, but it was better than the alternative."

"What was the alternative?" Cade asks, studying me.

I press my lips together, not willing to go into every sordid detail of my past with complete strangers. The guys catch my hint and fall into soft conversation with each other. Unable to sit still as my nerves continue to flow through me, I stand and make my way around the slight bend to the mouth of the cave. Malakai and Cade are just visible, sitting in the light from the flashlights. The sight of the ocean, although painful, is a balm in the craziness that has become my life. I wish I had my phone. I really need to hear my bestie's voice—something normal in this highly abnormal circumstance.

A soft sound outside the cave puts me on high alert. I glance behind me, but neither Cade nor Malakai seem to have heard. On instinct, I fall into a fighting stance. Feet spread, knees bent, and fists protecting my face. I inch forward just as a man enters the cave. Tightening my core, I rotate at my hips, and my right hand flies forward. My fist connects with the nose of an incredibly naked man.

"Fuck!" he growls, clapping his hands to his nose.

His silver hair is wild about his shoulders and I know instantly who it is. I cover my mouth with my hands and my eyes widen in shock. Somehow, Sterling still manages to glare at me with icy blue eyes while he tips his head back and pinches the bridge of his nose.

"Oh shit," I breathe. "I'm so sorry! I didn't know it was you!"

"Fucking hell, woman. I think you broke my nose." His words are muffled but I can still hear the nasally tone to them.

Blood leaks from his nostrils and down his lips, dripping off his chin and landing on his chest. His very bare chest. I watch in fascination, unable to tear my gaze away, as the drop of blood slides down between the grooves of his pecks and over a tattoo I don't have time to look at. The drop of blood slides lower over his rippled abs. Lower, toward the V pointing my eyes to a truly impressive specimen hanging between his legs.

Holy shit. I don't notice my mouth hanging open until Sterling clears his throat.

"You're drooling." The faint humor in his rumbly voice snaps my mouth shut.

I whirl around with my eyes squeezed shut, a strange fluttering in my stomach. However, the image is imprinted in my memory, and it flashes behind my closed eyelids. Are all shifters blessed like that? Or is it just him? Heat suffuses my cheeks and I mentally scold myself. *Get your mind out of the gutter, Ellis.*

Sterling prowls around me, head still tipped back. I can't keep my gaze from sliding down his muscled back to his tight ass. When he enters the circle of light, Cade and Malakai look at him with identical quizzical expressions.

"Why are you bleeding?" Cade asks with a frown.

Malakai glances at me, a slight grin tugging his lips. "And why is Ellis blushing?"

This only makes me blush harder, of course. I wish my hair was down so I could hide my cheeks behind the curls.

"It would appear the kitten has claws," Sterling growls.

CADE

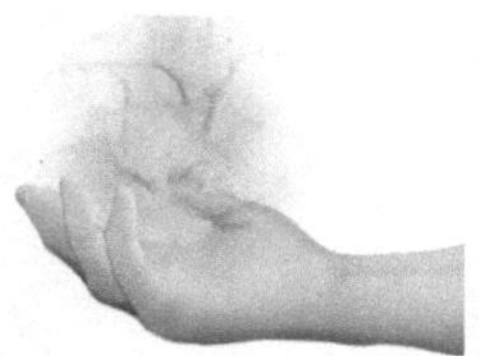

I GLANCE FROM STERLING TO ELLIS, AND BACK TO
Sterling.

"Come here," I say, waving Sterling my way and trying to hide
my smile.

He kneels next to me and removes his hand from his face.
Blood immediately dribbles out of his now crooked nose. I run
my finger down the bridge as my magic surges forth to find all the
broken pieces to put back together.

"Ellis broke your nose?" I ask, glancing at the girl again.

She crosses her arms over her stomach and hunches her
shoulders, making herself smaller. "It was a reflex," she mumbles.
"He startled me." The toe of her shoe scuffs the dirt on the cave
floor as she shuffles her foot back and forth.

"A reflex?" Kai drawls and leans back on his hands, studying
Ellis intently. "Interesting."

"You're good." I pat Sterling on the arm, and he moves to a
bag along the wall.

Ellis tracks his movement as he pulls out clothing. The glint
of lust in her eyes is not quite hidden. Her gaze travels to me and
our eyes meet. I give her a knowing smile, and she flushes further,
a delectable blush crawling up her neck and into her cheeks.

Sterling is a sight to behold when he's naked. Hell, he is a sight to behold when he isn't naked. But all that tan skin over layers and layers of muscle is certainly distracting. Of the three of us, Sterling is the bulkiest. I joke with him that he should wear plaid shirts—with his long hair, scruffy beard, and scar, he'd pull off the lumberjack look perfectly .

I notice Ellis cradling her fist against her belly and motion her over. She settles next to me and I grab her right hand, shoving down the weird swooping in my stomach as her skin touches mine. Nothing is broken, but I let my magic flow over her, anyway. She jumps as the purple light weaves around her fingers and quickly heals her bruised knuckles. When I'm done, I pull back, and she studies her hand as if she's never seen magic at work before. Which is crazy, because her dad is a mage.

My eyes take in the poorly concealed bruising on her face. I noticed it when I lowered her from the window, but I didn't have time to study her then. Underneath the thick layer of makeup, faint bruising is noticeable around her right eye and along her jaw. A small scab is barely visible in her eyebrow, and her lower lip is slightly puffier than it probably should be.

Someone has hurt her, and I'm unprepared for the rush of emotion that surges forth at that thought. Protectiveness, sadness, and righteous fury burns through me. Without thinking, I cup the side of her face and she flinches from that gentle touch. I grit my teeth and push down the anger that begs to be let loose on whoever did this to her, letting my magic flow through her again, healing her cuts and bruises.

I keep it flowing, going further than her face, scanning for any other injuries, and just as I suspected, I find two broken ribs and more bruising. What the fuck has happened to her? Who hurt her this badly? I let my magic heal those injuries as well.

She jerks, and her gaze flies to me as if she's surprised—or maybe ashamed. Shadows linger in her amber eyes and she quickly looks away, mumbling her thanks, and rotating her trunk to test for any lingering pain. There isn't any. I made sure of that.

On the other side of the cave from us, Sterling and Kai watch like eagles with their prey in sight. The flashlights on the floor make their eyes glow, and they look just like the predators they are. I hold in a snort at their expressions. I have a feeling this is going to get more interesting than just a contest for fun and training purposes.

Kai snaps out of it first with a shake of his head. "We should rest while we can. We move at dusk."

Sterling tosses me another blanket and I wad it up to use as a pillow, it's too hot to actually need to cover up with one. The cave is plunged into darkness when Kai flips off the flashlights, and I hear him and Sterling settling in. I tap into my magic to allow myself to see better in the dark. With no natural predator instincts like Sterling or Kai, I have to resort to using my magic. Usually, it's not a problem. Using too much of it will drain me, but I have such an outrageous amount rolling through my blood, I frequently need to burn off extra, anyway.

Ellis looks around with uncertainty, trying to see into the darkness, and I tug her down. I hear her small gasp of surprise and smile to myself as I tuck the blanket under her head and use her discarded hoodie for a pillow instead.

I have so many questions for her. This entire situation is unreal and confusing. Why is her dad hosting this contest? What happened with her engagement to Sam? And underneath those, there is a burning desire to know more about her. Who is this tiny, mysterious woman who is fierce enough to throw a punch at a naked shifter, but is clearly hiding something dark, and most likely heartbreaking? As she settles in as best as she can on an uncomfortable cave floor, I give in to my curiosity.

"Tell me about yourself," I ask her quietly, though I know the others will listen in with their heightened hearing.

She stills and draws in a breath before releasing it. "What do you want to know?"

"Anything. Favorite color? Job? Hobbies? ... Boyfriends?"

She shifts again, her arm brushing against mine. "Purple. My dad won't let me work. I enjoy boxing and reading."

I noticed she skipped the last question, but I let it go. "Boxing? I assume that's how you knew how to break Sterling's nose without breaking your fingers. Tell me about that."

"My best friend and I started boxing about seven years ago. She was almost raped and the owner of a gym happened to be there. He stopped it and offered us free gym memberships if we took him up on some boxing lessons. We've been doing it ever since."

I hum in the back of my throat. "That's probably a good skill to have. Being able to protect yourself in this city may one day save your life." She doesn't respond, so I think of another question, something else to keep her talking. "What's your favorite animal?"

"Sloth."

I turn my head in her direction. "Sloth?" With my magic-heightened vision, I see her shrug.

"They look like they give really good hugs."

While the answer is cute—and true—based on the bruises, ribs, and fear of human touch, I suspect that reason hits deeper for her.

"If you could work, if your dad let you, what would you want to do?" I ask.

"Honestly, I would love to open a training center of some sort," she says somewhat bashfully. "Offer classes to women— human women—on how to defend themselves. I hate how vulnerable we are."

Her answer is quiet, but I hear the determination in her voice, and my respect for this woman grows. Clearly, she has been battered and bruised, but I can tell she hasn't let it beat her down. There's a quiet strength to her I admire.

"Why won't your dad let you work?" I have my suspicions. Working for the man has shown me his true colors, and it doesn't surprise me to hear about the control he holds over her.

She snorts in an unladylike fashion, and my lips curve up in a smile. "He claims it's to keep me safe after what happened to my mom and sister." She pauses and takes a breath. "But I know it's just another way for him to control me. Another way for him to keep me hidden. A way to hide his constant disappointment and embarrassment at me being human."

I clench my jaw at the bitterness of her tone. It's what I expected to hear, but hearing her say it that way hits a nerve I wasn't even aware I had. Without thinking, I reach out and grab her hand, lacing our fingers together. At first she holds herself stiffly, but eventually her fingers relax and curl around mine.

"What about you?" she asks timidly.

"I'm sure you already know everything about me. It's all over the internet."

"I don't follow social media too much. I really only know the basics. Your name, your affinity, your job."

"Hmm. Well, my favorite color is blue. You know my job. I like anything to do with technology and electronics. No girlfriend." I answer the questions I initially posed to her. "Oh, and my favorite animal is a cat."

"A cat?" A smile laces her question.

"Yeah, a cat. What? Is that not manly enough for you?" I ask with mock outrage.

"No, it's just ... unexpected?" She shrugs. "I would think a powerful mage would like something more ..."

"Powerful?"

"Well ... yeah."

I chuckle. "I like how one second cats are cute and cuddly, and the next they are complete assholes. Keeps you on your toes."

She hums. "And what would you do for a job if you didn't work for my dad?"

Damn, that's a loaded question. She probably doesn't even realize how hard it hits. "I'd like to be a healer. Specifically, for animals."

We both fall silent. It isn't too long before her breathing evens out and her hand loosens around mine. I slide my fingers free and tuck my hands behind my head.

The thoughts racing through my mind are troubling. I'm not sure why I feel the need to make sure she feels safe with us. The burning desire to know more about her is overwhelming, and I have no clue where it came from. And I feel an intense need to protect her from any danger. I shake my head and close my eyes, trying to shut off my thoughts and fall asleep, but it takes longer than I would like.

———

There's a warm blanket draped over me, and it's so hot in this cave it's making me sweat. I slowly come awake only to find it's not a blanket at all. In her sleep, Ellis rolled over on top of me. Her head rests on my chest, her hand dangerously close to the waistband of my pants, and one of her legs is thrown over mine.

I barely breathe as I take in the weight and warmth of her. It's devine, and I could stay like this forever, despite the heat. My arm is wrapped around her back with my palm near the nape of her neck. A few loose strands of her riotous curls tickle my knuckles, and I desperately want to wind one around my finger.

A weird sensation settles in my stomach—something akin to butterflies, but stronger. It's a tugging sensation that makes me want to squirm. I don't, though. If Ellis wakes and finds us in this position, it would mortify her, so I keep my eyes closed and soak in the feeling, as I let her wake on her own and gently remove herself.

The cool air hits the parts of my body she had been covering, and I miss the warmth of her on top of me instantly. I lay still for a few more minutes, listening to her shuffle farther away. When enough time has passed, I stretch and yawn. Sitting up, I find Ellis against the cave wall with her legs drawn up to her chest. Her head is resting on her knees, and her gaze is trained on the cave entrance. Never have I wanted Kai's empath abilities more than I do at that moment. The image she paints is one of extreme loneliness and hurt. Mistrust and fear line every part of her body, and I want nothing more than to make everything disappear for her.

"Good morning," I say, my voice thick with sleep. Clearing my throat, I grab a bottle of water and take a large gulp.

"Morning," she whispers, not turning to look my way while she tucks herself into a smaller ball.

Kai stirs and I look over to find him slowly sitting up. The spot next to him where Sterling slept is empty. The crazy wolf is probably already out scouting and checking our trail. Kai's gaze travels to Ellis and he frowns. I assume he's using his abilities to read her and he doesn't like whatever he's picking up on. He glances at me with a raised brow and I shrug my shoulders. All things considered, I think she's handled everything pretty well. From her comment last night, I know this wasn't something she signed up for, but was rather forced into it.

Kai clears his throat. "Ellis, are you okay?"

She keeps her head turned away but huffs a laugh that's lacking in humor. "Yeah, just fucking peachy."

Kai's lips press together tightly, and I can see the tension in the line of his jaw. Sighing, he stands and slowly approaches her, handing her an unwrapped protein bar and bottle of water. "You should eat. As soon as we get to my place, I'll make sure you get some real food."

She says nothing, but she reaches for the protein bar and takes a bite. The act eases Kai's muscles and his shoulders relax. The quiet of the cave is oppressing and it's obvious neither Kai nor myself know what to do to make her happy. It's almost comical because as much experience as we have with women, none of us have actually had a lasting relationship. So knowing what to do in a normal situation would be stressful enough. And this situation is anything but normal.

"Is Sterling out scouting?" Kai asks, breaking the silence and glancing at me.

"I assume so. He was gone when I woke up." I stand and walk past Ellis to the cave mouth. The urge to look at her is strong, but I keep my focus forward to give her as much privacy as can be found in a cave.

It's a breathtaking view as the sun sets. The orange ball of light reflects off the surface of the ocean in a stripe that ripples with the waves. Oranges, pinks, and purples streak the rapidly darkening sky, and a few wispy gray clouds float past. I watch the sun fall below the horizon with a measure of peace I haven't felt in awhile. In the city, we never get to see this sight through the buildings, despite the ocean only being on the other side.

When the sun is gone and the moon has replaced it with a pale silver glow, Sterling lopes into view. The moonlight reflects off of his pelt as he shifts, his fur disappearing under his skin, and his bones lengthening. A few pops sound in the quiet that always make my stomach roil. It happens fast, in the blink of an eye—where a giant silver wolf was standing, now a giant naked man stands, instead. He steps next to me and pulls his wild silver hair into a man bun with the hair tie he keeps on his wrist—the only thing that ever stays when he shifts, for some reason.

"Is everything clear?" I ask, glancing at him from the corner of my eye.

"Yeah," he nods. "We're good ahead and behind. Before I went out, I scrolled through social media. I have an idea of who is taking part in this contest, so we'll be able to better plan for the challenges."

"Great. That would be helpful."

"You looked awfully cozy before I left."

I can hear the smirk in his voice, and I quickly turn my head toward him. "Don't say anything," I whisper. "I doubt she wants everyone to know she rolled onto me in her sleep."

Sterling snorts. "You are always such a gentleman." He turns and heads back into the cave, buck ass naked.

Ellis gasps as he strolls past her, and I grin to myself. I know if I were to look at her, there would be a rosy blush gracing her cheeks. After spending most of our lives with Sterling, his nakedness doesn't phase Kai or me anymore, but I have no doubt it will continue to affect Ellis.

"It's dark enough for us to head out," I say to Kai as I head back inside the cave.

He nods and packs up the blankets and the flashlights while glancing at Ellis. "Do you have a darker shirt to wear?" he asks her. "You can keep wearing my hoodie, but I assume it's a little hot."

"Yeah, I do." She looks around for her bag and I hand it to her.

Once she's decent, we set out for the path that leads down to the beach. Carrying her bag, I follow behind and keep my eye on her. We've only gone about ten feet when I notice her breathing. It's quick and irregular. She's plastered to the wall as much as she can be, and her eyes are squeezed shut. I assume the faint sheen of sweat glistening on her forehead has nothing to do with the heat.

Without thought, I use my magic to brace her back, an extra layer of protection, just like I did the night before. And just like the other times my magic has touched her, a spark zaps through me. It's almost addicting—the feeling of my magic touching her. It's almost as good as the feeling of her laying on top of me. She gives me a grateful look and takes a few deep breaths before continuing down the trail.

When we make it to the beach, I pull my magic back and I swear I have to fight it. It isn't sentient, but when it touches her, it almost becomes a living thing. And it wants to be with her. As it settles back inside me, it seems cold and alone, like it's mourning the lack of her.

An ugly emotion, like jealousy, rears its head as Kai takes Ellis's hand to help her into the boat. I shove it down and climb in after them, sitting so I'm across from Ellis and can watch her. Not to make sure she's okay, but just to watch her. I want to catalog every expression and every nuance of her face. The strength of that desire knocks me to my ass, and I collapse on the bench, rocking the boat roughly.

Kai sits in the back and lowers the motor into the water, steering us away from the beach. My gaze is glued to Ellis. Her eyes are closed, her head tipped back. The wind rips curls out of her bun and she smiles. It's a small smile, but it's real, and it makes my heart stutter. She looks beautiful with the moonlight painting her cheeks and hair. She looks like a goddess.

Kai is watching her from his place behind her, and I glance behind me and see Sterling looking at her, too. Their expressions must mirror my own. This woman we know nothing about has completely enamored us. I'm determined at that moment to learn everything I can of Ellis Kennedy. A determination I'm positive my brothers feel as well. A smile grows across my lips and I don't hold it back.

ELLIS

Somehow I make it down the cliff, around the coast of Lustros, up the delta to the River Altair, and dock near an abandoned building on the outskirts of the city. My body is on autopilot the entire time, following the guys and obeying their commands without second thought. Numbness crept in sometime during the night, and I woke with despair weighing me down and making my limbs heavy. My body doesn't seem like my own. It's like it belongs to someone else who is in charge of the movements, and I'm just along for the ride. All my energy is concentrated on lifting my arms and placing one foot in front of the other.

As we wind our way through the city, we keep to the shadows in an attempt to remain anonymous. I don't think we're doing the best job, and I'm drawn out of my funk watching the guys try to hide their identity. They duck behind streetlamps and parked cars, sidle up to the side of buildings to peer around the corners, and tug their hoods down low over their eyes. It's like I've fallen into some bad spy movie, and it lightens the weight on my chest.

Even at night—especially at night—the streets are busy and people take notice. Makalai, Cade, and Sterling are the most well known magicals in Lustros. The deadliest, sexiest, most dangerous predators of our city. And they have abducted me. So far, they haven't given me any reason to fear them, but I'm sure it's all just an act to get my guard down. The idea of slipping away occurs to me, and I debate it for half a second. But I don't know where I would go, or what would happen to me if I left. I assume someone else taking part in this contest would snatch me up, and not knowing who else is participating, this seems like my best choice at the moment.

The guys all relax as the gates to Thorne estate appear ahead. In the moonlight, the tan bricks of the house appear to be silver. Spotlights light up the four-story facade and warm golden light spills from many of the windows. It's boxier looking than my dad's mansion, giving off elegant, antiquated vibes. I can't see it in the dark, but I know from pictures that beautiful gardens surround the grounds.

Malakai leads us up the driveway and around the left side of the estate to a patio with wrought-iron tables and potted plants. A thumb pad next to the sliding glass door blinks red until he places his thumb on it, then it beeps softly and flashes green. Sterling and Cade enter first, while Malakai holds me back with a hand on my wrist.

"Is everything secure, Cade?" Malakai asks.

Cade takes a moment to look around with his brows drawn down before he nods. "Yeah. Everything is how it should be. Nothing has been tampered with."

Malakai exhales and his shoulders relax. "Thank the gods." He ushers me inside, arms spread wide as he turns in a circle. "Welcome to our man cave," he says with a smile, fangs on display.

The corners of my lips tug upward as I glance around the room. It looks like it was a library once, or rather still is. The room is two stories tall, and the second story hasn't been touched—a balcony with a gold railing wraps around the second floor with shelves and shelves of books. On the first level, more bookshelves are shoved to the side, but I notice there is still enough space to walk between them.

The walls are dark wood, and the floor is a beautiful white marble. A large, ornate fireplace takes up much of one wall, and the large screen TV perched above it looks so out of place I can't help but laugh. I see a table next to the fireplace with various gaming consoles, and there are a few leather sofas for lounging. On the opposite side of the shelves, a pool table and workout equipment take up the rest of the space.

"Well, what do you think?" Malakai asks, watching me take it all in.

"It's ... unique?" I'm not sure what to say. The clash of original features with modern touches is quite the juxtaposition.

Malakai and Cade laugh, and Sterling just grunts. My cheeks heat, and I immediately regret my statement.

"Sorry," I say quickly. "That was rude."

"Nah, it's true," Malakai says and approaches me.

His prowl reminds me of his appearance when he broke into my room, ready to whisk me away. There had been blood on him. The crimson liquid had dripped down the dagger he'd held in his hand. Once again, the realization that I'm at the mercy of these guys, floats to the forefront of my mind. None of them are known for being good men. Breathing suddenly becomes difficult as my lungs tighten. It's as if an elephant is sitting on my chest, preventing me from taking a deep enough breath. I take a step back, then another. My gaze never leaving the predator before me.

Those gray eyes are intense as he tracks my movements, cataloging every step, every breath, and every blink of my eyes. His nostrils flare, and like he did in my bedroom, and his steps falter. But he doesn't stop his approach. When his fingers wrap around my wrist, I flinch. Fear of him bringing my arm to his mouth and sinking those fangs deep in my vein has my heart pounding, sending my blood rushing through my body. He tugs me forward slightly, and I stumble closer to him, my legs suddenly forgetting how to work. Being vertically challenged, my head barely reaches his shoulders and I have to crane my neck to look at him.

"You are safe here, Ellis." He says with such sincerity I almost believe him. "This room is warded. Cade has magic and technology surrounding every inch of this space. No one will get in without us allowing it. And we won't allow it."

I swallow, and as he watches the movement of my throat, his eyes dilate and his hand grips me tighter. *Oh, gods.* I bet he can hear my heart racing and blood flowing. There is no way I could ever forget this man before me is a vampire.

Malakai's grip tightens on my wrist before he releases me. "You are safe with us," he reiterates. "We won't hurt you. You have my word."

I want to believe him. I really do. But every instinct in my human body is telling me to run. I'm prey to these guys, that's all I am, despite how they've treated me so far.

Malakai frowns before stepping away. "Sterling, can you go to the kitchen and get us some food? Cade, take her to my room to shower while I check in with my dad."

Leave the library and the wards? I've never met Malakai's dad, and I have no desire to do so today. "Is it safe to leave the library?" I ask. My voice trembles, and I swallow, hoping to hide my nerves.

Malakai turns from the door to look at me, his gray eyes shining brightly. "Cade will make sure you're safe."

As a mage, I suppose he can. I remember my mom using her magic to monitor for danger one night we got stuck downtown after the sunset. So I nod, and watch Malakai and Sterling exit, leaving me with Cade who gives me a reassuring smile and motions with his head to follow him. I hesitate, but of all the guys, Cade is the one I feel the most comfortable with. Something about him is less threatening. Maybe it's the fact he is more human than Malakai and Sterling.

I follow Cade through the estate, and try to catalog my surroundings. Knowing how to get around could end up saving my life. Unfortunately, my head isn't in it. I'm exhausted, hungry, and scared. My thoughts are spiraling, each one heavier and scarier than the one before. The barrier I have learned to erect around my mind, the one that keeps the memories at bay, is failing. My vision morphs, turning the red carpet lining the hall darker, more like dried blood. It sends the wall around my mind crumbling to the ground, and the memories I try so hard to forget crash into me.

Time blurs. I don't know if what I'm seeing is real or a product of my trauma from ten years ago. Phantom liquid squishes between my toes and I glance down. That can't be real, I'm wearing gym shoes. The copper scent of blood floats in the air and I rub my nose. *Not real. Not real. Not real.* Shaking my head, I squeeze my eyes shut, but when I reopen them, the bloody carpet is still there.

By the time we reach Malakai's room, I'm sweating. It runs down my back and between my breasts making my shirt cling to me uncomfortably. My hands shake with fine tremors that vibrate my arms, and my heart is pounding so hard the echoes of it can be felt all the way to my fingertips. Breathing is becoming more difficult. I can't draw in a full breath, it's like my lungs are constricted by my rib cage. The more I struggle, the fuzzier my vision becomes. I stumble into the room and Cade catches me around the waist.

"Whoa. Ellis, what's wrong?" His violet eyes take me in and a crease forms between his brows. "Hey, are you alright?"

He leads me to a window seat and gently pushes me into it. I dimly register him kneeling between my legs, his big hands resting on my thighs. Usually, just the *thought* of a man touching me would terrify me, let alone him *actually* touching me. But I can't breathe, and all my focus is on trying to get oxygen into my lungs. I'm going to suffocate. The ghosts won't leave me alone. I can't escape them, they chase me wherever I go. I'll never be free.

Cade grasps my face in both of his hands, and he forces me to meet his gaze. The color of his eyes draw me in, and I cling to them like an anchor. They shimmer and glitter, like an oil spill, but the only color is purple—a myriad of shades of purple, swirling together. It's mesmerizing. Beautiful. He is beautiful, with his scratchy beard and brown hair ruffled and falling over his forehead. His lips, that look so seductive when he smiles, are pulled down in a frown.

His thumb rubs back and forth on my cheek, a gentle touch I don't know what to do with. Keeping our eye contact, he scoots closer, further into my legs.

"Can't ... breathe ..." I manage between small gasps of air.

He takes one of my hands and places it on his chest, while his other hand keeps rubbing along my cheek. "Breathe with me." The low and melodic tone of his voice is soothing. "Feel my heart beating, nice and steady."

I do as he says, narrowing my focus to his chest under my hand, where a steady *thump thump thump* echoes. It's calming, the repetitive and expected rhythm something I can focus on instead of my restricted breathing. His chest rises and falls under my hand with his controlled inhales and I breathe with him, shallow at first, but growing stronger with each breath and each beat of his heart.

"That's it," he says softly. "You got this. Keep breathing." He stares at me like I'm the only thing in the room. A lifeline I desperately hold onto. "You don't have to be afraid of us, Ellis. I swear we won't let anything happen to you."

We stay locked in this position for several minutes. Eventually, my breathing slows and I take a deep, shuddering breath. The panic has passed, but the shame of him seeing me break down like that quickly takes its place. Tears prick the corners of my eyes and I try to blink them back, but one slips free and slides down my cheek. Cade brushes it away with his thumb.

"Please don't cry," he whispers, the brightness of his eyes dimming slightly. "I don't want to see you cry."

"Why are you being so nice to me?" I whisper back. It doesn't seem right to break the silence surrounding us.

He gives me a small smile that makes my stomach do a funny little flip. "Why wouldn't I? I know what people say about me— about us. It's not true." He cringes and nods his head from side to side. "Mostly."

"Why are you guys taking part in my father's challenge?" *Which one of you wants to marry me* is what I really want to ask, but I'm too scared.

"It was Kai's idea. He gets bored easily and was thinking it would be a fun change of pace. I don't think any of us really thought about the deeper implications of this whole thing. We didn't think about what it means to you, or how it would affect you. For that, I'm sorry."

His gaze roams over my face, lingering a second too long on my lips. Butterflies erupt in my belly, and it's such an unusual sensation for me I gasp. There are no razor tipped wings this time, cutting into my insides and making me bleed. It's the soft flutter that makes my blood sing and my heart race for an entirely different reason than panic.

He slides his hand lower on my cheek, the warmth of his skin traveling with it, and his thumb moves to rub along my bottom lip. His other hand is still pinning mine to his chest, and under my palm, his heartbeat kicks up a notch, right before he leans forward. My gaze drops to his lips and I freeze. A mixture of fear and excitement swirl together in my stomach, making me nauseous and hopeful at the same time. Cade closes the distance between us before I can decide if I want to stop him. The kiss is so gentle, barely a brush, a feather soft caress.

My breath catches in my throat as I try to figure out how to handle this. The kiss is not entirely unwelcome in its gentleness, but my mind conjures images of not so gentle kisses. I don't understand how I can simultaneously want him to kiss me more and want him to stop. The awful memories that rear their ugly head take away from the moment.

Cade pulls back, and when he notices my uncertainty, his eyes shutter. "I'm sorry, Ellis. I'm so sorry," he apologizes. "I shouldn't have done that. It won't happen again. I promise."

I say nothing, because while his promise comforts me, it also makes the butterflies in my stomach cease their fluttering, and I don't understand how I can feel both things at the same time. Do

I want him to kiss me again? All I know is that at this moment, I want to crawl into a hole and hide away from the world.

"The shower is through there." He won't meet my gaze as he nods toward a door I hadn't noticed in my panic attack.

"Thank you," I whisper. *Thank you for all of it.*

I stand in a daze with my hand touching my lips. They're tingly, like they're waking up after a long slumber. Cade Campbell kissed me. And I'm not sure if I liked it or hated it. What the hell does that mean? Has Sam ruined me forever?

Those questions stay with me as I stand in the spray of the shower with steam floating around me. I'm still standing under the water as it turns cold, but I still have no answer when I eventually step out and get dressed.

CADE

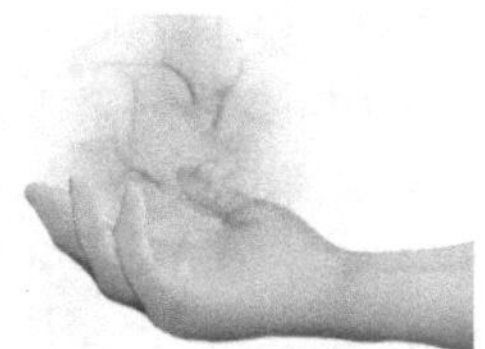

I FUCKING KISSED HER.

That had not been part of the plan, but seeing her falling apart did something to me. It physically hurt me to see her upset and struggling. My heart ached and my limbs trembled. The urge to make it all go away was so strong I had a hard time keeping my body in control. I couldn't stop myself from leaning in and stealing a kiss. And how fucking horrible of a person am I that I never even thought about how she would react? I don't know for certain that she's been abused, but I'm willing to bet everything I own on it. What kind of asshole doesn't even think about that before kissing someone?

Fuck.

I run my hands through my hair and mentally kick myself. *Fucking moron, thinking only with my dick.* I shouldn't have done it. But even knowing that, I can't help but want to do it again. I hadn't been prepared for the rush of emotions that swept through me as my lips touched hers. Excitement, hope, desire, a strange feeling of rightness. Even my magic reacted to the kiss, sending a jolt of electricity through my blood that did nothing to ease the temptation to kiss her again.

I can still picture her hand on my chest, the heat from her body soaking through my shirt, her fingers digging into the muscle. Trying to erase the memory, I rub the spot. It doesn't work. Fuck. What now? While she showers, I pace Kai's room, trying to think of anything but her lips. And I fail miserably. She takes a while, and I don't blame her. I can't imagine what she is going through right now, and my idiotic actions probably made everything worse. By the time she steps out of the bathroom with her curls wet and heavy on her head, I still have no answer to my question.

"Hungry?" I ask, offering her my hand and holding my breath, hoping she takes it. "The cook here is phenomenal."

That little time we touched—my hand on her cheek, my lips on hers—was addicting. I want more. She hesitates a second before placing her much smaller hand in mine, her fingers trembling slightly. It feels so good, so … right. I release a relieved breath, holding back a nervous laugh.

There are a million questions in my head I want to ask her, but sudden nerves dry my mouth, and I can't bring myself to ask them. I've never been shy or nervous around a girl before, but I'm so scared to say or do something that will spook her. So instead of voicing my thoughts, we walk silently through the halls, hand in hand, and I memorize the way her fingers wrap around mine, like a puzzle piece.

In the library, Sterling is unloading a tray of food onto the coffee table in front of the massive fireplace. The smells of roasted meat and savory sauces permeate the air and my mouth waters. I wasn't lying when I said the cook here was amazing. I walk Ellis to the couch by the coffee table and she sits down.

"Is meat okay?" I ask. When she nods, I grab a plate and fill it full of meat and veggies, and pour one of cook's special sauces over all of it. "Would you like something to drink? We have everything here. Wine, vodka, beer, soda, water."

"Water is fine," she says, as she takes the plate from me. "Thanks."

"Sterling?" I ask over my shoulder, snagging a bottle of water from the fridge by the bar.

"Beer," he grunts around a mouthful of food.

I grab three beers and take my haul back to the coffee table. The silence is oppressive and unusual for us in this room. In our sanctuary, we typically have music playing, or are joking and laughing with each other. Rarely is it so quiet. I know Sterling doesn't mind the stillness. He is the most reserved of the three of us, opting to watch and keep his focus on our surroundings. But my mind tends to wander when it's quiet. And right now, the wandering leads me right back to Ellis.

Again, I wish I had Kai's empath abilities. What I wouldn't give to know what Ellis is feeling right now. With her shoulders curved in and her eyes on her plate, I can only guess she's trying to stay as quiet and out of sight as possible. Like she's hoping we'll forget she's here. Not for the first time, I wonder what's happened to her to make her act this way.

Halfway through our dinner, Kai comes back. He's pissed, with his brows drawn down and his jaw clenched. I know his fangs will have descended before he opens his mouth to talk. But, him being mad after talking to his father is nothing unusual. I'm just glad he's back, because he won't let the quiet linger.

"So," I ask, grateful to be able to break the silence, "what's Pops have to say?"

Kai snorts and sits next to me on the couch. "The usual bullshit. No new missions, though." He grabs the last beer off the coffee table and twists off the top.

Ellis tenses next to me, and I quickly change the subject. "Does he know you're doing this contest?"

"Yeah, and he's pissed, but fuck him," he shrugs. "And speaking of, I text the number in the email and said Ellis is safe. So, now we wait for the announcement of the first challenge."

"Do you have any idea what these challenges may be?" Sterling asks Ellis, leaning forward and resting his elbows on his knees.

She sets her empty plate on the coffee table and shakes her head. "I don't. I'm sorry." Her eyes remain on her lap, where she fiddles with the lid to the bottle of water.

Kai clears his throat and leans around me to look at her better. "I know this is probably hard for you to answer, but can you tell us why your dad started this contest? It might help us with our planning."

The blood drains from her face, her usually tan complexion turning ghostly. Moving slowly enough to give her time to back away, I set my plate down and reach for her hands, trying to ignore my magic that rushes to the surface as our skin touches.

"If you can't tell us, that's okay," I say. "We just want as much information as we can get to keep you safe through this." I see Kai and Sterling nod in my peripheral vision.

Ellis swallows and closes her eyes, visibly preparing herself. "I did something bad." Her voice trembles as she speaks. "It's a way for my dad to punish me, while also solving the problem of finding someone who will marry me even though I'm only human."

My jaw clenches at her bitter words. I've heard her saying something to that effect before. That she is *just* human. It doesn't sit right with me, but I let it go for now. Instead, I gently ask, "What happened?"

Wide amber eyes open and latch onto mine. I keep my face relaxed and encouraging. Still, she hesitates. Uncertainty and fear line her features. She doesn't trust us, understandably.

"We won't tell anyone," Kai says next to me. "All three of us have our own secrets. Yours are safe with us."

She looks to me for confirmation and I nod my head, squeezing her hand gently.

Her shoulders rise as she takes a deep breath. "I hurt someone. I almost killed him. It was self-defense, but my dad doesn't see it that way. He thinks I should have let the guy do whatever he wanted to me." She shudders and closes her eyes again. When she speaks next, it's barely a whisper. "I just snapped. I couldn't take it anymore, and I had to do something."

Her hands tremble in mine, and tears cling to her lashes. Was this the same person who broke her ribs and gave her the bruises? Was this the guy who makes her flinch any time someone tries to touch her? I have to fight to keep my expression neutral, even though all I want is to get the information from her and pay this bastard a visit.

"So he set up this contest to punish you for defending yourself?" Kai asks incredulously. "And I thought my dad was an asshole. That's some serious bullshit."

"I thought you were engaged to someone in your dad's company?" I'm cautious with this question because in the cave, she avoided it.

"Not by choice," she whispers. The pain is evident, even in the hushed volume.

When she looks at me with haunted amber eyes, my heart stutters and cracks. She looks so small and sad sitting on the couch. Like a lost child desperate for someone to care for her. I can't stand that look. Again, moving slowly, I wrap my arm around her shoulders and pull her to me, tucking her in close. She holds herself still, barely breathing with muscles tense, before relaxing just a bit. I take it as a win.

Silence settles throughout the room again as we process what she said. It's not really a surprise to any of us. Kai and Sterling are the only ones born to privileged families, but because of my friendship with Kai, and having more power than other mages, I get to enjoy the privileges of living an elite life.

Of course, with those privileges, come disadvantages as well. Like Kai's arranged marriage and our jobs. We all know too well the kind of people who rule our world and the things they do to remain in power. People like Ellis, humans and weaker magicals, get shafted.

Sterling clears his throat and breaks the heavy silence around us. "I have a list of everyone competing in the contest." He rattles off a list of ten names, all of them we've heard of—few will be true competition for us. "And Samuel Morris," Sterling ends the list.

Ellis stiffens under my arm, and a startled noise escapes her lips. "No," she whispers.

She pushes away from me with jerky movements and walks around the couch, arms clutched around her middle. Tremors work their way through her body, despite how she tries to control them by squeezing herself tighter. Her eyes are wide and terrified, and her breath comes faster and faster, just like it did in Kai's room.

"Fuck." I hurry around the couch, grabbing her shoulders and turning her to face me.

While she looks at me, I can tell she isn't really seeing anything. It's more like she's looking right through me. Her eyes move from side to side as tears build along her lashes. Under my palms, the skin of her arms has gone clammy and cold.

"What the hell?" Kai says as he comes up behind her. "What's wrong? Do you know Samuel Morris?"

When he says the name, Ellis flinches—actually flinches—and the dots connect in my head.

"Sam works for your dad," I say slowly. "He works really closely with him."

She doesn't comment on my statement. Instead, she appears to draw further into herself. I hate the sight of her cowering.

"I heard rumors just before the contest was announced," I continue. "He missed a few days of work. People were saying he was in an accident. He wasn't, though, was he Ellis?"

Wide, wild eyes focus on me. Her pulse jumps in her throat, and I don't need Kai's abilities to sense the fear rolling off her.

"I had to," she whispers. "I had to do it."

"What did he do to you?" Kai growls behind her. The words are distorted as his fangs descend.

Sterling stands from his seat and crosses his arms, a frown pulling his mouth into a snarl. His icy blue eyes never leave Ellis, and his muscles tense and relax as he flexes them.

She whimpers, and the sound seems to break her open. Tears pour from her eyes and she falls to the ground. I wrap my arms around her before she hits the floor, and haul to my chest, cocooning her from the world around her. Her entire body is trembling like a leaf, and I squeeze her tighter, trying to hold her together. She is so tiny in my arms, her face hitting the spot between my shoulder and chest perfectly. How the fuck anyone could ever hurt her is beyond me.

"It's okay, Ellis. We're here now." I breathe into her hair.

Like a damn that has broken, she spills the entire story, keeping her head buried in my shirt. "My dad arranged for him to marry me, so he could have a son who was a mage. I didn't know at first, and everything was fine. He was sweet and caring. But when I found out the truth, everything changed." Her muffled words hitch as if they get stuck in her throat. "He ... he threatened me when I tried to break things off. He became violent and possessive. He ..." she stops and shudders. A small, helpless sound comes from her.

I press her tighter to me and her arms slowly wind around my waist. Sobs climb up her chest, wracking her body. She clings to me like a lifeline, and I glance at Kai over her head. Red rims the gray of his irises, a sure sign he is on his way to losing control. I can't imagine the emotions she is putting off that he's reading.

"You don't have to tell us this," I say to her, even as a nasty suspicion grows in my gut.

She takes another deep breath and shakes her head. "He raped and beat me every time I saw him," she says brokenly, crying so hard it's difficult to make out the words. "I was so strong at first, but it was too much. I couldn't do it anymore."

It's deathly silent in the room, the two predators gone supernaturally still, so much so even their chests have stopped moving. The only sounds are Ellis's sobs as she cries into my shirt. I struggle to wrap my mind around what she just told us. The torture she's been through. The suffering and abuse. This beautiful goddess with clipped wings and a broken soul. My mind empties like the tide receding from the shore and I just stare at Kai over the top of Ellis's head, at a loss for what to do.

Eventually, Kai breaks the silence. "Fuck!" He yells and throws his beer bottle. It shatters against the wall, beer and glass spraying everywhere.

Ellis jumps at the outburst and tightens her hold on my waist. The door slams behind Kai as he storms out of the room. I glance at Sterling, silently communicating with him to go check on Kai. As he walks through the door, I see the look on his face. He's as torn up at Ellis's story as the rest of us, and for some reason, he looks slightly guilty, too.

"Come on, love." I lead Ellis to the couch again and pull her into my lap.

She curls up tightly to me, and I hold her as her body shudders against mine. It's hard for me to act calm and collected with her, when on the inside, I'm a raging storm of anger. White hot fire burns through me, desperately seeking an outlet, and my magic is a wild torrent in my veins. I've met Samuel Morris a few times, never thought anything about him, except that he was stuck up Thomas Kennedy's ass. Now, I want to tear him limb from limb for what he did to Ellis. Her dad, too. I don't want to ask her, but I don't doubt her dad knew what was happening and did nothing to stop it.

Fuck. How could anybody treat someone that way? How could a father let his child go through that, over and over? I realize I'm squeezing Ellis too tightly and loosen my grip. My body trembles with the need to protect her. The urge to tuck her away from the world and do whatever I can to make her happy is so strong it's impossible to fight.

When she runs out of tears, I lean back and look at her. Her face is splotchy, her eyes are swollen and red, and exhaustion lines her features, but she's still beautiful.

"What can I do?" I ask, needing to do something to help her. "What do you need?"

"I want to talk to my friend, Allie. I need to talk to her, but

Malakai didn't let me bring my phone." She hiccups and wipes her hand over her face to dry her tears.

I dig my phone out of my pocket and hand it to her. "Use mine." I gently lift her from my lap and stand before placing her back on the couch. "I'll give you some privacy."

She looks up at me with wide eyes, panic clearly written on her face.

"I'm not leaving. I'll just be over there." I point to the shelves on the other side of the room and she nods.

It's easy to tune out her conversation since I don't have the supernatural hearing Kai and Sterling do. I browse the books on the shelves, not really seeing the titles, while I keep one eye on Ellis. She's crying again; I see her wiping her eyes. Each one is like a brand on my soul, painful and scarring. Why does seeing her upset hurt me so much?

When Kai and Sterling return, I wave them over so they don't interrupt her. "You good?" I ask Kai.

"Yeah, sorry." He rolls his shoulders like he's trying to ease his stress. "I don't know why that hit me so hard."

"I think it hit all of us pretty hard." Sterling stares at Ellis across the room.

"This changed everything, didn't it?" Kai asks, quietly.

Sterling and I nod. I cross my arms over my chest and say, "Yeah, I think it did."

"This isn't just for fun or training anymore. We have to keep her safe. We can't let Sam get his hands on her ..." Kai pauses before adding, "or anyone else." He glances at me. "Is this going to impact your job? I don't want you to get involved in this if it does."

I shrug my shoulders. "I don't think I have a choice."

"What about your mom and sister?" he asks.

Fear hits my system like a freight train. Fuck, I didn't think about that. I take a deep breath and run my hand down my face. "I don't know," I say honestly. "I'll have to play it by ear. But I can't walk away now."

Kai nods in understanding. "Okay, but if you need to step back, do it. Don't risk them."

I appreciate his words, but they give me no comfort. How the hell do I choose between my family or Ellis? It should be an easy choice. My family should always come before someone I just met, but I can't bring myself to say the words. It feels wrong, making my skin itch just thinking about it.

"Cade, can you lay some extra wards in my room?" Kai asks. "No more staying in the library. I want her to be comfortable here."

I nod and glance at Ellis. She's smiling through her tears, soft laughter filtering through the silence to us. I guess that is the magic of a best friend. I glance at mine and think they would be the only ones to pull me out of something dark like that. In fact, they have done it in the past. I look at Ellis again, and think maybe I'll be able to add someone else to that list, too.

ELLIS

I can't believe I just told three strangers about my life. I've never even really told Allie everything. She just assumed and I never confirmed or denied her suspicions. But tonight, I just spilled it all. I couldn't stop once I started. It was like someone reached inside of me and grabbed all that ugliness and pulled it out. If I'm being honest, I feel a little lighter having shared one of the darkest secrets of my life.

There's something about Cade that I find comforting. I don't really know him, but I feel safe with him near. And Malakai and Sterling have had plenty of opportunities to hurt me but they haven't. As hard as it is for me, I think I may be able to trust them. I sure as hell hope I can, after everything I shared with them.

Being able to talk to Allie helped lift my spirits as well. Hearing her voice and letting her know I'm safe-ish took a load off me. I can always count on her to make me laugh, even in the middle of a crisis.

As soon as I set Cade's phone on the coffee table, all three guys come back to the sitting area. Malakai kneels in front of me and places his hands on my thighs. Red rims the pupils of his gray irises, and his black lashes fan across his pale cheekbones as he closes his eyes.

His voice is low and soothing when he speaks. "I know you don't trust us, and you have no reason to, but I will say it as many times as I need to until you believe me."

He opens his eyes, and I suck in a breath. Something travels through my body, something I can't explain. It's a subtle warmth spreading from my chest outward, but goosebumps break out on my arms and legs, and I lean forward without realizing I even moved.

"I will never hurt you," Malakai continues. "The three of us will never hurt you. We are going to do everything we can to keep you safe."

Swallowing thickly, I nod my head. I believe him. There is sincerity in his gaze and truth ringing in his words. Maybe I'll regret it later, but I'm running out of options. I need something or someone to hold on to. So far, they have kept me safe and treated me well. I have to believe they will keep doing that. If Sam is really taking part in this contest, having these guys as my champions might be the only thing that saves me.

Malakai stays kneeling in front of me for a moment longer, our gazes locked on each other, before he gently squeezes my thighs and stands. "Obviously, Sam will be our biggest threat. Anyone else on that list we need to prepare for?" Malakai asks Sterling as he reclaims his spot on the other end of the couch.

Cade sits next to me, and I lean into him. It's a pull in my middle that makes me do it. Nerves flutter in my belly, but I tell myself I can always move away if I need to. His arm comes around me immediately, and those butterflies return.

"A few could be problematic," Sterling says, running his fingers through his tangled hair. "Uriah and Josh are both powerful shifters; panther and wolf. Carson is ... well, you know." He shrugs and falls silent.

"Carson is a dick. I want to rip his fangs out every time he opens his damn mouth," Malakai growls.

I try to stay awake as the guys continue talking strategy. I really do. But the events of the past day and night are catching up with me, not to mention how emotionally draining it was to share my story. My eyelids get heavy and each blink takes longer for me to open them again. Cade is like a warm blanket wrapped around me, further lulling me to sleep. I can't remember the last time I felt relaxed in someone's arms. His scent, like cedar and lilac, settles my nerves, and it doesn't take long before I fall asleep.

———

Quiet voices wake me. I stretch and quickly realize I am not on the couch I fell asleep on. Panic sends me bolting upright. Black sheets pool around my waist and I almost knock heads with Cade, who leans back with wide eyes.

"Whoa," he says gently. "It's okay. We moved you to Kai's room. Figured the bed was more comfortable than that couch."

Glancing around calms my heart's frantic rhythm in my chest. I recognize the room from when Cade brought me here to shower. It's minimally furnished with a couple of black leather chairs, a small cart with bottles of alcohol, a window seat, and the enormous bed I'm currently laying in. The bed. I almost groan at how comfortable it is. Like sleeping on a cloud. I run my hands over the black silk sheets and it's like my hands are skimming over water.

A silvery moon glows in the dark sky behind Malakai sitting on the window seat. It gilds his black hair and makes the dark strands shimmer. Either I haven't slept long, or slept through the day into the next night.

I brush my wayward curls out of my face and glance at Cade. "What time is it?"

He gives me his classic sweet smile. "It's almost 9:30. You slept all day."

I guess it doesn't really surprise me. The past couple of days and nights have taken a toll on me. And some part of me must have recognized the safety offered by these guys, because it feels like the first full night's sleep I've had in years. Even my own bed in my own home was never truly safe. But I'm more rested and ready to face whatever challenges await us.

"Any news on the first challenge or anything to do with the contest?" I ask.

Both guys shake their heads, and I realize Sterling isn't here.

"Rumor is the email will go out around 10:00 tonight," Malakai says.

When I look at him, I fall away. Time seems to stop while we stare at each other. His black hair is long on top and styled in messy perfection. Red still rims his pupils, just the barest tint encroaching on the gray. In the window seat, with the moonlight shining down on his pale skin, he looks like he's carved from marble. My heart flutters in my chest and my breath catches at the sensation. Or rather, it catches because of the reason my heart reacted that way: the sexy vampire currently giving me bedroom eyes.

Malakai's eyelids lower and he smiles at me. It's not a sweet smile like one of Cade's. It's dark, silken, and bears the promise of pleasure edged with the slightest bit of pain. *Oh shit. I forgot.* He's an empath and can totally read what I'm feeling right now.

A slight flutter of wings in my belly makes me look away. What am I doing? I kissed Cade the other night. And I'm not interested in any kind of relationship, especially not with one of these three guys.

Cade takes my hand and rubs circles on the inside of my wrist with his thumb. Goosebumps spread across my arms at the sensation. A sensation that doesn't make me nervous. I marvel at the lack of fear. In fact, I kind of want more. And that is terrifying. What is going on with me? Why am I not crawling out of my skin? How can I possibly want more when the very thought usually makes me want to puke up my guts?

"Kai and I were just talking about the best way to keep you safe during the challenges," Cade says, oblivious to my inner turmoil. "One of us will stay with Kai while he does the challenge, and the other will stay here with you. We will keep our phones on us, and we have a system in place that I created where we can immediately let the others know if we're in danger. We'll be using that as well."

I nod, relieved I'll be able to stay here and not have to see Sam. And it's a relief to know I won't be alone. I wouldn't put it past Sam to use the opportunity to abduct me.

The door to Kai's room opens and Sterling walks in with his hair loose around his head in a silver tangle. He's shirtless, and his pants hang indecently low around his waist. All that tan muscle is like a magnet for my eyes. I latch onto the sight and my gaze travels south to that deliciously deep V pointing the way to what I know he's hiding behind those sweats.

The bed dips as Cade leans closer to me. He runs his thumb under my lower lip and whispers in my ear, "You're drooling again, love."

I snap my gaze away from Sterling, who is now smirking, his ego getting an extra boost I'm sure it doesn't need. Without thinking, my eyes land on Malakai. I swallow roughly when I see his hooded stare on me. Heat creeps up my chest and neck, and I look down at my lap, only to realize one of my hands is still clasped in Cade's grasp. I take a shuddering breath and try to force away all thoughts from the three gorgeous guys in the room, but I'm having a hard time ignoring the mix of masculine scents and the testosterone in the air.

What the hell is happening? The soft throbbing in my core is not something I've felt in a very long time. But, I can't be turned on. I don't think my body even knows what that means anymore. The idea of a man touching me, in any way, only brings me fear. So where is that fear now? Why am I suddenly feeling the desire to squeeze my legs together to ease the growing ache between them? I'm saved from my confusing mix of emotions when Malakai's phone beeps.

"Email," he says. "Looks like it was sent out early." His eyes move side to side as he reads the details of the first challenge. A frown forms and a crease appears between his brows. "Fuck. Didn't plan on that."

"What's up?" Sterling asks, sitting in one of the black chairs, legs spread and looking entirely too inviting.

"The first challenge is an extreme obstacle course taking place the entire length of the city, complete with assassins." He looks up at the guys with a wicked grin. "No big deal. However, it says Ellis is to be present for each challenge. In order to prove a worthy husband, the contestants must, and I quote, 'maintain their possession of her' while completing the challenges. If you can't do both, you are not worthy of her." He snorts at that last bit.

The blood drains from my face. I won't be able to stay safe here. Instead, I'll be front and center where anyone can grab me. Where Sam can grab me. I don't think I can handle seeing him without having a full-blown panic attack. Just thinking about it makes my heart pound and my breath come faster.

Cade's hand tightens on mine. "This is still okay," he says, his violet eyes pinning me to the spot. "It's not ideal, but we can still make it work. Kai is the only one who has to compete in the challenge. Sterling and I can stay with you on the sidelines. We'll keep you safe, Ellis. This changes nothing."

"He's right," Sterling says, rubbing a hand down his face. "Having two sets of eyes on you is better than one. Obviously, I would feel better if you weren't there, but we don't have a choice. We'll adjust our plans accordingly."

I nod my head. There is nothing else to do. We don't get a choice in this matter, so I just have to roll with it. I have to trust that these guys will keep me safe. Can I do that? Can I let myself trust them?

"Do you have any weapons I could borrow?" I ask, looking at each guy in turn.

All three of them look at me with wide eyes. Malakai's grin spreads displaying the tips of his fangs, Sterling pulls his lower lip between his teeth, and Cade's gaze is pure desire as it roams over my face.

"What weapons are you good with, love?" Cade asks, his voice low and gravelly. "We already know you can throw a punch."

Sterling grunts, and I feel an ounce of shame for that punch. "Any, really," I reply. "Guns and knives. I've trained with a lot of weapons at the gym."

At first, silence meets my answer, then Sterling groans a barely audible, "Fuuck, that's hot."

Malakai laughs and says, "Then guns and knives you will get."

"When does this challenge take place?" Cade asks.

Malakai looks at his phone and curses. "Tomorrow morning, 10:00."

"Well, that sucks," Cade says. "But you've trained for this. You can handle the sun long enough to complete this challenge."

Malakai agrees. "Okay. We have some time to rest and prepare. Sterling, my dad requested a meeting with us."

Sterling sighs, but he stands, and he and Malakai leave to take care of business with Malakai's dad.

"You okay?" Cade asks me after they leave.

"I don't really have much of a choice but to be okay." I refuse to meet his eyes. If I do he'll see my answer for the lie it is.

"Not true," he says. "It's okay to not be okay. This is not an ideal situation."

He scoots closer to me and places his free hand on my cheek, turning my head so I'm looking at him. In the lamplight, his purple eyes glitter, and my stomach flip-flops at the intensity of his gaze and his touch on my cheek. I welcome it. For the first time in years, I welcome a man's touch.

"I won't let anything happen to you," he whispers.

"Why?" I ask, desperate for answers. "Why promise to keep me safe? It would be easier and safer for you guys to just wash your hands of this whole thing."

He shrugs one shoulder, keeping his hand on my cheek. "We're not quitters. And we would never leave someone in a situation like this when we can help. Especially not you."

I want to ask 'why' again. Why do they care so much about

someone they don't even know? But my questions are forgotten as Cade leans in and presses his lips against mine. It's just as gentle of a kiss as the first one we shared, and just as life altering. I'm torn in two different directions: pull away or lean in. Tell him to stop or ask for more. I want more, I really do, but I'm terrified. What if it drags up memories I want to forget? What if I can't get past the dread and fear?

He pulls back and his eyes search mine. "I'm sorry. I shouldn't have done that."

"Don't be sorry," I whisper. "I ..." I can't continue. The words get stuck in my throat. I want to ask him to kiss me again, but how do I tell him the thought of a man touching me is paralyzing?

"Ellis," he whispers back. His gaze seems to peer directly into my soul. It's so intense it makes me feel as if I'm sitting naked before him. "When was the last time someone touched you without hurting you?"

I can't answer him. The words are too heavy to drag forth, and I'm scared I'll start crying if I force them out. I don't want to cry right now. The bed dips as he shifts so he's facing me fully. With slow and controlled movements, he lifts his other hand to frame my face in his strong, but gentle, grasp, and he leans closer.

"Let me make you feel good." He rasps, his gaze searching mine. "Please, Ellis. Let me do that for you. I want ..."

I'm positive I'm not breathing. How could I be when he asks me with such desire burning in his violet eyes and ringing in his words? It's almost contagious. The butterflies swoop low in my stomach and the throbbing builds in my core.

I suck in a shuddering breath, and his scent hits me. Lilacs and cedar, nothing like sandalwood. Something in me calms at the realization. I stare into his eyes and see nothing but his pleading with me to trust him. Jerkily, I nod my head, fighting the urge to run.

His shoulders lose their tension, and one hand slides from my cheek into my hair to cup the back of my neck. My heart is pounding so fast I'm positive it's going to beat right out of my chest as he leans forward, his breath fanning across my mouth.

"Just say the word, Ellis. Tell me to stop, and I will." His lips are inches from mine as he speaks. "No questions asked."

I give another jerky nod, and that's all he needs to close the distance between us. The kiss rings throughout my entire body. My skin tingles. My heart races. The butterflies in my stomach erupt into furious flight. Fire flares to life inside me, heating me and making me melt under Cade's touch.

He pulls away, eyes glowing and swirling with his magic. "Was that okay?" he breathes.

I swallow. Was it okay? My body is telling me yes, and it wants more. My brain is still not sure about all of it. "Yes?" I reply.

He smiles. I really fucking love that smile. It's so sweet and gentle, and it puts me at ease.

"Yes," I say more confidently.

"Can I ... can I kiss you again?"

This time, I don't hesitate. "Yes."

ELLIS

THIS KISS IS STILL GENTLE, BUT THERE IS SOMETHING more to it. More need. More desire. I don't realize my hand has moved until the fabric of his shirt is clenched in my fist. The hand in my hair gently tugs the strands and tips my head back as Cade deepens the kiss. His lips part mine, and his tongue slides in to brush against my own. Those butterflies I thought had died come to life in full force. Swooping and fluttering so fiercely my whole body tingles.

When I gasp against his mouth, he starts to pull away. But I don't want him to stop. I want to drown in him. So, I wrap my arms around his neck and keep him there, desperately hoping he can wash away all the pain and fear I live with every day of my life.

His free hand settles on my waist, and a small noise climbs up my throat as his hand slips under my shirt. His skin against mine, his calluses scraping against my flesh, is too all-encompassing. My body is burning. My heart beats a frantic rhythm, and my brain tries to keep up with what is happening. Someone is touching me and it doesn't hurt. No, not just someone. Cade. Cade is touching me, and I love the way he makes every nerve in my body light up.

He tastes like mint, and his scent is all around me. I'm dizzy from all the sensations—sensations I haven't experienced in so long. A gentle touch, a burning kiss. It suddenly isn't enough.

"Fuck," he mutters against my mouth before pulling away. "Is this too much? Do you want me to stop?"

He's breathing as fast as I am. Just under my bra, his thumb rubs back and forth on my ribs, and my mouth answers his question before I even have time to think about it.

"Don't stop," I breathe.

Those violet eyes flare with heat and he gently pushes me down on the bed, his gaze never leaving mine. When he positions himself so he's straddling my hips, fear plows through the haze of lust he'd built in me. Ice floods my veins, extinguishing the fire, and I freeze. It's no longer Cade sitting over me. My nightmares become reality, and it's Sam staring back at me, pushing me into the bed before he forces himself on me. I can't breathe, each breath gets stuck in my chest. I can't move. All I can do is lay under him, frozen in terror.

Cade pulls back. "Hey," he whispers. "Don't do that. Don't go there. Stay with me. " He brushes hair from my forehead and searches my eyes.

There is no way I can mistake those purple eyes for the muddy green ones that haunt my nightmares. His touch remains gentle, soft strokes on my skin that creates goosebumps wherever he touches. I blink, clearing the nightmare from my mind.

"That's right, love," Cade breathes. "It's me. I won't hurt you."

His words soothe some of my fear. I swallow and nod my head. When was the last time I ever felt anything good? Determination sweeps through me. No more. I won't let Sam rule my life anymore. Forcing the remaining fear aside, I try to bring back all the things Cade made me feel.

"Do you want me to stop?" he asks gently.

"No," I whisper, shaking my head vehemently.

He slowly leans down, giving me time to change my mind. I

don't. He kisses me again, drugging me into the euphoria I so desperately want.

"Tell me if you want me to stop," he says with his mouth hovering over mine between kisses.

Shivers travel over my body as his voice, husky and breathless, settles along my skin. He kisses me again, but doesn't linger on my lips. He moves to my jaw and peppers kisses along my neck. His thumb finds my nipple and rubs it through my bra. It's pure instinct when I whimper and arch my back, seeking more contact.

One corner of his mouth pulls up in a smirk as he pinches the peak between his thumb and middle finger.

"Fuck, Cade," I say breathlessly, my chest rising and falling as I gasp for air. My hands grapple with the sheets and I ball them in my fists.

"You like that?" he says, his face buried in my neck.

I can't answer his question, especially as his mouth closes over my other nipple through my shirt. The heat from his mouth soaks through the fabric, and his teeth gently bite down. My hands land on his head, and my fingers tangle in his hair. It feels so fucking good, and the only sound I can make is a strange mewling noise.

Cade lifts his gaze, desire glazing his eyes. "Do you want me to keep going, love?"

"Yes. Please, yes, yes." I barely recognize my own voice. It's so breathy and husky. But I need him to continue. There's an ache building between my legs. An ache I haven't felt in such a long time. It's foreign and exciting, and I need him to keep fanning the flames.

He moves his hand down my abdomen. Nerves ignite, but they aren't entirely unwelcome. It's a mix between uncertainty and excitement. His fingers tease the skin above my leggings with soft, gentle brushes back and forth. The desperation to feel his touch lower is driving my hips up, and I'm not even ashamed. I need this. I *want* this.

Instead of diving into my leggings, he runs a finger down my center over the leggings. It's not enough pressure. He's so close to where I need him to touch, but he's holding back. The teasing drives another whimper from me.

"So fucking wet, I can feel it through the leggings." Cade's eyes glitter and he smiles seductively.

He bites my nipple again, harder this time, and I moan. The whisper of pain shoots straight to my core and my inner muscles clench around nothing. My body lifts off the bed, begging for him to continue.

Just as he hooks a finger under the top of my leggings, the door opens. We both whip our heads in that direction, breathing as if we'd just run miles, only to see Malakai saunter in. He pauses as his gaze roams over the scene on his bed and a slow grin spreads across his face. *Oh gods.* My cheeks heat, and I try to wiggle my way out from under Cade.

"Don't stop on my account," Malakai drawls, a soft growl lacing his words.

"I think he wants us to put on a show, love," Cade says as he returns his attention to me. "What do you say? Should we keep going?"

Let him watch? My gaze travels over Malakai's body and lands on his hips, where his erection is tenting the front of his sweatpants. He runs a tattooed hand down his bare chest—when did he lose his shirt?— and grabs himself through his pants. A quiet moan leaves his lips, and the sound settles low in my gut, making more liquid heat pool between my legs. Do I want him to watch? Do I want Cade to continue?

I clench my thighs together, and the slight pressure is good. So good. But it's not enough.

"Keep going," I rasp, and the heat in my cheeks fans higher.

Cade laughs darkly and he slowly teases my pants and underwear down my hips. In seconds, I'm laying on a bed with no pants and a man straddling my legs. Too exposed. I'm way too exposed. My heart stutters in my chest and I swear the world starts spinning. When his gaze travels over my torso and down to my pussy, I instinctively try to cross my legs.

He stops me with his hands on my thighs. "Don't do that." His words are low and filled with lust. "Don't hide yourself. You are fucking perfect."

Looking into his eyes, I remind myself who I'm with. Cade. This is Cade and he's done nothing to hurt me. In fact, he's done the exact opposite. He's made me experience something I haven't in years. I don't want him to stop. *I want to keep feeling.*

I relax my body as much as I can, and Cade takes that as a sign to keep going. Slowly, he trails his fingers along the inside of my thigh. It's terrifying and exciting all at once. The closer his fingers get to my center, the more the anticipation builds. My legs are trembling, and my heart is pounding in my chest when he finally slides a finger through my folds. His touch is so different from Sam's. He's gentle while still giving enough pressure to turn me on. Any uneasiness I may have had disappears as he pushes one finger inside me.

My head falls back on the pillows and I breathe through the pleasure Cade is giving me. The wet sound of his finger sliding in and out is erotic as fuck. I never got wet for Sam. He always had to use lube. In the past two years, I don't think I've ever been wet. I appreciated looking at guys, but I would never let myself feel anything deeper. It was always a moot point.

But this ... this is pure pleasure.

My gaze slides to the right, toward Malakai. For a moment, I tense, unsure how I should feel about someone watching this, but that fear quickly evaporates. Sitting in a chair with pants pulled down to his thighs, Malakai's gaze is glued to Cade's finger and what he's doing to me. My inner muscles clench at the sight of him lazily stroking up and down his cock, the tip glistening in the lamplight. It's surreal to think these guys are turned on by me, and that realization eases my discomfort at having someone watch.

Cade follows my gaze, and he smiles darkly. "I think Kai is enjoying this. How about you, love? Are you enjoying it?" He punctuates his question by adding a second finger.

My hips lift, desperate to meet his thrusting fingers. "Yes," I breathe. "Please, Cade. Please don't stop." I need him to keep going.

It's been forever since I've actually enjoyed any kind of pleasure. I never even touched myself. It was always too much of a trigger. Now, there is an ache between my legs that I need taken care of. Cade has pulled me from my fear, at least for this moment, and given me everything I've ever needed.

"I like when you beg, Ellis."

I moan again when he says my name, all deep and throaty like that. With my eyes squeezed shut, I'm not prepared when he removes his fingers just before he licks up my center, all the way to my clit. Lightning shoots through my veins, and I grab Cade's head on instinct, trying to push him harder against me.

"Uh uh, I'm in charge here," he says, words muffled with his face buried between my legs.

Looking down and seeing his head between my thighs, violet eyes meeting mine, is an image I'm not soon to forget. He smirks, like he knows exactly what thought just went through my head. With a roguish wink, he goes back to work. Licking and sucking and lapping at me like a starving man.

"You taste divine, love," he growls.

I'm writhing on the bed and my thighs are quivering when I glance at Malakai and see him stroking the length of his cock, twisting his wrist at the tip. The light catches the underside of his dick, and I realize he has piercings all along the length. Holy shit. What would that feel like inside me?

There is nothing lazy about Malakai's movements now. His gaze is locked on what Cade is doing with his mouth, and he reaches between his legs with his free hand and grips his balls. With a groan, he comes all over his chest, his hand working his cock until there is nothing left.

The sight pushes me to the edge, and Cade's tongue rubbing my clit throws me over. There is no room in my head for anything except the pleasure roaring through my body. I toss my head back and squeeze Cade's head between my shaking thighs as I come. He draws every last rolling wave of ecstasy out of me. When I eventually still, my breathing uneven, he looks at me with his mouth and chin glistening with my orgasm. His eyes are shining so brightly, with so much emotion, and it hits me right in the chest.

"That was so fucking hot," Malakai groans.

I'm not going to lie, I think I agree. I've never done something like this with an audience. And watching him watch me, seeing how turned on he was? It was a powerful feeling. One I've never felt before. I'm so weightless, my mind so happily dazed, the fact I just had an orgasm for the first time in a really long time barely registers. I let someone touch me, and instead of pain, my body felt immense pleasure. The thought is enough to pull me out of my post-orgasm bliss.

Cade crawls up my body and kisses me deeply, and I can taste myself on his lips. It's hotter than I thought it would be. Thinking I need to do something for the hardness currently pushing against my thigh, I reach down to grab Cade but he stops me with a gentle grip on my wrist.

"This was about you, love," he says, brushing a sweaty curl from my forehead.

"But what about you?" I ask, suddenly unsure. Sex has always been about the other person. Sam couldn't have cared less about my pleasure. As long as he got off, he was happy. If I cried, it only made him happier.

Cade gives me a wicked grin and turns to look at Malakai. "Kai can take care of me. Right?"

"Fuck." Malakai jumps up and prowls to the bed. "Yeah, I can."

Cade lays down next to me and I watch in fascination as Malakai crawls up the bed to hover over Cade. He isn't going to do what I think he is, is he? Yep, he sure is. Malakai leans down and roughly kisses Cade. As their tongues clash, Cade grabs Malakai's hair and tugs. The deep groan that Malakai emits makes me squeeze my legs together, somehow already turning me on again.

Malakai breaks away and glances at me with a wicked look. "I can taste you on his tongue." He licks his lips and smiles. "Fucking delicious."

My mouth dries out at his words. Why was that so hot? Malakai tugs Cade's sweatpants down, freeing his rock hard erection. What is it with these guys and having such gloriously thick cocks? I bite my lip as Malakai wraps his hand around Cade's dick and slowly pumps up and down.

Cade leans his head back against the pillows and closes his eyes. My eyes are glued to Malakai as he licks up the length of Cade's cock. It twitches, and Malakai smirks, his eyes never leaving mine. I'm helpless to break eye contact as Malakai opens his mouth and sucks Cade's length as deep as he can go.

"Fuck," Cade groans and lifts his hips, seeking more contact.

Malakai places a hand on Cade's lower belly to hold him in place. He picks up his pace, licking and sucking, taking Cade until he is gagging. All the while, Malakai's eyes never leave mine. It's so fucking hot to watch and my belly flutters.

Malakai releases Cade long enough to say, "I think she enjoys watching me suck your dick, Cade."

Cade opens his eyes and looks at me through his hooded lids. Even with Malakai giving him a blow job, he gives me the sweetest smile. "Kiss me?"

My body comes to life with those words. The way he kisses me like I'm precious to him, like he's dying and only I can give him life—it's addicting. So I push myself up onto my elbow and lean over him, my hand resting on his chest. It amazes me how easily I let myself touch him.

He grins eagerly. "We could have a lot of fun with this," he says, then pulls me down and kisses me.

He kisses me until we both are starved for oxygen, and he only pulls away to throw his head back as he comes. I bite my lip and watch him, his body tensing and moving with each wave. It's beautiful and sexy at the same time, and it makes my heart do a weird thump in my chest.

Malakai sucks every last drop from Cade before lifting his head with a grin. "So much fucking fun."

Cade tucks himself back into his sweatpants and tugs me down until my head is resting on his heaving chest. "Was that okay?" he asks, lazily drawing random patterns on my arm with his finger.

I bury my face in his shirt, inhaling his scent, and smile. "It was more than okay."

"As amazing as all that was, we need to get moving. We have a challenge to prepare for." Malakai grins at us and winks before heading for the door. "Meet in the library in ten minutes."

Cade rubs my back in gentle circles. "Are you sure that was okay?"

"Thank you," I say, and have to swallow. My throat is tight and the words hurt as I force them out. Not because I'm not thankful. Not because I don't want to thank him. They hurt because I have to say them in the first place.

Sam took so much from me. My trust. My pleasure. My ability to feel safe in my own skin. Tonight, Cade gave a little bit of that back to me. I'm not sure I'll ever be able to thank him enough for that.

"Don't thank me, love. It was my pleasure." He grins. "Literally." His grin turns into that sweet smile I can't get enough of. "I feel like I should be thanking you. For trusting me, for letting me do that. I hope we can do it again sometime."

I duck my head, and whisper, "I'd like that."

MALAKAI

IN THE PARKING LOT BEHIND THE KENNEDY BUILDING, the four of us gather around Sterling's Land Rover. I tell myself I'm just making sure everything is secured properly, as I approach Ellis and check the holster at her back where her gun is resting. I'm not doing it to get my hands on her, not at all.

She looks like she was made for us, wearing black leggings and a tank top. Somewhere Sterling found her a pair of black knee-high boots, and I have to adjust myself when she isn't looking. Her ensemble is topped off with a black leather jacket. A few loose curls frame her face, having already escaped the braid she attempted to tame her hair into. The image she paints is of a sexy avenging angel, and it makes me want to get her on the back of my bike. How fucking hot would it be to have her body pressed against mine as we speed through the city? Damn. I really need to make that happen.

I don't need to reach deep into my power to feel her nerves and fear. It washes over me like a current, electrical pulses I can't tune out like I usually do. She shifts back and forth on her feet, her gaze darting around the parking lot, never settling on one thing for longer than a second.

I grasp her hand in mine, her fingers trembling slightly, and wait for her to look at me. "Everything is going to be fine. Sterling and Cade won't let anything happen to you."

Cade wraps an arm around her shoulders and gives her a squeeze. She doesn't look convinced, but she nods anyway.

I tug on my black gloves and adjust the hood of my jacket. With the hood, gloves, and a pair of sunglasses, there is minimal sun that can reach my skin. The whole vampires can't go out in the light theory is a bunch of shit. We can and we do. It won't kill us immediately, but it also isn't comfortable. Typically, we stick to the nighttime hours, like the vampires in the stories.

If we have to go out during the day, wearing long sleeves and hoods provides a layer of protection against the energy drain of the sun. That's what happens when we're exposed to direct sunlight. It drains our energy. One massive energy suck. If we stay in the sun for too long, we will die. But it would take hours.

I have extensively trained my body in direct sunlight. As a result, I have built up a tolerance to the sun that most vampires don't have. I'm counting on that during this contest to give me a leg up against the other vampires and to let other non-vamps think it's a weakness they can use against me.

"Everyone ready?" Sterling asks, rolling his shoulders and stretching his neck.

The three of us—Sterling, Cade, and I—exchange a look, a silent conversation passing between us, reminding ourselves what's at stake. Something shifted for all three of us after her admission of what Sam has done to her. This is no longer just a fun training exercise. We all agree, our priority now is to keep Ellis safe. The fierceness of that conviction makes me swallow. I shouldn't feel so strongly about her when I barely know her, but the incessant tugging in my gut makes it impossible to ignore. And I won't even be able to help protect her as I complete the challenge. But I trust these guys with my life, so I know I can trust her life with them as well.

As we make our way around the building, I'm assaulted by emotions. It seems like the entire city has turned up to watch this, and the onslaught of their excitement slams against my mental barriers, even though I've had a lot of practice shutting it down. I have to grit my teeth as I fortify my mental shields. It disgusts me. Did anyone even think about Ellis and how all of this affects her?

The rest of the contestants gather at the bottom of the steps of the Kennedy building. I spot Sam and Ellis's dad immediately, both of them radiating a commanding presence that's impossible to ignore. Ellis's fear scrapes against my mind. It's so strong I can feel it amid all the other emotions, and I'm amazed she's still standing. I glance at her, and a mixture of anger and sadness wash through me. No one should have to go through what she did, and the fact that it was *her,* my Ellis, makes it so much worse. Ignoring the wave of shock that pauses me in my tracks at the thought of Ellis being mine, I step toward her. With her face drained of color and slight tremors vibrating her body, she looks utterly petrified.

I grasp her face in my hands, forcing her gaze away from her tormentors. "Ellis, look at me."

"Don't let them take me," she pleads, fingers gripping my shirt tightly enough to leave wrinkles. Her voice is a hoarse whisper, her eyes wild and fear-filled.

The words cut through me. The desperation and terror like a knife sharp enough to slice to the bone, and I swear my heart bleeds from them. Cade tightens his arm around her shoulders, tugging her closer.

Letting a tiny bit of my power rise to the surface, I make sure she's looking in my eyes as I say, "Relax, Ellis. You are safe with Sterling and Cade." I know my eyes are glowing. They're reflected in hers.

Using my compulsion is not something I enjoy doing. I don't believe people should be forced into doing things against their will. But her fear is overpowering her. She needs to stay focused and alert, and the terror is impeding her ability to do so. Her shoulders lose some of their tension, and I know my compulsion hit the mark.

An official-looking judge approaches and hands me a map of

the city. "The course will take place in the circled area," he says. "Expect any kind of challenges and tests during the course. There are medics stationed throughout, however, they will only treat life-threatening injuries until you make it through to the other side." His gaze lands over my shoulder on Ellis. "When it comes to Ms. Kennedy, everything is fair game. If someone takes her while you're on the course, it will be your responsibility to get her back. Whoever has possession of her at the end of the third challenge will be awarded her hand in marriage."

A rumbling growl from my left side tells me Sterling's wolf is making his presence known. I second his feelings. Ellis isn't a possession. This entire situation is seriously fucked up.

The judge looks slightly uncomfortable, and I don't blame him. I know without looking at Sterling that his ice-blue eyes are glowing, and he's staring at the judge like an animal with its prey in sight.

I nod acknowledgement and he swiftly walks away. Before I can even blink, I notice Thomas Kennedy approaching. Ellis's apprehension grows behind me.

"Ellis," the man says, ignoring the three predators surrounding her. "I hope you keep your eyes open during all of this. I would hate for something to happen to you." His tone is oily and it's obvious he truly doesn't care what happens to her.

Sterling growls again. "Is that a threat?" His words are almost impossible to make out around his rumbling voice.

Thomas slides his gaze to Sterling and his lip curls in disgust. "No. Simply a warning."

Ellis says nothing, but her hands wrap around my bicep, squeezing tightly.

"What the fuck is wrong with you?" I ask, bewildered that a father could so nonchalantly threaten his daughter's life.

He narrows his eyes on me. "Enjoy your time with my daughter. It will be short-lived." His blue eyes sparkle with amusement. "Oh, yes. I forgot to mention. Sam misses you. He can't wait to win this contest with you in tow."

With a truly evil smile, Ellis's dad walks away. Red explodes in my vision and my fangs descend so quickly they slice through my lower lip. Through my rage, I dimly hear Cade turning to Ellis and speaking quietly to her, calming her growing fear. It's taking all of my self-control to not launch myself at Thomas Kennedy and draining him dry. Motherfucker.

"Contestants to the starting line." A booming voice over a speaker announces.

"You got this bro," Cade says as he steps into my line of sight. He wraps his hand around the back of my head and brings our foreheads together. "Be safe out there."

I nod against his forehead, running my tongue along my lower lip, licking away the blood there.

When Cade steps away, Sterling approaches. He grabs my shoulder in a bruising grip. "Don't worry about Ellis. Focus on yourself." He reminds me.

"Thanks." I shake out my arms and roll my head from side to side.

Adrenaline courses through my veins and I let the crowd's emotions filter through my mental shields to amp me up further. Before the guys can lead Ellis away, she tentatively approaches me.

She bites her lower lip, indecision flickering through her amber eyes as she looks up at me. I'm so tempted to tug that lip from between her teeth with my thumb, but I restrain myself and instead give her a reassuring smile. A small shiver runs over her as her gaze drops to my mouth, *my fangs*. As in tune as I am with her emotions now, it's easy for me to pick up on the desire winding through the fear and it settles low in my gut, enticing and delicious.

She takes a deep breath before standing on her toes and pressing her lips to my cheek. "Be careful, Malakai."

Her concern does something funny to me. It threatens to throw me off my game, so I give her a roguish wink and say, "Don't worry about me, baby girl. I'm Malakai *fucking* Thorne."

Her lips pull up in a small smile, remembering what she said when we first met not too long ago.

I'm grinning when Cade and Sterling pull her away to watch the start of the race. A voice booms over the speaker again, but I tune it out. I check my weapons to ensure everything is within reach. With my eyes closed, I sink into myself, to the place I fall before a mission. I detach from my conscience and let myself become someone I hate. Someone who doesn't give a fuck about life or death—mine or others.

I become the monster everyone believes me to be.

At the sound of the gun, the group of guys at the starting line take off. Everyone goes their own way, hoping to avoid the others. I hang back slightly and keep my eyes on Sam, not trusting the fucker not to do something to me or Ellis. Dammit, I need to push her out of my mind. She is a distraction that will cost me if I let my mind linger there.

I watch Sam disappear between two buildings across the street. With the skill of a predator, I scale the lowest building. At seven stories tall, I get a decent view of the city and the other contestants as they make their way through the course. There is no way I can keep to the rooftops, although that would be ideal. The buildings in general are too tall and it would take too long to climb each one.

Perched on the edge, I contemplate the best path that will get me to the end the quickest and with relatively minimal contact with others. In my mind, I picture the city laid out and I think I can keep to the roofs for a short time before the buildings get too tall. With this plan in mind, I stand and jump to the next building.

It's a couple stories taller than the one I'm on, and I have to grab the edge to pull myself up. Even my supernatural abilities can't make me jump that high over such a large distance. I continue across the roof, keeping my senses open to any dangers. It's not until I make the fourth jump to the fifth, and last, building that danger finds me.

Just as my feet hit the roof, a knife comes from nowhere and embeds into my left shoulder. Lightning shoots down my arm, spreading outward from the wound. Immediately, my fingers tingle and I know the blade must have hit a nerve.

"Fuck," I hiss as I grab the handle and yank it out. It burns like fire as it slides out with a wet sucking noise, and I grit my teeth at the onslaught of blood that dribbles from the wound. Ducking down to keep covered, I press my hand to the injury and will my abilities to kick in and speed up the healing. This is where being a mage with healing magic would come in handy.

I look around for any sign of my attacker, but all I see are empty windows in the taller buildings around mine. Cautiously, I scooch to the opposite side of the roof, keeping low and close to the short wall. From the direction the blade came and how it was stuck in my shoulder, the attacker had to have been in front of me and to my left. I crawl my way to the right side of the building, the side that faces Main Street. Not ideal, but better than going down the side in plain view of the dick who threw a knife at me.

I slip the blade between my teeth. The metallic taste of my own blood reminds me I haven't fed in a while. I purposely avoided it to give myself an edge during this challenge. A vampire on the verge of hunger is more dangerous than a well-fed one.

A quick glance over the edge tells me I can jump about halfway down and land in a window. From there, it's another jump to the ground. Across the street is an alley. It's too dark to see what's inside, but I'll risk it.

I move quickly to avoid being hit by another dagger and throw my legs over the ledge. Hanging on the side of the building, I check the distance to the window one last time before letting go. I mentally calculate my fall and grab onto the window ledge I was aiming for. The impact jars my shoulders, the injured one screaming in pain as my body jerks to stop.

"Fuck, shit, gods damn," I gasp through the fire burning in my shoulder.

I collect myself before letting go and dropping the rest of the way to the ground, landing in a crouch, my hips and knees popping at the contact. Jumping to my feet, I sprint across the street and into the alley.

Before I'm ten steps inside the dark cover between the buildings, a net of magic snares me around my legs and arms. I stop before I topple over, keeping my balance purely from my supernatural abilities. Running footsteps approaching the alley has me turning my head in that direction and I see a shifter approaching—a dagger matching the one that had embedded in my shoulder in his hand.

A scuff of a footfall in front of me whips my head forward, only to see Sam emerge from the depths of the alley.

Motherfucker.

Sam grins at me as he prowls forward. "That was too easy," he croons. "I'm a little disappointed. I thought for sure the mighty Malakai Thorne would be harder to take out, but I really shouldn't be too surprised." His hands hang loosely at his sides, his green magic sparking at his fingertips.

I give him a feral smile, making sure my fangs are visible. What I wouldn't give to rip out this fucker's throat. "Glad to disappoint." I'd bow, but his magic holding me in place prevents me from doing so. Instead, I nod my head and give him a wink. I glance behind me, keeping tabs on the shifter with the dagger. "Thanks for the blade," I say to him. "I was in the market for a new one."

His soft growl makes me chuckle. This is too much fun.

A secretive smile plays about Sam's lips. "You shouldn't be so cocky. Even if you crossed the finish line now, you wouldn't win. You'd be missing the key piece."

Dread forms like a lead ball in my stomach. The key piece. *Ellis.* What is he saying? I keep my cocksure smile in place, not giving him any sign of my worry. Shrugging my shoulders the best I can in his magic net, I say, "You couldn't keep her before. Why do you think you could keep her now?"

Sam's grin slips, and I see him for what he really is. The man who raped and abused Ellis. It's in his eyes and the lack of emotion in them. It's in his smile and the chilling curve of his lips. It's in the over inflated ego and lack of conscience. This man is a real monster.

My friends and I may get that label. We may do things that border the line between humanity and evil, but we're not monsters. Sam is. And if he somehow got his hands on Ellis again, it's time for me to go. As much as I want to stay and drain him of his blood, I need to move.

Fingering the rings on my thumb, I subtly twist one metal band until it clicks into place with another. A burst of energy erupts from the ring, interfering with Sam's magic, and giving me the opening I need to move.

"As pleasant as this has been, I have a challenge to win." I grin at Sam as I say, "See you on the other side."

I flip him off and jump, putting as much power as I can into it, and I'm barely able to grasp the edge of the six-story building next to me. Grunting, I pull myself up and dash across the roof, leaping to the next building as fast as I can.

Sam's curses and shouts follow me from below. "Motherfucker!" he yells. "Track him. Do not let him get away."

Sam's insistence on catching me gives me hope. If he had Ellis, there is no way he would waste time hunting me down. If he's trying so hard to stop me, it has to mean he's trying to keep me from crossing the finish line and winning this first challenge. Unfortunately, that also means I now have to evade him and his shifter friend.

I crouch low on the roof, listening to their footsteps and angry muttering below me. Different plans form in my mind as I try to figure out the best course of action. Jumping from roof to roof is too noticeable. My best chance is to get back on the ground and in the shadows. But how to get there?

I spot a random brick on the roof, and an idea comes to me. Snagging it in my gloved hand, I carefully peer over the edge. Both Sam and the shifter are looking away. Perfect. I throw the brick with all my strength, aiming for the roof across the street. It lands with a thud and draws both of their attention away from me and the building I'm on. As they rush to the other building, I run to the other side of the roof and throw myself over the edge.

It's a rough landing, the jump higher than I should have made. It's like being hit by a freight train, and as the impact reverberates through me, I curse. *Fucking hell*, I'll be feeling that later, fast healing or not. Forcing myself from my crouch with gritted teeth, I peer around the corner before running for the next. I continue this way for three blocks, with no sign of Sam, or anyone else for that matter. It's not until I slip into an alley that I run into more trouble.

My senses pick up on movement, and I skid to a stop a second before a blade flies past my head and clatters against the stone wall. Chest heaving, I glance around and spot a man standing in the shadows, dressed in all black with a hood casting his face in darkness. Black blades, strapped to every inch of his body, glint the sunlight streaming between the buildings. Assassin. Excitement bubbles up in me, my adrenaline kicking into high gear. Sam was a worthy appointment, but an assassin? It must be my lucky day. If only I had time to play.

The assassin moves, gliding through the shadows like he owns them. A second blade appears in his hand as if by magic, and I grin, letting my heart rate slow down and emptying my mind of all other distractions. I pull my own daggers from my thigh sheaths, and rush forward, throwing a dagger at the same time. The assassin bats it from the air with his blade like it was nothing more than an annoying gnat. Impressive.

When I'm within striking distance of him, I drop to my knees, ignoring the bite of pain, and let my momentum pull me past him. With supernatural speed and strength, I twist my body backward, swiping out with my blade, and slicing through his hamstrings. He falls, and before he can throw his own dagger, I'm on him. My teeth sink into his neck, his warm blood coating my tongue and sliding down my throat. I don't let myself feed, though. As much as I need to, I don't have the time. And his blood tastes like shit. I rip out his throat and spit onto the pavement before I turn back to the mouth of the alley.

I'm only one block from the finish line. Scanning constantly, I keep to the shadows and slink down the street. Movement to my left catches my attention, and I slip into the darkened doorway of an office building. Another contestant emerges from the shadows across the street and makes a dash for the finish line. He doesn't make it. A massive dog is upon him before he can react.

Holy fuck. A faerie dog. Kennedy wasn't joking when he said this would be dangerous.

A faerie dog is the size of a bull and looks like a rabid wolf. Their red eyes and poisonous fangs are used by parents as bedtime stories to scare their children into behaving. They are incredibly rare, and how Kennedy got his hands on one, is beyond me. The man is insane to let that thing loose in the city.

I don't waste any time. With the faerie dog distracted, I make a break for it. I use all my supernatural strength and push myself to run faster than I ever have in my life. My muscles strain and my heart pounds behind my ribs as the finish line draws closer, and I'm pretty sure I'm not breathing as I race for it. With an extra burst of speed, I cross the line right before a force barrels into me from behind.

The ground rushes up to meet me, and I put my hands out to catch myself. Thinking it's the faerie dog, I flip over, dagger at the ready, only to be frozen in place by magic. Not the faerie dog, but Sam.

He presses a dagger to my throat and growls. "It doesn't matter that you crossed the line first. She. Is. Mine." Spittle flies from his mouth, and he looks like a rabid dog as he stares down at me.

I shove him hard enough to slide out from under him, and I jump to my feet. *No.* That can't be true. My hands shake as I fumble in my pocket for my phone, my breath stuck in my chest. A notification for a missed call and voicemail from Sterling turns my blood to ice in my veins.

STERLING

Kai scaling the building momentarily distracts Ellis from her nerves. If it wasn't something I was used to seeing, I would probably be distracted, too. She is getting a first-hand glimpse of the badass Malakai is.

I shake myself and push my wolf aside, refocusing on the task at hand. Seeing Ellis kiss Kai raised ugly feelings in my gut. It's getting harder and harder to control my wolf when I'm around her. He's tugging on his leash more and more. It's why I stayed away as much as I could at Kai's place. He's itching to claim her, and I can't let him do that.

Focus, jackass. We need to keep her safe. Keep your dick in your pants. Not that my wolf wears pants. Maybe I should have said fur?

Cade and I are pressed against her as tight as we can get, constantly scanning our surroundings and using our senses and magic to search for any kind of danger. It's distracting as hell having her touching me as much as she is. Her scent, an intoxicating combination of vanilla and lavender, is driving my wolf crazy.

"Let's make our way to the finish line," Cade says once Kai is out of sight.

"We should drive there," I reply. "Being out in the open like this is making my skin crawl."

We've only taken a few steps when Ellis screams. One second she is pressed against me with Cade's arm around her shoulders, the next she's gone. How the fuck that happened, I don't have time to figure out. Cade and I whirl around to find her held against someone's front with their arm banded around her chest and a knife pressed to her throat. The terror that courses through me at the sight leaves my legs weak and shaking. I sense Cade tensing next to me as his arms stretch out in front of him. Purple light shimmers around his hands and he takes a step forward.

The knife at Ellis's throat presses tighter to her skin. She whimpers and looks at us with wide, fear-filled eyes. The sound incites my wolf and it takes all my willpower to keep him from taking over. My fingers extend into claws and my teeth lengthen. As blood wells along the edge of the blade and slides down her slim neck, my control on his leash slips. He pushes against my mind, trying to force the shift on me. The desire to destroy the man hurting *his* Ellis echoes along with my own.

"Don't make another move," the man says in a low, gravelly voice. He steps back, pulling Ellis with him.

I don't notice the other two men next to him until they break away and head for Cade and me. I grit my teeth, a low growl rumbling up my chest.

"Please," Ellis whispers, her voice wobbly. "Don't do this."

Tears well in her eyes and my skin itches as fur ripples under the surface as my control slips a little more.

"Shut up!" the man holding her yells. He jostles her, causing the blade to bite deeper into her skin.

She cries out and Cade reacts. He hurls a blast of magic at the guy approaching him. Dude avoids it, moving unnaturally fast. If his pale skin hadn't told me what he was, his inhuman movement sure as hell did.

Cade rushes forward and engages the vampire. Over his shoulder he yells, "I got these guys. You get Ellis!"

Before I can make a lunge for the guy holding Ellis, the second guy charges me. I try to dodge, but he anticipates my movements and grabs me by my throat. Over his shoulder, I see the guy holding Ellis dragging her away, and my wolf loses his mind.

I can't control him as he takes over, pushing me to the background as he surges forth and forces the change on me. Huge paws replace my hands and feet, and I land on the ground on all fours. A few pops and the tearing of clothing, and we're standing as a wolf in front of the guy who attempted to strangle us. A low, menacing growl reverberates up our throat and we bare our teeth in a snarl. The guy steps back, then shifts himself, now a sleek, black panther.

Fuck this. We don't have time to fight this guy. Behind the panther, we see Ellis being dragged around a building, out of sight. We howl and launch forward, snapping for the panther's neck. He dodges our jaws and swipes his paws across our chest, but we don't feel the pain through our terror. The thought of losing Ellis sends us into a rage.

We hear Cade curse but we can't spare attention for him. One of us has to get away. We step back to re-evaluate, and Cade takes the opportunity to hit our opponent with a blast of purple light. It sends the panther skidding across the concrete. The distraction must have cost Cade, though, because we hear flesh meeting flesh and another curse from Cade.

We're torn. Cade is pack, and he's hurt. Instinct tells us to fight, protect, kill. But Ellis needs us. Our priorities shifted as soon as she came into our lives. We take off in the direction Ellis was dragged. Our sense of smell is heightened in the wolf form and we use it to track Ellis's scent. We can't miss the mingled scent of fear and blood with her vanilla and lavender, and it pushes us faster, harder. We wind our way through the buildings of the city, heading farther away from the obstacle course.

A scream echoes in the air. We know immediately it's Ellis, and we run faster than we ever have. We round a corner, skidding in a slick patch of who the hell knows what. For a moment, pride wells in our chest as we watch her fight her attacker. She throws her elbow back, connecting with the guy's abdomen.

He loses his hold on her, and she reaches to the small of her back and grabs her gun, but the guy is faster than her—and apparently a mage. His magic whips out of him and wraps around Ellis's wrist and tightens. A scream tears from her throat, and her body contorts as she falls to the ground in pain, the gun falling from her limp hand.

We dart forward, but we're not fast enough. The mage wraps his magic around Ellis and her body convulses on the ground. The scream that comes from her freezes our blood in our veins and ignites a fire inside of us. Her head is thrown back, her neck stretched, causing the knife wound at her throat to open further. Popping sounds reverberate off the buildings, and we have to fight the bile rising in our throat as we realize he is breaking her bones with his magic.

The mage is distracted by torturing Ellis, and he doesn't see us coming until it's too late. We barrel into him, knocking him to the ground. His head hits the concrete with a sickening *thunk,* and his magic disappears. Wasting no time, we close our jaws around his throat and tear it out with a force that shocks even us. Blood and skin and muscle hits the concrete with a wet slap, and we go back in for seconds, just to make sure.

When we're sure the mage is no longer a threat, we pad to Ellis. She's laying too still on the ground and we have a moment of fear thinking we're too late. We hold our breath as we lower our muzzle to her chest. The wet rasp of her uneven breaths sends relief crashing into us so fiercely it causes my wolf to step back. I take advantage of him being thrown off balance and I push forward, shifting to my human form.

I crouch in front of her and hesitate before touching her, afraid I'll do even more damage. She's unconscious, her body bloody and bruised with her limbs lying at unnatural angles where her bones have been broken. The uneven breaths making her chest rise and fall are wet and labored. It sends my wolf howling inside me.

"Fuck. Ellis, I'm here," I say shakily. "I'm so sorry, but I'm here now. Please, kitten. Please be okay," I beg.

Something in my chest physically hurts. Seeing her injured, broken, and in pain is tearing me in two. It's hard to breathe, and I want nothing more than to curl up with Ellis and let her know she's not alone. My wolf paces inside me, his anxious energy feeding into my own. I've never felt like this before.

I reach for my phone in my back pocket, only to realize I shifted and lost my clothes, so I have no way of reaching Cade or Kai. Fuck. Cade. I hope he's okay, but there is nothing I can do about that now. Refocusing my mind, I know I need to get Ellis to safety. My hands hover over her, hesitating before I touch her. I don't want to move her, but I don't have a choice. Looking around to get my bearings, I make a plan in my head.

As gently as I can, I slide my arms under her and lift her to my chest. Even as gentle as I am, she still groans, and it breaks my heart. "I'm so sorry, kitten," I mutter. "I need to get you to safety. It's going to be alright. I promise."

I silently curse myself for making that promise. We promised her she would be okay today, and look what happened. Moving as quickly as I can without jostling her too much, I make my way through the back alleys of the city, keeping to the shadows and using my wolf to keep alert for danger.

The place I'm heading to is a secret apartment the guys and I have in case of emergencies. It's on the top floor of a corner building in the most derelict area of the city. It's run down and gross, but it's not meant for comfort. Until we can safely move Ellis back to Kai's place after this first challenge, it will have to do.

I make it to the building, but wait in the shadows for a moment, letting my wolf get a read on what's happening around us. When he determines it's safe, I quickly duck through the half-rotted door that opens up to a set of equally-rotted stairs. They groan ominously under mine and Ellis's combined weight, but I make it up the five stories without falling through.

As soon as I'm through the door to our apartment, I make sure it's locked behind me. The one bedroom contains a full sized bed with clean sheets pushed against a wall. The place is sparsely furnished, with only the necessities stocked in case of emergency —medical supplies, non-perishable foods, weapons, water, and a few pieces of clothing.

I gently lay Ellis on the bed, wincing as she groans again. She hasn't regained consciousness and I'm at a loss for what to do. The worst of her injuries are internal and without Cade, I can't heal them.

"I'm sorry, kitten. I have to take your clothes off." I tell her, even though she can't hear me or respond.

There are multiple scrapes and cuts on her body, which I can take care of with our medical supplies, but I want to make sure there are no other major wounds. I get her jacket and tank top off, and the amount of bruising on her torso makes me think she must have some broken ribs, which would explain her shallow and labored breathing.

I unzip the boots I bought her when I left Kai's for a few hours because it was too hard to be near her. The constant fight with my wolf, the incessant need to be in her orbit, and the desire that only grows with each passing day. It's all so exhausting. I saw the boots in the shop window, and I knew they were exactly what she would need during this ridiculous challenge, and I couldn't stop myself from buying them.

When I get to her leggings, I find a pocket. *Stupid idiot!* Of course, Cade insisted on giving her a burner phone. In my fear and anxiety, I didn't even think to check her for one. I thank the fucker and take it out, dialing his number while I pull off her leggings.

He doesn't answer, and I try not to draw conclusions that will only make me worry more. I pull a sheet over Ellis and head to the bathroom to get our medical supplies. When I return to the room, the sight of Ellis lying motionless on the bed causes my heart to skip a beat. She looks so small and fragile. And we failed her.

I take a quick inventory of her cuts, making my wolf growl with each one I find. The sound echoes through the small apartment. I've made it through about half of her injuries when the burner phone rings. I lunge for it.

"Hello?"

"Sterling, thank fuck." Cade says breathlessly. "Where are you?" A harsh cough comes through the speaker.

"I'm at our emergency apartment. I need you here, now. Ellis is hurt."

"How bad?" He coughs again.

"She's not conscious. A lot of broken bones." I run my hand through my hair, wincing as it gets caught in the tangled strands. "I don't know what else. It was a mage."

"Motherfucker," he curses. Shouting coming from the background makes Cade let out a string of curses Kai would be proud of. "I'll get there as soon as I can shake these bastards from my tail. Have you heard from Kai?"

"No," I sit on the edge of the bed and brush a curl from Ellis's forehead. "Shit, Cade. She's burning up."

"Son of a bitch. I'm trying, Sterling."

He hangs up, and I sigh. I get a cool, wet washcloth from the bathroom and place it on Ellis's forehead. There isn't much I can do besides continue treating her outside injuries. When I'm done, I pull on a pair of sweatpants and sit on the bed next to her.

"I'm right here, kitten," I say softly. "Cade is on his way. He'll get you all fixed up."

I try not to lose myself to my thoughts. There's nothing positive floating through my head at the moment, and it would only bring more fear and uncertainty. I let my wolf closer to the surface to monitor our surroundings, and I try to call Kai, but he doesn't answer. I assume it will be another thirty minutes or so until he finishes the race, so I leave him a brief message telling him we're at the apartment, but nothing else.

After what feels like hours, someone knocks on the door hard enough to rattle the entire apartment. "Open up, it's me."

I hurry to the door and let Cade in. "Fuck, brother. What happened to you?" I ask.

He's sporting a black eye and claw marks cover his arms and chest. His shirt is bloody, torn, and hanging in rags. One arm is pressed tight across his middle, and his whole body is hunched over like it hurts to stand straight.

"Another fucker joined the fray after you left," he wheezes. "Even with my magic, I couldn't take a vamp *and* two shifters."

"Can you take care of Ellis?" I ask, worry creeping in.

"Yeah. At least, I should be able to."

I follow him as he shuffles his way into the bedroom and falls to his knees by the bed.

"Shit. Ellis," he groans. "I'm so sorry, love." Purple light wreaths his hands and they hover over her body as he takes inventory of her injuries. "What the fuck happened to her?" he grunts. "Almost every bone is broken. Her lungs and a kidney have been punctured, and she's bleeding internally."

The room wobbles and I have to steady myself on the doorframe. "You can heal her, though, right?" I ask.

"I'm fucking drained, but I can take care of the life-threatening injuries."

I watch as he gently places a kiss on her forehead before he sets his hands on either side of her head. Violet magic flows through her body, lighting up under her skin and healing the broken bones and internal damage. When the light fades, Cade sways on his knees. I jump forward and grab his shoulders.

"She'll be fine," he slurs. "Just needs rest." He exhales heavily, and his breath is a wet rasp as it leaves his chest.

His eyes roll up in his head and he goes limp in my hands. I gently lay him down on the floor next to the bed and shove a pillow under his head. After taking care of his injuries, I sit on the bed to keep an eye on both of them, while my wolf remains on high alert.

I itch under my skin. The urge to shift is so strong—my wolf wants to protect. Cade and Kai became my pack after I lost mine, and the day Ellis came into my life, my wolf knew she was part of the pack as well. I have to fight him to keep my human form. Sitting still on the bed isn't working, so I stand and pace the length of the room, trying to ease the jittery feeling that has settled in my muscles. Five steps from one wall to the other.

Another knock on the door draws me from the room.

"It's Kai."

I open the door and find Kai, bloody but alive.

"Why the hell are you here?" he asks, shoving into the apartment. As soon as he sees Ellis and Cade, both unmoving and injured, his body goes preternaturally still. He whirls to face me. "What the fuck happened?" His words are distorted as his fangs descend and his eyes turn more red than gray.

I quickly explain, and he only calms down once he knows both of them will be okay. Still, he curses Cade and me for failing to keep Ellis safe, and I let him. We deserve it.

With Kai here, I feel safe enough to let myself go. I yank my sweats off and my wolf surges forward and takes over. We brush past Kai and nuzzle Cade's neck before hopping up on the bed. A soft whine escapes our throat as we gently lay our head on Ellis's thighs, gaze trained on the bedroom door.

There will be time later to discuss how the challenge went. Right now, we both settle in to watch over our pack and keep them safe.

ELLIS

THE RED CARPET UNDER MY FEET SQUISHES WITH EACH step. Red carpet? I glance at the rug in confusion. It's supposed to be cream with flowers. Why is it red? I take another step and watch the crimson ooze between my toes. It's thick and sticky, and cool against my skin.

My gaze follows the rug, climbing the stairs. More red is puddled on the treads. I step in each one, fascinated by the contrast of the bright color against my tan skin. At the top of the stairs, two bodies lay sprawled on the wooden floor, a floor now soaked in the same red liquid.

I recognize the blond hair splayed out around the first body's head. The curls are the same as mine. But, they're stained crimson.

"Mom?" It's so quiet in our house. My voice echoes, reverberating off of the wooden floors and walls. "What are you doing?"

I kneel next to her, the red soaking into my pants. It's so cold. I brush my mom's hair from her face. The sight is so unexpected and so gruesome. Her neck is split open, so wide I can see inside her throat. A scream tears from my chest.

I scream, and scream, but my mom doesn't open her eyes. I'm scared to look at the other body, but I force myself to take in the *brown curly hair, the blood that's pooled around the body, and the unnatural angle of the limbs.*

"Gracie?" I whisper, my voice trembling.

I bolt upright in bed, gasping for breath, heart pounding in my chest. The sweat coating my skin feels so much like the blood in my dream I have to lean over the side of the bed to heave as my stomach tries to empty its contents. Shivering and stomach roiling, I'm pulled from the visions left in my mind as puffs of warm air wash over my shoulder.

I look behind me and almost scream. There is a wolf in bed with me, and the damn thing practically takes up the entire space. It's not just any wolf, though. Even if I hadn't recognized the eyes, something inside me would have told me with absolute certainty that it was Sterling.

He pushes my shoulder with his nose again and whines, looking into my eyes with concern.

"I'm okay," I breathe. "Just a bad dream."

I shiver again and realize I'm wearing only my bra and panties. It doesn't take long for me to remember what happened. The challenge, the mage. The excruciating pain. I scan my body for injury and see only minor scrapes. Twisting my torso, I expect the knife-like agony of broken bones, but there's only the dull sting of skin stretching around the many cuts.

Sterling whines again, and I glance at him. It's amazing I can read his expressions so clearly. His eyes shine with worry, his head low between his paws, tail tucked in close. I'm momentarily distracted by his beauty. Icy blue eyes and silver fur that I'm itching to touch. Where his scar is in his human form, the fur is missing. He nuzzles my abdomen and makes a chuffing noise that I assume is his way of telling me to lay back down.

"What happened?" I ask, even knowing he can't respond in wolf form. "Have you been laying here this whole time?"

Another chuffing sound, and this time, he pushes his nose under my hand. I run my palm up his nose and into the fur between his ears. Holy shit, he's so soft. I want to rub my face in his fur, curl up against him, and go back to sleep.

Ignoring my aching body, I lift my other hand to rub along his neck. His eyes close and he tilts his head to the side, inviting more scratches. It brings a smile to my lips. This massive, snarly wolf is complete putty in my hands. When he rolls over on his back and exposes his belly to me, I giggle at the sight of him looking up at me with his tongue flopping out of the side of his mouth.

I rub my hand along his belly, reveling in the silken texture of his fur between my fingers. "You are so beautiful," I whisper.

His tail thumps against the bed in answer.

Cursing and banging coming from another room draws me from the moment, and I glance around to take in my surroundings for the first time. I'm in a small room with a bed and a chair as the only furnishings. It's dingy and run down, but the sheets on the bed are clean.

More cursing and banging, and I look to Sterling for an answer. He doesn't seem alarmed, so I assume it's nothing to be worried about. Gingerly, I slide to the edge of the bed, exhaling through the stinging and aching. I don't even care that the sheet slides away and exposes more of my almost naked body. It's surprising I don't feel even an ounce of embarrassment that someone—most likely Sterling—undressed me down to my bra and panties. Maybe it's the fact they are cute, lacy black scraps of fabric, but I suspect it's because there is this strange level of comfort around these guys.

Sterling hops off the bed and grabs a black tee from the chair in his jaws. He brings it back to me and I quickly slip it on. It's huge on me and will cover everything without having to put on more clothes.

I cling to Sterling's back as I stand up, groaning at the pull of cuts and bruises. He is so large, his paws are bigger than my hand, and his head comes up to my belly. It's not just his size that seems to take over the entire space. His energy is palpable, a crackling dominance that radiates from him. Alpha energy.

With Sterling pressed against me and my hand on his head for support, we make our way out of the bedroom into a short hallway that opens into a kitchen. The image before me stops me in my tracks, amusement and a sense of contentment settling in me.

"I don't know what the fuck I'm doing," Malakai grumbles, his back to me as he drops an ancient-looking pan onto an equally ancient-looking stove.

Sterling huffs and nudges me forward with his nose.

"Four hundred years old and you can't cook real food." Exhaustion laces Cade's voice. Even his posture, slumped over a rickety table, screams fatigue.

If I could walk any faster, I'd rush to his side. As it is, I can barely shuffle forward with Sterling's prodding.

"I'm a fucking vampire. I don't need to cook. My food comes straight from the tap." Malakai points to his neck, but keeps his back turned to us.

"That's off-putting," I say as I shuffle further into the room.

Both Cade and Malakai whip around. Malakai rushes forward and wraps his arms around me. It throws me off guard, and instead of panicking, I lean into it. Behind Malakai, I see Cade struggling to stand from the chair.

"Thank fuck, you're okay." Malakai buries his face in my neck.

A trickle of fear drips through me when he inhales my scent, but I quickly relax as his hand cups the back of my neck in the most gentle way. I melt into his arms and let him carry my weight as he wraps an arm around my waist and turns to the table.

"Sit the fuck down, Cade," Malakai growls. "You're going to fall over."

"Are you okay, Cade?" I ask him.

He looks rough, and concern bubbles up inside of me. Dark circles line under his eyes, and strain brackets the corners of his mouth. I let Malakai help me into a chair, and I tense as it shifts under my weight, scared the entire thing will fall apart in a shower of dust. Cade's chair scratches across the floor as he scoots it closer to mine.

He grabs my hands and holds them tightly in his own. "I'm okay. Just wore out from using so much magic."

Even as he says this, pale violet light flows from his hands and into me. It's warm and tingly as it passes through my body, like fireflies fluttering through my veins. I jerk my hands back from his grasp.

"Then why are you using more?" I ask. The question makes room for another, and they continue to pour out, one after the other. "What happened? How long have I been out? And ... what are you doing, Malakai?"

The vampire turns to look at me with a spatula in his hand. "Trying to make some real food for you and Cade. But I don't know how the fuck to cook, and this useless heap of fur refuses to change back into a human." He glares at Sterling and points at him with the spatula like it's weapon.

Sterling growls and bares his teeth at Malakai. Without thinking, I put my hand on the scruff of Sterling's neck and he instantly calms, laying on his belly at my feet.

"Daaamn," Cade says with one brow raised in appreciation. "Having you around will be useful in keeping that dog under control."

Sterling lifts his head, and while I know wolves can't glare, I swear he does.

"To answer your other questions," Cade says, "I was just making sure you're okay. And you were out for about a day."

A day? Holy shit. What have I missed during that time?

"As for what happened?" He barks a humorless laugh. "Where to begin?"

"How about what happened after that mage took me?" I offer tentatively.

All three guys—well, two and a wolf—tense at my words.

"Well," Cade drawls, "I fought off a vampire and two shifters, leaving me mostly drained by the time I got here. Sterling tracked you down and he brought you here." He glances around the dingy kitchen. "This is a safe house of sorts. No one knows we have it, but we keep it in case of emergencies. I had enough magic left in me to heal your worst injuries. I passed out and only woke up a couple of hours ago."

I take a closer look at him and under the exhaustion lining his features, I spot a black eye and what appears to be claw marks on his arms. Bandages peek out from under the collar of his shirt, as well.

"Are you okay?" I ask. My hand raises without me thinking of it, and my fingers graze the white bandages.

"I'm fine, love." Cade, grasps my hand and places a kiss on my knuckles. "Just need to rest and recharge. Some food would do wonders for that," he mocks-yells at Malakai.

"Fuck off," Malakai growls.

"And Sterling? Was he injured?" I look at the wolf but see no injuries.

"He's fine. No injuries. Just stubborn." At my curious look, Cade explains. "His wolf tends to take control when he feels his pack is threatened. It's usually easier for Sterling to ride it out rather than fight the wolf."

Interesting. I don't know a lot about shifters, just the main facts. Everything else, all the intricate details that make up being a shifter, I know nothing about. I make some mental notes to ask Sterling when he's human again.

"Malakai? How did the challenge go? Are you hurt at all?" I run my gaze over his back and down to his ass. He's still wearing his leather armor, and *holy moly*. Those pants make his ass look *gooood*.

Malakai turns to face me, appearing grateful to quit fumbling around at the stove. "Nothing major. A few cuts that will heal or have already healed on their own." He rubs at his left shoulder, like it pains him. "As for the challenge, I won. No thanks to that wonderful ex of yours."

I stiffen at his words, my heart stopping for a second. "My ex?"

He studies me before quietly asking, "How much do you want to hear about him?"

While the mention of Sam triggers me, I want to hear everything. "I don't want to be left out of the loop. I think I need to know what's happening."

Malakai nods. "He cornered me in an alley and used his magic to tie me up. Luckily, Cade spelled some pieces of jewelry for me and they came in handy. I broke his hold on me. Unfortunately, I was in a hurry to finish the race, so I couldn't do anything to take him out of the picture. I did enough to get my ass out of there and to the finish line."

"So, Kai won the first challenge while still maintaining 'possession' of you." Cade uses finger quotes to signify his disgust at the word. "Now, we wait for the second challenge."

"Which," Malakai says, "I suspect will come later than planned. Your dad wasn't too pleased to see me cross the finish line first. When I sent him a text with a picture of you to prove you were still with me, he said nothing. If I were to guess, he's probably planning something extra nasty."

"Great. So what happens now?" I ask and look around at all three guys. Not for the first time, I marvel at the strangeness of everything. How I ended up here, in this situation with the Triad protecting me, and the unsuspecting butterflies. It's enough to make me think it's all some grand dream.

"Everyone knows we have you now. So, there will be no hiding anymore." Malakai crosses his arms and leans against the counter. "Every moment not spent at my dad's will be dangerous. As soon as you and Cade are well enough, I want us all back there, where we have protection."

"Why don't we stay here?" I ask. "It seems like no one knows about this place."

"While that's true," Cade explains, "We lack the extra protection of the wards, the cameras, and the security guards the estate provides. Plus, all of our gear is at the estate."

I chew my lower lip while I ponder our situation. When my dad announced this contest, I knew I was going to be in danger. I didn't realize how *much* danger, though. If Sterling hadn't found me in time, I'm sure that mage would have killed me. I don't think it was his intention, but when I started fighting back, it pissed him off. The fact I got a couple of hits in probably messed with his ego, and he took it out on me.

I don't want to even think about how the guys will be in even more danger now, too. The thought does funny things to my stomach, and I don't want to look too closely at the reason why. Instead, I stand and make my way to the counter next to Malakai.

"How about I help you make us some food?" I ask. "What the hell were you attempting to make, anyway?"

The counters are covered in a white powder, and a lumpy tan mixture coats the inside of a cracked measuring glass. He mumbles something I can't understand, and I look at him with a raised brow.

"Pancakes," he says. If vampires could blush, Malakai would be blushing. It's adorable.

I look over the mess he's made on the counter and stove top and purse my lips. "Riiight. Is there any more pancake mix?"

Malakai hands me the box. "Are you sure you're up to it?"

Sterling, who followed me to the counter, tries to push me back to the chair with his body. I hold in my wince as I bend down and kiss the top of his head.

"I'm fine. And I'm hungry." I rub my belly for added effect. "And no offense, I don't think anything you cook will be edible."

"Thank everything holy," Cade breathes, turning his gaze to the heavens. "It would be completely inedible."

"Bite me." Malakai throws the spatula at Cade, who smoothly catches it out of the air.

"I believe that is your job." Cade winks at Malakai. "One you are quite good at, too, from what I've heard."

"Umm, yes, well," I say, clearing my throat. "Pancakes."

I try to ignore the way my stomach flip-flops when Malakai brushes against me as we work at the counter. Small talk flows freely and quietly between us. No mention of Sam, my dad, or this ridiculous contest. It's light and drama free, and for the first time in a while, my mind is relaxed. I'm in the moment and enjoying every second of it.

The batter is everywhere by the time we're done. There's even some on my face, which Malakai licks off. I freeze as his tongue slides up my cheek, all wet and warm. Tingles shoot down my spine and settle in my pussy. I squeeze my legs together and take deep breaths, trying to clear my mind. Now is not the time for that.

His chuckle is dark and seductive, and I can't help but look at him. The red circling his irises is more prominent than when he started the obstacle course. His thick black lashes cast shadows that make his eyes look darker than they are. The paleness of his skin is offset by his black hair, and I reach out to brush a stray lock off his forehead without thinking about it.

As close as we're standing, it's not hard to miss the breath hitch in his chest as my fingers graze his temple. I always thought vampires would be cold, but his skin is only slightly cooler than mine. My fingers trail down the side of his face until my hand is cupping his cheek, and his eyes close as he leans into my touch. I swallow. It was easier than I thought it would be to touch him. There is no fear, only the slightest bit of nerves flutter in my belly, and I'm not sure if it's because I'm scared, excited, or turned on.

A low growl breaks us out of the moment. Malakai pulls away and winks at me. Disappointment settles over me and my fingers itch to touch him again. Instead, I shake my head and bend over to pat Sterling's head.

Together, Malakai and I made decently edible pancakes, and with the stack loaded onto two plates, we join Cade at the rickety table. Sterling plants his massive paws on the edge and the wood groans alarmingly under his weight. He stretches his neck over my plate and, with his teeth, snags three pancakes from Cade's before settling once again at my feet.

Cade stares at his plate, now minus three pancakes, and grumbles. A giggle bubbles up my throat, but I swallow it down. With a sigh, Cade rolls his eyes, and we both dig into our breakfast like starving animals.

"Are you hungry?" I ask Malakai. The red in his eyes has grown, and I know enough about vampires to know that is a sign of hunger.

Cade stiffens next to me, and Sterling presses himself against my leg.

Malakai carefully blanks his face. "Not for food, no."

I roll my eyes. "Well, yeah. I know that. Do you need to feed?" I notice the small muscles of his hands and forearms tense on the table.

He closes his eyes and breathes deeply for a moment. "I'll be fine for a few more days."

I want to ask him who he feeds from, but that seems like a deeply personal question. Instead, I nod and push my plate away. "I think I'm going to lie down. Cooking took a lot out of me."

Sterling follows me to the bedroom and hops up on the bed with me. When he curls against me, I bury my face in his fur like I wanted to before. I cling to him, partly because I want to, and partly because if I don't, I'm afraid I'll fall off the bed.

"You're so soft," I whisper as I run my hand over his side, petting him. "I have so many questions for you."

He nuzzles my neck before his tongue flops out of his mouth and he licks up the side of my face, the same cheek Malakai licked. I giggle at the feeling of his rough tongue and wrap my arms around his neck. There is something comforting about having a giant, warm, soft wolf in bed with you.

He puts off enough heat that I don't need the sheets. Instead, I let my eyes drift shut, knowing I'm safe for now, curled up with my wolf.

ELLIS

THE NEXT DAY, THE GUYS DECIDE TO HEAD BACK TO Thorne estate. I'm relieved to be back here. Somehow, the place is comforting to me. Maybe it's all the security, or maybe it's because my time here has been a sort of awakening for me. Whatever the reason, I feel more like myself than I have in years. So much so, I'm able to lounge on the couch in the library and read a book.

"What are you reading?" Sterling's voice echoes through the library.

The book falls from my fingers and lands in my lap as I jump, my heart attempting to eject from my chest. I was so absorbed in my reading, I didn't notice him joining me. He sits next to me on the couch, and I'm acutely aware of how close he is to me. With my cheeks burning, I pick up the book and show him the cover.

He laughs. "Is that a sexy book? Getting some ideas in that pretty head of yours?"

I'm not sure how to answer his question. So far, Sterling has been the one to keep his distance from me. I feel like I bonded with him in his wolf form, but flirting has never been our thing.

"Maybe," I say shyly. He chuckles and I duck my head to hide the blush heating my cheeks.

"So, you said you had questions for me," he says. "Is that true?"

"Yeah, I have lots of questions, actually." I set the book in my lap and look at him.

"I have a question for you, too," he says.

"What's your question?" Nerves flutter in my belly. I don't want to talk about Sam or my situation before Malakai abducted me.

"You've trained at the gym. You can throw a punch to match the best of them. And you've shown us you're able to use a gun and a knife." He levels his blue eyes on me, staring straight through me to my soul. "What happened yesterday? That mage grabbed you, and you did nothing to fight back at first."

I fiddle with the pages of the book and take a deep breath. Embarrassment burns through me, and I'm unable to look him in the eyes. "Um, I ... I froze. He grabbed me, and I panicked. It's hard to forget two years worth of ..." I trail off, not wanting to finish that thought. "In all my training at the gym," I say instead, "I never really learned self-defense. I can shoot a gun, preferably at a stationary target. I can stab someone standing in front of me, and I can punch someone who startles me. But I never learned how to break a hold if someone grabs me." I shrug and finally look up at him.

He nods like that is what he expected to hear. "I'll make you a deal, then. You train with me and the guys, and I'll answer your questions."

I grin at him and watch in fascination as a slight blush creeps up his tan neck. "Deal."

"Good," he says and clears his throat. "We'll start now."

"Now?" I ask, setting the book on the coffee table. "Where are Cade and Malakai?"

"Kai's dad needed them to do something. They'll be back later tonight."

"Okay. Well, let's do this, then," I say with bravado I'm not completely feeling.

I'm already wearing leggings and a tank top, as I only brought a few items of clothing with me when this whole contest began. Most of those things are comfort clothes that are easy to move in. Perfect for training, I guess.

Sterling moves to the area of the library that's been transformed into a gym. Weights and exercise equipment line one wall, and mirrors have been set up for optimal muscle ogling. Realistically, I know those mirrors are for making sure your form is on point, but I also know guys. Those mirrors are more for flexing and checking themselves out.

Padded mats cover the floor, which is where Sterling stops and turns to face me. His muscles shift under his tight t-shirt as he ties his long hair back in a bun. I watch him, loving the silver color and the way it makes his icy blue eyes pop.

"Alright," he says. "We'll start with the easiest grip to break. Once you show me you understand it, I'll answer one of your questions." He holds out his hand and instructs me to grab his wrist. "If someone were to grab you like this, you need to remember you're trying to break the grip through the opening of their fingers. You want to rotate your wrist until your palm is facing the ground, step in close and bring your hand to your chest. As you do that, slice your elbow forward over their hand and it will break their grip."

He demonstrates with me holding his wrist, before we switch and he grabs mine. I follow his instructions slowly, getting the feel for the movements and correcting where he tells me to. Once he thinks I have the move down, he increases his speed and strength to make me work for it.

"Good. That's really good." His eyes shine as he looks at me. "I think you have that one. Ask a question."

"Okay," I say as I gather my thoughts and try to think of the first question I want to ask. "The guys made it sound like you didn't have control of the wolf after you shifted. You don't control it?"

"My wolf is separate from me. He is his own entity, and he has his own thoughts and feelings and urges. It's like we share each other's bodies. Does that make sense?" His brows furrow as he tries to explain it to me. "When I'm human, he's tucked away in my consciousness, always there looking out through my eyes. Same when I'm in the wolf form—I'm tucked away in his consciousness. We can communicate with each other, and offer suggestions, but ultimately, whichever form we are in has the control."

"That makes sense." I say slowly.

"As for control," he continues, "I've lived with my wolf for a very long time. We have come to an understanding of each other. When I was younger, we fought a lot more over control."

"So, when you shifted when I was hurt and stayed in your wolf form?" I prod.

"I know how much my wolf needs to protect those he considers pack. I could have wrestled control back from him, but in the end, I knew it was easier for me to let him protect you in wolf form."

I hear his words, but my mind gets stuck on one word in particular. "Your wolf considers me pack?" I ask quietly, unable to look into his pretty blue eyes.

He gives me a little grin that causes those elusive butterflies to stir in my belly. "Next move," he says instead. He walks me through how to break a hold if someone grabs my hair, and once I have that move mastered, he steps back. "Next question."

While I'm dying to ask him what he meant by his wolf considering me pack, something else has been nagging me. "Do you have a pack? I've never seen you with another shifter, even on social media. It's always just Malakai and Cade."

He stiffens, and his eyes shutter. I realize my mistake and regret asking him such a personal question.

"I'm sorry," I say quickly. "I shouldn't have asked that. Of all people, I should understand family issues and not wanting to talk about it."

"No, it's okay." He shrugs. "My pack became corrupt,

basically. I was kicked out for not complying with the alpha on things I didn't agree with. Malakai and Cade are my pack now."

And apparently me? Just as I'm opening my mouth to ask, he stops me.

"Next move."

This time, he shows me how to break a hold if someone grabs me from behind in a bear hug. It's hard to concentrate on what he says as he wraps his massive arms around me. He steps in close until his chest presses against my back, and instead of fear, a thrill of excitement moves through me. He's talking, walking me through the steps, but all I can focus on is how his words vibrate deep in his chest against my back.

He's so warm, his shifter magic burns off energy faster than a human. I fight the urge to melt into his arms. With him being so much bigger than me, it makes me feel so small in his embrace. Protected and safe. It's a strange sensation, one I'm not used to, and I find that it's not unwelcome. The thoughts that pop into my mind are surprising, for so many reasons. What would it be like to feel his body wrap around mine with no clothing between us? What would he feel like, covered in sweat and moving against me? Inside me? Fear and curiosity battle as each thought crosses my mind.

His breath stutters, and he leans forward until his mouth is against my ear. With a deep inhale, I know his animal senses are sharp enough to catch whatever scents I'm putting off.

"Kitten," he practically purrs. "What are you thinking of right now?"

He smells like pine and the night air. It settles inside me, like a missing piece of my soul has snapped into place. I can't help it, with the way his warm breath fans across my cheek, his arms pulling me tighter to his chest. My back arches and my ass rubs against the growing bulge in his pants. The moan that slips past his lips emboldens me, and I do it again.

"Fuck," he growls. "You need to stop, Ellis."

But I don't want to stop. Part of me is waking up. Something inside me has been dormant for two years, and these guys are bringing it back to life with each look, each gentle touch, each kind word. It's invigorating, scary, and exciting all at the same time. I turn in his arms and rest my hands on his chest. Under my palms, his heart pounds behind his ribcage. He's breathing heavily and his eyes are hooded, the pale blue darker than usual. Knowing that I am the reason for his body reacting that way is a powerful thing.

I bravely stand on my tiptoes to reach his lips, but before I can mold my mouth to his, he grabs my wrists and gently pushes me away. Reality slams back into me so fast it leaves me in a daze. Cold flushes through my system, tempering the heat that built because of Sterling.

"I can't ... I ..." He curses under his breath and storms out of the library.

I'm left standing on the mats, alone and shaking. Confused by my actions. Confused at his reaction. Just ... confused. *What just happened?* I rub my arms, cold in his absence, and I replay everything that happened between us. The longer I think about it, the more my anxiety grows. Why did I do that? Why did I try to kiss him? Before I know it, I'm shaking so badly I have to sit on the couch or risk falling over.

Alone with just my thoughts is never a good place for me when my panic hits. I shakily pull out the burner phone Cade gave me and dial Allie's number. I need her to talk me down before a full-fledged panic attack hits.

"I'm so confused," I admit after telling her everything—what had happened with Cade and Malakai, the first contest and how I was almost abducted again, the self-defense lessons and how Sterling bolted. "How can I be attracted to anyone, let alone three guys, when Sam still haunts me? The thought of someone touching me makes me want to crawl out of my skin. But the thought of one of these guys even looking at me makes me hot and flushed, and ... needy."

"It makes sense to me," Allie says. "Not only are they all

incredibly attractive, but they have been nothing but kind to you. They have protected you and cared for you. Not one of them has hurt you, and most importantly, they have made you feel good again. That's huge, El. They've shown you it's okay to trust again. Everything they've done has proven that there are still good men out there, and you happened to stumble upon three of them. I'm crazy jealous."

I huff a laugh. "So, it's okay? I can be confused and sometimes scared, but still want them?"

"Of course! Hell, I went on that date with Connor, and I was terrified. I wanted him to to kiss me so fucking bad, but the thought made me want to puke at the same time. It's a natural reaction, and you have extenuating circumstances that make it even harder."

With the reminder of her date with Connor, I change the subject and we chat for another hour. With the magic way of hers, she calms me down and makes me see reason. There is nothing wrong with my confusing emotions, but maybe I need to talk to the guys about them? Or should I just ignore it? Ignoring has always been my go to, so maybe I'll just stick with that. No point in bringing something up and making everything awkward.

After we hang up, I'm too antsy to read, and my mind won't stop circling back to Sterling. I know the library is warded, and Malakai would be pissed if I left, but I can't sit here a moment longer with only my thoughts for company. Cautiously, I open the door to the hallway and take a step outside.

I wander through Thorne estate, keeping my eyes and ears open for any sign of Salvatore Thorne, Malakai's dad. I really don't want to run into him. The place is gorgeous. Elegant opulence speaks to how long the Thorne's have been in residence here. Gold trim and vaulted ceilings. Plush carpets and fancy artwork. Portraits hang on the walls, depicting members of the family through the ages.

I spot a portrait of Malakai as a young boy with an older woman. He has the same features as her. High cheekbones, plush lips, arching brows over beautiful gray eyes, a face framed in black hair. It has to be his mom, but I can't remember a time I have ever heard about a woman living here, besides Salvatore's mistresses.

I keep wandering down the halls until my stomach grumbles, and I make my way to the kitchen. It's been renovated into a modern style with marble countertops, white cabinets, and large stainless steel appliances. Surprisingly, the space is empty. I had expected to find people cooking, even at this time of night. Vampires are nocturnal, after all. It takes me a moment to remember vampires don't need food, so the only people in this house eating would be the human servants.

I open the fridge and find a ton of food. It all has to be prepared, though. Rather than fumble my way around an unfamiliar kitchen and piss off the cooks, I grab a container of strawberries from the fruit drawer. In the pantry I find the sugar and pour some in a bowl. Strawberries and sugar has always been one of my comfort foods.

I sit at the island on a barstool, and only make it through two strawberries when I hear male voices. My heart stops and I try to listen to see who it is. All I can hear, though, is my blood rushing through my ears. I scan the island for some kind of weapon and find nothing but the strawberries. The image of me throwing strawberries at an attacker almost makes me laugh.

The kitchen door opens and the light from the hallway back lights the two men so all I can see is their silhouette. Somehow, I still know who they are. I relax as Cade and Malakai stalk into the kitchen.

Malakai stops short when he sees me sitting at the island. "What are you doing awake?"

I shrug my shoulders. "Couldn't sleep." I watch him carefully. This would be the first time I've ever disobeyed his orders, and I have no clue how he'll react.

"Where's Sterling?" he asks, glancing around. "You shouldn't be here by yourself." No anger in his voice, just disapproval that I didn't listen to him.

"He didn't want to be around me, apparently." I cringe at the bitterness in my tone.

My gaze travels over Malakai, then Cade as he steps around his friend. The blood drains from my face when I get a good look at them, leaving me dizzy and lightheaded. They're both wearing black leather armor and black boots. Weapons are strapped to every inch of their bodies—knives, guns, throwing stars, even a couple of swords. It's not the weapons that give me pause, though.

"Is that blood?" My voice is barely a whisper as I voice the question. The visceral reaction I have to blood is something I'm not sure I'll ever get over.

Their leathers are covered in brownish stains. Red drops are splattered on Cade's neck and they both have dried blood crusted in the creases of their hands. Malakai even has a trail of it from his mouth down his chin.

Cade freezes as he realizes what they must look like. His eyes widen and he raises both hands to pacify me, only to notice the blood on them and shove them behind his back instead.

"Not ours," Malakai says as he smoothly walks toward me. His hands make quick work of the weapons strapped to his body as he drops them on the counter, the metal clanking against the marble.

My gaze locks onto him, and I watch him prowl to the island. He moves like a lethal cat. If it weren't for the pale skin and fangs, I could easily mistake him for some kind of feline shifter. I don't know why, but my body reacts to the sight of him in leather and weapons. He's dangerous, and he looks every inch the predator he is. But I know—some primal part of me knows—he would never hurt me. The conviction of that thought gives me pause.

Malakai reaches for a strawberry, and my gaze is transfixed on his mouth as he slowly wraps his lips around the fruit and bites down. Red juice dribbles down his chin, mixing with the blood. I run my tongue along my lower lip, so tempted to lick up the juice, and his gaze follows the movement. When his eyes meet mine, they are hooded and dark with arousal. A thrill travels through me as I remember the scene that played out in Malakai's bed before the first challenge. I really want them to make me feel that good again.

Cade enters my field of vision, weapons still strapped to his body, and I'm snapped out of the moment as Malakai's words finally sink in through my lust-addled brain.

"If it's not your blood, whose is it?" I have to clear my throat —that husky sound is not what I sound like at all.

Malakai glances at Cade, who nods. A purple light settles around the kitchen, coating the walls and doors like a second layer of paint. Malakai hops up onto the countertop and leans back on his hands.

"What we say here cannot leave this room." He levels a stare at me, and there is no amusement glittering in his eyes like usual. "Cade just set wards so no one can enter or listen in. If it ever gets out, Cade, Sterling, and I will be killed. And probably you, too."

I swallow but nod my head. When Malakai is this serious, I know better than to second guess his judgment.

"My father has trained us to do his dirty work," he says. "Anyone he needs taken out of the picture, we are the ones who do it."

A stone drops in my stomach. Those few strawberries I ate threaten to come back up. I had always heard the rumors about the guys, but after spending time with them, I couldn't imagine them killing people for no reason.

"You're assassins." I whisper. Fear causes my heart to race in my chest, and I have to clasp my hands together to hide their trembling.

"For a while, we did what he said. No questions asked." Cade says as he picks up where Malakai left off. His hands move over the straps of his weapons, removing and adding them to Malakai's pile on the counter. His movements are effortless and speak to the many times he's probably done it. "It's not something any of us are proud of, but at the time, we didn't have a choice. If we didn't do as he asked, he tortured us. Threatened to kill us. Threatened my mom and sister."

I blink. I didn't realize Cade had a mom and sister. It gets added to my list of questions.

Malakai leans his elbows on his knees. "It took us some time to make the connections and get the resources we needed, but eventually, we found a different solution to my dad's missions. Something other than the deaths of innocent people."

"If the people Salvatore asks us to kill are innocent, we offer them a choice." Cade crosses his arms over his chest and leans his hips against the island. "They can die by our hands or they can disappear. Become different people. Pack up, move away, and never return. All of them choose to disappear."

"We give them money, new identities, and tickets on the next boat out of Lustros." Malakai looks at me, his eyes so serious it's unsettling.

"What about the blood?" I ask, gesturing to them.

Cade grimaces. "We have to set the scene to make Salvatore believe we followed his orders."

"We take criminals from the prisons," Malakai explains. "Men who truly deserve the death we end up giving them."

"It's messy and gory." Cade's eyes are trained on me, like he's trying to read what I'm feeling. "But, in order to fool Salvatore, there can't be anything left to identify who was really murdered."

Holy. Shit. What they are doing is so incredibly dangerous. Malakai wasn't lying. If his dad ever finds out what they do, they will all be killed.

Cade rubs the back of his neck, dried blood flaking off and falling to the counter. "Does this change your opinion of us?"

I let myself really consider this. Do I like that they murder people? Not particularly. Is what they do better than murdering innocent people? I guess so. They don't have a choice. I understand that, and I know what it feels like to not have a choice in your life decisions.

I remember Cade telling me he wanted to be a healer when we

first met. Instead, he is taking people's lives. How much does that hurt him? I glance at him and see the shadows in his eyes, the regret and hate and despair hiding under the shimmering violet.

"Does it bother you? What you have to do ... does it bother you?" I ask. I already know Cade's answer, but Malakai, I can't read.

"I hate it," Cade says, unsurprisingly. "Even though the men we kill are the worst of the worst, I don't enjoy taking a life. Each one is a mark against my soul. A black stain that will never go away."

My heart aches for him. My body acts on its own, standing and walking around the island to him. I wrap my arms around his middle and hug him tightly, offering the only comfort I know. He hesitates briefly before hugging me to him, resting his head on top of mine. As he releases a breath, his body shudders around me.

When I pull away, I move to Malakai. He opens his legs and I step between them without hesitation. His hands land on my ribs, and he pulls me closer.

"What about you, Malakai? Does it bother you?" I ask quietly, staring into those multi-colored eyes.

"You want my honest answer? It bothers me more that my dad is asking for these people to be assassinated. He's asked for entire families—parents and children—to be killed. Solely for the fact they don't agree with him or stand in his way of his glory. It bothers me that my brothers have been roped into this when they deserve so much more." He pauses and a muscle ticks in his jaw and his fingers tighten on my sides. "Does the killing bother me? No. These guys are murderers and rapists. People like Sam who deserve worse than what we give them. I will gladly spill their blood, and revel in it."

I release a breath at his words and the raw honesty in them. It should scare me. He has admitted to being a bloodthirsty monster. But the fact he wishes something different for Cade and Sterling? There is something soft and light under all that darkness.

It's thrilling to think this vicious creature handles me with such tenderness. I look into his red-rimmed eyes and let them draw me in and wash away my fear and anxiety. The way he looks at me gives me the strength to want him. My conversation with Allie helped me to realize I don't want to keep letting Sam control my life. I got away. Now it's time to reclaim everything he stole from me. I'm determined to reclaim who I am and the pleasure I can find in life.

My hands slide up Malakai's thighs, the leather warm and smooth under my palms. He pulls me closer until there is no space between us. His muscular legs tighten on either side of me and I stand on my toes, stretching forward until our mouths touch.

MALAKAI

I HOLD BACK. AS MUCH AS I'M DYING TO DEVOUR everything about this woman, I make myself be gentle. Ellis has had to deal with too much shit from that asshole, Sam, and I'm determined to make her feel like a queen.

When she pulls away, she glances at Cade on the other side of the island and red creeps into her cheeks. A grin spreads across my face. I figured after the little incident in my room before the contest, she would realize there are no barriers between me and Cade.

With an equally amused grin, Cade steps around the island and in between my legs, sandwiching Ellis between us. He pulls her back against his chest while reaching around her and grabbing a strawberry off the island. He brushes kisses along her neck and her head falls back against his chest, releasing a little gasp. The sound makes my cock twitch in my leather pants.

Cade brings the strawberry to Ellis's mouth, and watching her lips close around the fruit is one of the hottest things I've ever seen. Her gaze meets mine and I know she can see how much this is affecting me. Cade presses the last bite of strawberry to my lips and I don't break Ellis's gaze as I take it.

Her tongue sneaks out to lick the juice off her bottom lip and something in me snaps. I need to taste her now. Sliding my hands into her hair, I cup the back of her head and draw her mouth to mine. This kiss isn't gentle. After a night of killing and being bathed in blood, adrenaline pumps through my veins. Ellis's desire brushes against my shield. It's tentative, almost curious, but I also sense her determination, and any lingering thoughts of taking my time are blown away.

The taste of strawberries is still on her tongue, and I can't get enough. The little sounds she makes drive me wild. Cade presses against her, pushing her harder against me. When she gasps into my mouth, I open my eyes to see his teeth latched onto her neck. My gums burn as my fangs descend. Fucking hell, I want it to be my mouth at her neck. I want to ... no, *need* to ... taste her blood.

She distracts me from that urge when her hands slide under my shirt. Her skin is warmer than mine, and her fingers practically burn as they travel up my sides. I break our kiss and help her pull the leather shirt over my head—it's tight, and it takes a moment to remove.

"Your turn," Cade whispers in her ear.

A brief flash of hesitation in her eyes, then she blinks and it's gone. Cade draws up the hem of her tank top, exposing her delicious tan skin, inch by excruciatingly slow inch. I trail my fingers up her sides just like she did to me, smiling as she shivers at the touch.

"What about you, Cade?" she asks breathlessly.

"Patience," he breathes, as he whips his leather shirt off as fast as he can.

Cade takes her chin in his hand and tilts her head back so he can kiss her. Her lacy black bra teases me, and I reach out with both hands to palm her breasts, rubbing my thumbs over her nipples. A noise climbs up her throat, and I watch the peaks pebble behind the fabric. Cade unhooks the clasp, and the material slides down her arms. The sight steals my breath.

As soon as the bra hits the floor, I slide off the counter so I can wrap my mouth around one of her nipples. The sound she makes goes straight to my dick confined in my leather pants. With my hand, I roll her other nipple between my fingers, urging it into a tighter peak.

"You guys," she moans.

"Yes, Ellis?" Cade asks.

I don't let her answer. Instead, I wrap my arms around her waist and pick her up, setting her on the island. Gently, I wrap my hand around her neck, and push her down until she is laying on the marble surface. She gasps and arches her back as her heated skin meets the cool marble.

"Is this what you want?" I ask, as I trail my hand from her neck down between her breasts. When I reach the waistband of her leggings, I pause with my fingers curled around the edge.

"Use your words, Ellis." Cade unbuttons his leather pants but stops, waiting for her answer.

"Yes. Yes, please," she begs. "I want more."

Her chest is heaving, and her fingers are scrambling on the marble. I'm hard as a fucking rock, watching her breasts rise and fall with each breath. Her flushed skin is mouthwatering, and I can't keep my gaze away from her pulse throbbing in her perfect neck.

Always the considerate one, Cade rounds the island and grabs Ellis's face in his hands. He looks down at her and rubs his thumbs along her cheeks. "Are you okay with this?" he asks gently.

She hesitates for the barest second. "I want to feel good," she breathes. "Please."

"Please, what?" Cade asks, his voice low and gravelly. "What do you want, Ellis?"

I unbutton my leathers while Cade makes sure Ellis is game for this, and slide them down my legs, baring my cock. Already, precum glistens at the tip, and I rub my thumb over it. Ellis watches with hungry eyes.

"I want you to make me feel good." An embarrassed blush joins the rosy tint of her flushed skin.

"We'll always make sure you feel good, baby girl," I reassure her. "You never have to ask us for that."

Cade tilts her head back until she's looking in his eyes. With complete earnestness in his gaze and voice, he says, "You say stop, and we stop. No questions asked."

She nods, and Cade takes that as his cue. His leathers hit the floor in record time, and he hops up on the island, kneeling beside her head with his cock in hand.

"Open that pretty mouth, baby girl, and take Cade's cock as deep as you can." I run my hand over her abdomen, her muscles tightening at the touch.

She obeys beautifully, lifting her head from the counter, and Cade slips the crown of his dick into her mouth, while supporting her neck with his hand. With her distracted, I pull down her leggings and panties. I run my hands up her legs, bending down to kiss along the inside of her thighs. Her breath stutters, and she releases Cade's dick. Uncertainty slides along my mental barrier, and that just won't do.

"Ellis," I growl, and wait for her gaze to slide to mine. "Spread your legs, baby girl. Let me see that pretty pink pussy." She hesitates, muscles locked in fear, and I run my palms up and down her thighs. "It's not fair Cade got to taste you already. I've been jealous ever since. You're not playing favorites, are you?"

She takes a deep breath and shakily spreads her legs, exposing her center already glistening with arousal.

My mouth waters, and there is no holding back at that sight. I dive in and groan as soon as my mouth makes contact. She tastes fucking divine. I lick up her slit, teasing her clit and making her hips lift off the island.

"Oh my gods," she says breathlessly.

I grin and lift my eyes, meeting her gaze. "We're not gods, baby girl. We're your monsters."

Her eyes roll back in her head as Cade slides his hand behind her neck to lift her head again, and he pushes into her mouth.

Watching her swallow his cock makes mine jump. I know how good he tastes. Almost as good as Ellis's pussy.

I lower my head again and really show her what I can do with my tongue. My fangs tingle at the need to be buried in her skin. I graze them along her most sensitive areas and her eyes pop open wide.

"Oh fuck, Malakai," she begs, hips lifting off the counter.

I wish I could. I really want to bite her and claim her as mine. I want to taste her blood on my tongue, mixed with her arousal. The image in my head spurs me forward and I slide my tongue deep into her. I use my thumb to rub circles over her clit and she screams around Cade's cock as she comes.

Cade pulls back, breathing as heavily as she is. "You are so beautiful when you come," he rasps.

She lays limply on the island with her eyes closed, a small blissful smile on her lips.

Cade brushes her hair from her forehead. "Do you want more, Ellis?"

Her eyes open, and she looks back and forth between us. Indecision, desire, anxiety. I sense all of it. She wants more, but she's scared. I rub my palms over her hips and back down to her thighs.

"Can we help erase those memories?" I ask. "Will you let us give you something to replace them?" I slide my hands back up, this time rubbing my thumbs over her nipples before pinching them between my thumbs and pointer fingers. "You have no idea the pleasure we want to give you," I whisper against the skin of her abdomen as I place gentle kisses there.

She whimpers, and I trail my lips down her belly to the apex of her thighs. I know the instant she decides she wants it. Not only by the determination and desire I pick up, but by the way she spreads her thighs and lifts her hips off the counter.

"Show me," she breathes.

Before I go any further, I grab her left wrist and run my thumb along the small scar on her forearm. "I assume this means you have an implant?" I don't think a vampire can get a human pregnant, but I'm not willing to take that risk. A baby Malakai running around? It's enough to make me shudder.

She nods and I wrap my hands around her thighs and tug her to the edge. Her gaze locks onto me as I slowly strip all the way out of my leather pants and take my cock in my hand.

"Are you sure about this?" I give her one more chance to say no. Once I'm buried deep in her, there will be no stopping.

"Yes, I'm sure." Her emotions match her words as they brush along my mental shields.

Cade plays with her nipples, and I rub the tip of my cock through her folds. The temptation to sink into her wet heat is so strong, I groan. Just the tip running through her wetness could bring me to my knees. I line myself up with her entrance and slowly push inside. Her inner muscles squeeze my cock, and I have to close my eyes and grab the edge of the island.

"Holy shit, baby girl. You feel so fucking good." I roll my hips and slip inside a little more. It's like the most exquisite form of torture. One more thrust and I'm seated to the hilt.

So lost in my own pleasure, I almost don't notice that she's not moving. She's barely breathing. I can hear her heart thundering in her chest, the blood rushing through her veins.

Cade rubs his thumb along her cheek. "Are you okay, Ellis?"

She nods, but keeps her eyes squeezed shut.

"Baby girl, look at me." I want her to know who is inside her. She needs to know it's not Sam, and I'm not going to hurt her.

I don't move until she does. As soon as her amber eyes lock onto mine, I rock my hips, sliding out before slowly sliding back in. We both groan, and I have to stop. If I keep going, I'll blow my load right now. Once I gain my composure, I watch Ellis as I pull out to the tip and thrust back in. I keep my movements gentle and slow. As much as I'm dying to slam into her over and over, I know I need her to trust me first. I need her to trust that I will never hurt her.

"Don't forget about Cade's cock, baby girl."

She opens her mouth, her gaze sliding to Cade. He cradles her head in his palm, supporting her, as he thrusts his hips until I'm positive he is hitting the back of her throat. When he looks up and meets my gaze, I know something big is happening between the three of us. He knows it, too. I see it shining in his eyes. The weight of it settles along my bones, and it grounds me. It's a sense of certainty and contentment I've never experienced before.

Cade and I keep our gazes locked for a moment more before Ellis moans and snaps both of our attention back to her. He reaches down and pinches a nipple in his fingers, as I bend down and suck the other into my mouth. My fangs graze the skin of her breast, and her pussy clenches around my cock.

It takes every ounce of self-control I have to not bite her. She's flushed and disheveled. Her back arching off the counter as she searches for more. Her lips stretched wide around Cade's dick. The picture of her like this will stay with me forever. I bite down on my lip, drawing blood and tasting the copper tang mix with Ellis's arousal still on my tongue.

Ellis releases Cade's cock and breathlessly says, "I want you two to kiss."

"Fuck," Cade grunts. Sweat drips down his temple and a lock of his hair falls to his forehead with his movements.

Ellis takes him in her mouth again, working him like a popsicle. He looks at me and I lean forward, powerless against her wish and my desire to kiss him. Between Ellis clenching around my dick, Cade's tongue in my mouth, and the sounds and scents of sex in the room, I know I can't hold on much longer. I reach between us and press hard on Ellis's clit. She bucks off the island as she comes, squeezing my cock with each contraction.

I groan against Cade's mouth as my orgasm barrels through me, filling her while her inner muscles milk every drop from me. I distantly recognize Cade grunting his own release, but I'm too focused on piecing myself back together.

"Are you okay?" Cade asks between heaving breaths.

She looks at us with tears building on her lashes, and my

stomach drops. Fuck. We shouldn't have pushed her. Before I can drop to my knees and beg her to forgive us, I catch her emotions. Amazement, relief, hope.

She gives us a small, satisfied smile. "Thank you," she whispers.

I bend down and kiss her gently. "None of that. Let's get you upstairs."

"I'm not sure I can walk," she mumbles, her words slurring together.

Cade grins smugly as he hops off the island.

"Why the fuck are you grinning like that?" I ask him. "I'm the one who fucked her senseless."

He grabs all of our clothing and laughs. "Pretty sure it was a team effort, asshole."

I scoop Ellis off the counter, and she wraps her arms around my neck effortlessly. As I carry her to my room, all three of us completely naked. I can't help but wonder how long this can last. Her head resting sleepily on my shoulder is something I could easily get used to, but at what cost?

———

I wake as the sun is setting the next night, and I'm incredibly uncomfortable. My fangs ache and my stomach is cramping. Ellis's vanilla and lavender scent surrounds me, tempting me, making my mouth water and my cock hard. I lay still, breathing deeply, and try to tune out the sound of her heart. It's hard when my fangs pulse in time with each beat, and I swear I can hear her blood pumping through her veins.

I need to feed. Like really fucking bad. I don't usually let it go this long, but after meeting Ellis, it never seemed right to feed off someone else. There are a couple of girls I use consistently, and yeah, feeding usually turns sexual, which is one of the reasons why I haven't fed this past week. Just the thought is enough to turn my stomach. I'm not even sure I could physically do it when the time came.

What the hell am I going to do? I can't hold back much longer. If I do, I risk hurting Ellis, and that is the last thing I want.

She stirs, and I clench my jaw and squeeze my eyes shut. When she runs her hand down my stomach, every muscle in my body tightens and the urge to pounce on her and latch onto her neck almost overwhelms me. I grasp her wrist, stopping her pursuit, straining to not squeeze so hard I break her bones. Not biting her is physically hurting me—fire runs through my veins and my limbs throb. I reach over her and punch Cade awake.

"What the fuck, man?" he grumbles as he rubs his shoulder and opens his eyes. As soon as he sees me, he understands. Wrapping an arm around Ellis, he pulls her against him. "Why don't you go hop in the shower?" He lowers his mouth to her ear and whispers, "I'll join you in a minute."

She grins sleepily and slides out of bed. As soon as the bathroom door shuts, I release a breath. The pain doesn't go away, though.

"How bad?" Cade asks.

"Really fucking bad." I'm sweating now, my hands shaking.

"Do you want me to call one of the girls?" He reaches for his phone.

"Hell no," I grit out. "I don't think I can use either of them again. It's not right."

"Okay ..." he says slowly, sitting up to look at me. "It's Ellis, right? The reason you haven't fed from anyone else."

I nod and it hurts my neck, making me grimace. The muscles tense and aching.

"How long has it been?" he asks.

My eyes burn and I rub them. "Four weeks?" I don't actually remember the last time I fed.

"Are you fucking serious, Kai?" Cade glares at me and crosses his arms over his chest.

"I didn't feed before we kidnapped Ellis so I would have an

edge. After I met her ... I just couldn't bring myself to use anyone else."

He closes his eyes and bites his lip, his typical thinking pose. "So, ask her. After last night, I'm sure she wouldn't say no."

Just the idea sends agony through my body because I want it so fucking bad. I curl up in a ball and groan. "I don't think I can."

"Why the hell not?"

"Because ... I think she's my beloved."

Cade's mouth falls open and he stares at me in disbelief. "Your ... how ... are you sure?"

I rarely see Cade stumble over his words, but I understand. I feel the same way. "I mean, I can't be sure until I taste her blood." Just the thought sends fresh waves of desire and hunger through me, and I groan again. "But, as soon as I caught her scent the first time, my heart sped up. Every time I touch her, my heart races." I place my hand on my chest, my slow and steady heartbeat thumping under my palm.

"But, she's human. Can a vampire have a human beloved?" he asks, brows drawn low over his eyes.

"I've never heard of it, but nothing about Ellis is normal," I gasp. "Both her parents were supposedly mages. Why is she human? Something doesn't add up." *Fuck.* Just those short sentences took my breath away, leaving me gasping for air.

"And I'm guessing you don't want to mention this to her?"

"For obvious reasons," I say dryly. "I would kill for her to be my beloved, but I can't let her tie herself to me. What the fuck can I offer her besides being stuck with an assassin prince who is engaged to someone else?"

"Your dad would never accept her," Cade muses.

"No, he wouldn't." That is definitely bitterness in my tone. No way would my dad allow me to marry a human.

Cade looks as defeated as I feel. Well, right now, all I feel is awful.

"What happens if we fail?" Cade asks quietly, his gaze trained on the closed bathroom door. "Do we just walk away from her? What if we win? What do we do at the end of this?"

"I don't think I can let her go," I reply. "I don't *want* to let her go."

"But what if it's the best thing for her?"

I clench my jaw against the pain that thought brings. It's different from the agony of needing to feed. This pain burns in my chest, like my heart itself is rebelling at the thought. "Then we'll cross that bridge when we come to it." More anguish builds in my gut and I double over, grunting.

"You need to leave," Cade says firmly. "I don't care where you go or what you do, but you need to clear your head. Get away from Ellis for a bit."

I nod my agreement. "Yeah, I do." I slowly climb from the bed and have to grab my stomach as lightning shoots through my veins. "Holy fuck, this is awful."

"Figure something out, Malakai," Cade snaps. "You can't put Ellis in danger."

Fuck if I don't know that. I just don't know how I'm going to figure it out. Before the door closes behind me, I turn to look at Cade, the room swimming in my vision.

"This changes nothing," I say as I glance at the closed bathroom door where Ellis is showering. "Between the three of us, I mean."

Cade nods, but the relief in his eyes is clear. For her—hell, for him—I don't mind sharing.

ELLIS

I'M JUST ABOUT TO TURN OFF THE WATER WHEN CADE steps into the shower.

"I didn't think you were coming," I joke.

"Sorry," he says as he wraps his arms around me and pulls me tight to his chest. "I was talking to Kai."

"Mmm. So Malakai is more interesting than a naked chick in the shower, all wet and soapy?" I rub myself against him to make a point.

He groans and laughs at the same time, and it rumbles in his chest. "Nothing is more interesting than you, naked and soapy in the shower." He kisses my neck, and I angle my head to give him better access. "Are you okay with all of this?" he asks between kisses.

"With all of what?" It's hard to focus on his words with his mouth on my neck sending little shockwaves of pleasure through my body.

He pulls back with a smirk, like he knows exactly what he's doing to me. "With this. The touching. The kissing. Me and Kai, and both of us together? I don't want to make you uncomfortable."

"I don't know how to explain it, but yeah, I'm okay with it," I say slowly, trying to figure out what I want to say. "I mean, the touching and kissing are fine. It's easy now. Natural. And the sex was great. It just took me a bit to relax." I shrug my shoulders and drop my gaze to his chest, tracing the drops of water that slide down his smooth skin. "Sometimes I get stuck in my head. Sometimes something triggers a memory and I need a reminder of where I am and who I'm with." I stop my babbling and bite the inside of my cheek, tasting blood.

He lifts my head with a finger under my chin. "I'll give you all the reminders you need. I just don't want you to feel pressured into doing anything. You always have the final say, Ellis."

"Thank you," I whisper. Having that power means everything to me. I've never been in control before—of my life or in the bedroom. Cade and Malakai giving me that control is exactly what I need. I trail my fingers down his chest and pull my bottom lip between my teeth.

Cade tugs it free with his thumb. "What are you thinking right now?"

"I just want to take my life back." I stare into his eyes, hoping I can make him understand what I'm trying to say. "He took so much from me. And I'm sick of letting him control me. I want to … I want to live again."

Cade says nothing. Understanding shines in his eyes, and I'm grateful I don't see pity. He has never once made me feel ashamed for what I experienced. He has never once made me think it was my fault. It has always only been understanding. And his desire to make it all go away. He holds me to his chest, and we stay like that in the warm spray of water and a comfortable silence as my words settle around us.

"Can I ask you a question?" I ask timidly after a few minutes.

"Always." His hands trail down my back and over my ass, cupping my cheeks and pulling my hips to his.

"Are you and Malakai a thing?" I grind against him and smile when he takes a shuddering breath.

"I wouldn't say we're a thing," he answers carefully. This time it's me who takes a shuddering breath as his hands slide up my sides, and his thumbs graze my nipples. "But we've had sex in the past. Many times. Neither one of us will deny we find each other attractive."

His hand slides south and slips between my legs. Suddenly weak, I grasp his shoulders to keep myself from collapsing on the shower floor at his touch.

A slow grin spreads across Cade's face. "That turns you on, doesn't it?" His sultry whisper sends shivers down my spine.

My legs try to close around his hand, desperate for more pressure. "I find it incredibly hot," I reply honestly. "Especially when I'm in the middle of you two."

He rubs up my slit with more pressure, but avoids anywhere near my clit. Frustration builds, and I rock my hips, chasing his fingers.

"Last night was one of the hottest nights I've ever had." He keeps his fingers just shy of where I need them. "Watching Kai fuck you while you choked on my cock." He closes his eyes and smiles. "So fucking hot."

"Have you ever shared a woman before?" My breaths are coming faster and faster, and pressure builds between my legs.

I reach between us and grab his cock. Teasing him like he's doing to me, I keep my pressure light, just grazing the head of his dick with my thumb. He hisses in pleasure and thrusts his hips forward. When he slides one finger inside my pussy, I bite my lip to keep from moaning out loud. The slight stretch, while heavenly, isn't near enough.

"Never," he answers, pumping his finger in and out at a slow, lazy pace. "But I guarantee that won't be the last time you find yourself between us."

I want to ask if Sterling would ever join in, but I'm scared the answer will wipe away the heat that has built between us. Cade adds a second finger and my hand stills as I get distracted by the euphoria pulsing through my veins. Fire builds in my core, and

Cade crooks his fingers, hitting that spot that makes my knees buckle.

Pleasure rushes through me, and I pant, "I want you to fuck me while Malakai fucks you." My eyes pop wide, shocked that I actually voiced that desire. I'm not one for dirty talk, but what Cade is doing to me now, and what they both did to me last night? It's like they've opened a door, and I don't think I want it to shut again.

Cade's eyes darken, and his pupils dilate, seconds before his lips crash against mine. I protest when he removes his hand from between my legs, but I'm cut off when he grabs me by the back of the thighs and lifts me up. Excitement flutters in my stomach as I wrap my legs around his waist, feeling his cock rub against my center. I grind against him, desperately needing to feel him on my most sensitive parts, and he curses as his head falls to my shoulder. The shower wall presses against my back, the cool tile contrasting sharply with Cade's hot body and the warm water falling around us.

"You are the most amazing thing to happen to us," he whispers against my skin.

With his hands around my waist, he lifts me up and slides me onto his cock. We both moan as he pulls me down until he is seated fully. Breathing becomes difficult as he moves his hips, drawing out slowly and thrusting back in hard. He is slightly thicker than Malakai, and the stretch pleasantly burns through me.

The emotions that bubble up inside of me as Cade fucks me against the shower wall are so strong. A week ago, I would have said I never wanted to have sex again. A week ago, I was bruised and scarred and traumatized. I wouldn't say that trauma is gone. I wouldn't say I'm completely healed. But, these guys make me forget my past experiences. They shine a light on the good things. They show me what it means to be pleasured. I feel protected and cherished for the first time in years.

Tears burn the corner of my eyes and I squeeze them shut. The fact I'm so grateful a man has shown me kindness, is devastating. Always expecting pain from other people has worn me down, and I had given up on ever experiencing anything different. I bury my head in Cade's neck, desperate to hide this side of me. If I cry, he'll stop, and I don't want him to stop.

Cade, being Cade, seems to get it. The movement of his hips slows but doesn't stop. His thrusts become deeper but more gentle. No longer is he fucking me against the wall, instead he is making love to me, and it's too much for me to handle emotionally. My heart stutters to a stop in my chest, and a sob crawls up my throat.

His lips trail over my neck and jaw until he reaches my mouth, and he kisses me deeply. "I've got you, love," he whispers. "This is all you're going to know from here on out."

His words and his actions undo me. My orgasm creeps up on me and crests like a wave. It's not earth shattering. It's not as mind blowing as last night. But it's almost ... healing. Cade's orgasm follows mine and we both still. He holds me against him, rubbing my back and kissing my shoulders and neck. There are no words spoken between us, but there is no need for them. The stillness in the air is calming and helps to ground me.

When the water cools, he sets me down. Unable to look into his eyes, too scared of what he'll see in mine, I keep my gaze trained on his chest. I don't know what to say or how to react after what just occurred between us. Luckily, I'm saved from having to think of something to say when my stomach rumbles loudly.

"Oh my gods, how embarrassing," I groan and slap a hand over my belly.

Cade chuckles and turns off the water. "Let's get you something to eat, love."

———

"Where's Malakai?" I ask between bites of my grilled cheese.

It turns out Cade is a much better cook than Malakai. When Cade said he was making me a grilled cheese, I expected your standard slice of american cheese between two pieces of bread. Boy, was I wrong. This man turned my grilled cheese into some kind of delicacy.

"He's burning off some energy," Cade mumbles.

I turn to look at him. "Is he okay? Why does he have to burn off energy?"

"Sometimes his empath abilities overwhelm him." He shifts on the couch, and he won't meet my gaze.

I frown, but say, "Oh, okay." I take another bite of my sandwich and change the subject. "This is seriously the best grilled cheese I've ever had."

Cade smiles. "Good, I'm glad you like it. You need to eat more."

I look down at the food in my lap. "Yeah, I lost a lot of weight the past two years."

A muscle ticks in Cade's jaw as he leans his elbows on his knees. When he looks at me, his smile doesn't reach his eyes. "Well, it's a good thing I like to cook."

"Grilled cheese?" Sterling growls as he enters the library. "You better have made me one."

Our eyes meet, but there's no acknowledgement on his face of what almost happened between us. Pain slices through my heart, and I press a hand to my chest. Why does it hurt so much? He's never once shown any interest in me. So why do I expect him to?

Cade grins and slides a sandwich wrapped in a paper towel across the coffee table. Sterling unwraps his sandwich and takes a massive bite.

"Is that meat?" I ask, eyeballing his sandwich. It's definitely not just a plain grilled cheese.

"Yeah," Cade snorts. "It's more of a turkey melt than grilled cheese, but we gotta keep the wolf fed and happy."

Makes sense he would eat a lot of meat. It actually sounds really good. A corner of Sterling's mouth twitches up, and I realize I'm staring at his sandwich.

"Is there something you want, Ellis?" His low voice slides over my skin and makes me shiver.

I bite my lip and notice his gaze zero in on the movement. "Can I have a bite?"

"You're going to take food away from the wolf?" Cade cries. "Are you crazy?" He shakes his head in mock dismay and runs his hand down his face.

Sterling makes his way around the table and sits next to me. It's the first time we've sat near each other, and he keeps his distance, making sure our legs or arms don't touch. He holds out his sandwich and I lean in to take a bite. As he watches my mouth, I know I don't imagine the desire burning in his icy eyes.

"Damn, Cade." I say around my bite of food. "You should be a cook instead of a healer."

He chuckles. "I'm glad you like my cooking. I enjoy taking care of people anyway I can."

We all finish our food in silence, savoring the yummy goodness too much to talk. When I'm done, I stand and walk around the library, taking in everything with new eyes. Now that I feel like I understand the guys better, I notice little things that make me smile.

On the mini fridge by the bar, a stick figure drawing of Malakai is proudly displayed. I know it's Malakai because of the fangs and detailed drawing of a pierced dick. If I had to guess, I'd say he drew it himself.

There is a little stuffed wolf on one of the leather chairs, and I don't fail to notice the glass eyes have been painted ice blue. There is also a collar around the wolf's neck. I can't read the name on the tag, but knowing these guys, I'm guessing it's not complimentary.

I look around for something that reminds me of Cade, and I actually laugh out loud when I see it. Hanging on the wall above the pool cues is a picture of Cade without his clothes. The picture is positioned perfectly, so it looks like a pool cue has replaced his cock.

"You guys really *are* like a family," I say quietly, not able to hide the longing in my voice.

Cade stands with a smile and walks to the pool cue in question. He runs his hand down it suggestively and winks at me. "They're assholes most of the time, but they're my pack. I wouldn't trade them for anything."

"That's how I feel about Allie," I say, leaning against the table. "She has been there for me through all the worst moments of my life. Starting when I lost my mom and sister."

A loud thump makes me jump, and I turn to see Sterling bending down to pick up a book he appeared to have dropped. He won't look at me but his cheeks are stained red and his movements are jerky. Nothing like the smooth animal prowess he typically exudes.

"Are you okay, Sterling?" I ask.

"Fine," he bites out before storming from the library without another word.

I turn to Cade, chewing on my bottom lip. "What was that about?"

He shrugs, brows drawn down and looking just as bewildered as I feel. "I have no idea." He stares at the door Sterling left through for a moment more before shaking his head. "Wanna play a round of pool?"

I glance at the cues hanging on the wall and green felt covered table. "I've never played before."

"Oh, well then," Cade says with an evil grin as he rubs his hands together eagerly. "This is every guy's dream come true. Teaching a beautiful woman how to play pool. It's the perfect excuse for getting up close and personal."

I laugh softly at his antics. It feels good to laugh. "Isn't it a little late for that? You've been plenty close to me."

"Never close enough," he says.

My stomach flip-flops. The way he said that, the way his eyes seem to pierce straight into my soul. I have a hard time drawing in a full breath as butterflies take flight in my stomach.

He grabs my arm and pulls me in front of him. Positioning me so I'm facing the pool table, he puts the cue in my hands. He goes over techniques, and moves my hands and hips so I'm positioned correctly. I'd like to say I was paying attention, but his hips pressed against my ass, his arms around me, and the heat his body is putting off are the only things I can focus on.

"I didn't hear a single word you just said," I admit. "I'm a little distracted at the moment." I emphasize my point by rubbing my ass against his hips. A thrill goes through me as he groans and his cock thickens behind his jeans.

"That is highly inappropriate behavior," he whispers in my ear while keeping his growing erection pressed against my ass. "I'm trying to be a good teacher."

"Maybe I don't want you to be a good teacher ..." I trail off suggestively.

Cade curses and spins me around. The pool cue falls from his hands and he presses my hips against the table, leaning me backward with a gentle hand on my chest. The edge of the table digs into my hip bones, but I barely notice it as his lips trail up my neck. He leaves little kisses over my jaw and the corners of my mouth. It's addicting. There is no such thing as too much Cade. I let my hands slide up his chest. His t-shirt is strained across his muscles and I love the softness of the fabric over the planes of his body.

His mouth is inches from mine, and I can already taste him on my tongue and feel his breath fanning across my lips. Right before his mouth meets mine, a loud screeching beep sounds from somewhere in the library. I jump at the sudden noise and look around. Cade curses and steps away.

"What is that?" I ask loudly over the noise.

Cade grabs his phone from the coffee table and silences it. As his eyes scan the screen, his face pales. I open my mouth to ask what's going on, but the library door opens and Sterling barrels in.

"It's Kai," he says, holding out his own phone as well. His icy blue eyes are wide and wild. The energy he's putting off is palpable. Nervous and chaotic. Scared.

"Get the car." Cade barks and heads for the little office off of the library where they keep their weapons.

Sterling dashes out the side doors, and a second later, his Land Rover's engine fires up. Standing next to the pool table, I stare at the patio door, mouth hanging open. What the hell is going on?

"Cade, tell me what's happening," I demand, loudly enough for Cade to hear in the little office.

He emerges with his arms laden full of guns and knives. "I'll tell you in the car. Let's go."

I open the door for him just as Sterling pulls the Land Rover around. As soon as the car doors shut, Sterling guns it around the estate and down the driveway. The gates are closed, and Sterling curses as he slams on the brakes.

"Shit. Hurry up," he mutters as the gates slowly squeak open.

When the opening is wide enough to fit the Land Rover through, he floors it again and takes off down the street. I lean forward between the front seats and look back and forth between the guys. Sterling is focused on the street, the lights from the dash casting a haunting glow on his face. Cade is doing something on his phone and a muscle ticks in his jaw as he grinds his teeth together.

"Okay, someone better start explaining," I say shakily. Suddenly nauseous, I press a hand to my belly. An uneasiness has settled within me, almost like some part of me already knows what's happened.

Sterling answers first. "Cade set each of us up with an emergency alert on our phones. If we are ever in trouble, we can press the button and it notifies the others that we need help."

I have to swallow to work moisture back into my mouth. "That beeping was a notification that Malakai is in trouble?" My voice breaks on the word *trouble*.

"It was," Cade answers gravely. "When activated, we are sent a GPS location of where the alert was initiated."

"Okay," I say, forcing myself to breathe evenly. "Where is he?" What's happened that a vampire like Malakai needed to call for help? I shut my imagination down, stopping the downward spiral of possible horrible scenarios.

"He was in the alley off of Court Street, when he signaled for help," Cade replies. "I'll hack into the street cams to find out what happened and if he's still there."

A tense silence fills the car as Cade does his thing. I chew on the inside of my cheek, a nervous habit I developed after my mom and sister's death. Sterling flies through the city, heading toward Court Street which follows the river Altair, and when he gets to the bridge spanning the expanse of water, he slows down.

"What do we have, Cade?" Sterling asks, his hands clenched tightly on the steering wheel.

"Fuck," Cade whispers.

I lean forward between the seats again to look at Cade's phone, but he angles it away from me. Frustration crawls up my throat, but I bite back the acidic comment that will do nothing but fan the already raging flames.

"He's still in the alley." He glances back at me, indecision warring on his face.

"Don't keep anything from me, Cade Campbell," I snap. "You brought me along, don't shut me out."

"Sam is there," Cade says tensely. "It looks like Kai crashed his motorcycle. Sam and his guys have him circled. He looks bad. Real bad."

My breath catches in my throat, getting stuck on the lump that forms at his words. Invisible bands wrap around my chest, slowly squeezing the air from my lungs, and the corners of my vision go blurry.

"Fuck!" Sterling screams and slams his hands on the steering wheel.

The noise jars me out of my head. I jump and suck in a huge breath. Gritting my teeth, I swallow down my fear. The last thing I need is for my anxiety to take over. I won't let that happen.

Cade leans down to grab a gun from the floor at his feet. He quickly checks the clip and passes it back to me. "You stay in the car. Don't even think about opening that door." His voice is firm, and leaves no room for argument. He turns back to Sterling. "Go up Court Street. When you get to The Black Crow, slow down. I don't want them hearing the engine. The alley is a block away from The Crow."

Cade loads his own guns and slides them into the pockets and waistband of his pants. Before we get to the alley, he turns to me again. "Please, do not leave the car. I will ward it so no one can get in. Stay down and out of sight."

"I won't leave." I promise. "Just, please, be careful. And get Malakai back."

Cade leans back and gives me a quick, hard kiss. In the rearview mirror, I meet Sterling's gaze. Something flickers in his icy blues, but he says nothing. Words bubble up inside me, but get stuck in my throat once again.

He turns to Cade. "Ready?" Sterling asks. His teeth are already elongating. His nose morphing into a snout.

Cade nods, and the car rolls to the alley. Sterling throws the car in park and both guys are out in a flash. I drop onto the floor in the back and hold my gun at the ready. As soon as the doors close behind the guys, the noises start. Gun shots, shouts, growls, the pinging of bullets as they hit the ground and the brick wall of the alley.

I want to look to see what is happening, but I know Cade is right. The risk is too great. If Sam sees me, who knows what he'll do. No, that's a lie. I know exactly what he'll do, and I also know I won't live through anything he has planned for me.

Moans and screams are added to the symphony of violence outside the car. Growls and roars sound from multiple shifters. Are the guys okay? Is Malakai okay? Cade only said he was real bad off. How bad is real bad? He's a vampire, so he should be able to heal from anything, except a stake to the heart or head. I don't let myself think that. I *can't* let myself think that.

The fear that overcame me when I found out Malakai was in danger confuses me. Intense terror flooded my system, so much so that it almost paralyzed me. Why do I have such fear of the guys getting hurt? Just because I've had sex with two of them, doesn't mean we're in any kind of relationship. Does it?

Still, the connection I have with them is so strong. There is an actual sensation inside me whenever I'm near them, a tug in my gut physically drawing me closer to them. I don't understand it, and it terrifies me. But, I don't know what to do about it.

Do I want to do anything about it?

The sounds outside get louder. A crescendo of gunfire and shouting. I curl tighter into a ball, trying to drown out the noise. My imagination goes wild, and I can't stop it. Images flood my mind, stopping my heart in my chest, and sending tendrils of fear oozing through my bloodstream. Malakai, with shards of metal piercing his chest. Sterling lying motionless on the ground, icy blue eyes staring unseeing at the sky above. Cade, grasping a gaping hole in his chest as he tries to save his friends. I squeeze my eyes shut tight until bright lights flare behind my eyelids from the pressure, trying to erase the awful images plaguing me.

The rapid fire gunshots finally dissipate, slowing until there's only silence. I wait a moment more before taking a deep breath and preparing myself to peek outside. Not knowing what I'll find or what I'll do if the images in my head are actually reality.

"Sterling! Leave him. I need your help with Kai!"

Cade's shout makes its way into the closed car, and I pop up to look out the window in time to see Sterling bound into view from a side alley. He approaches Cade and shifts into his human form. A twisted mess of metal lays at the mouth of the alley, and I dimly recognize it as Malakai's black motorcycle. I can't see Malakai, but Sterling and Cade's grim expressions tighten my gut.

As the guys heft Malakai into their arms, I hop out of the car to give them room to slide him in. I press a hand to my mouth to stifle my gasp when they pass me. Seeing Malakai, the strong, deadly, dangerous vampire, hanging limply in his friend's arms sends the world spinning around me. There is no smirk, no twinkling gray eyes, no ... *life*. I wait for Cade and Sterling to get him situated laying across the backseat before I hop in and sit on the floor by his head.

Afraid to touch him, my hands hover over his too still body. He's barely recognizable. His pale skin is gray. Cuts and bruises pepper his face. Dried blood is matted in his unruly black hair and oozes from multiple wounds. He looks dead. I shakily place my hand on his chest and almost collapse when his heart thumps slowly and weakly under my palm.

"Where are we going?" Sterling asks as he slides naked into the driver's seat and starts the engine.

Cade climbs into the passenger side and looks back at Malakai with a frown. "I don't know. We can't take him to a hospital. We'll be sitting ducks there. We really need to get back to the estate."

"He's going to be okay, though, right?" I ask, my voice shaking. "He hasn't been staked, so he will heal on his own."

Cade's eyes shutter, and he turns to look out of the windshield. "Take us to the estate," he says quietly.

"Cade. He'll heal on his own, right?" I ask again. He doesn't answer, and my heart pounds harder. "What aren't you telling me, Cade?"

He shakes his head and presses his lips together, refusing to meet my gaze. Ice floods my veins and something ugly writhes in my gut. An anger, not directed at Cade, but at the world. An untamed need to destroy those who did this. It's such a powerful thing it knocks the breath from me, and I have to blink back the rage turning my vision red. *What the fuck is happening to me?*

I snap. "Dammit, Cade! Answer the fucking question!" Terror raises my voice to a screech, and I wince. In my life I have experienced fear plenty of times, especially over the past two years, but this is like a different kind of fear. It's paralyzing. It consumes my thoughts and fuels my anxiety. I need to know that Malakai will be okay. The thought of him not being okay makes me sick to my stomach. It mixes with the anger and leaves me shaky and unsteady.

It's crazy how quickly these three guys have embedded themselves into my very being. Maybe it's because they are the first ones to actually treat me like a person. Maybe I latched onto them too tightly because I want so badly to be accepted and cared for. Whatever the reason, I know the feelings I have for them are growing by the day, and the thought of losing one of them is too much.

"Cade, please." Desperation makes my voice wobble. "Tell me he'll be okay." Tears slip out of my eyes and track down my cheeks.

Cade closes his eyes, as if he can't bear to see my reaction. "He hasn't fed in a month."

"What the fuck!" Sterling shouts. "What the hell was he thinking?"

"What does that mean?" I whisper, looking back and forth between Cade and Malakai.

"Vampires need to feed at least every other week, if not every week," Cade explains. "Malakai was on the edge of losing himself this morning. It's why he left. He was trying to clear his head a little bit."

Sterling picks up where Cade leaves off. "What Cade is trying to say is, Malakai doesn't have what he needs in his system to heal." I don't need to see his expression to know it's dire. His voice tells me enough, flat and dull.

Sterling's words echo in my head, bouncing and rebounding,

as I stare at Malakai's still form. The strands of his hair are like silk when I trail my fingers through them, brushing a stray curl from his forehead. I can't wrap my mind around this situation or what it means. He won't heal on his own because he hasn't fed? Everything inside me has gone numb, a stillness has settled over me, a white fog that stuffs my brain with emptiness.

I whip my head to look at Cade, an ember of hope bursting to light. "You can heal him, though, can't you? You can use your magic to heal him." The pain on Cade's face is all I need to see to know his answer before he says it. I'm already shaking my head when he opens his mouth.

"I could heal him," he says slowly, "But with his injuries and him not having fed in so long, he would most likely be rogue when he woke. It's not a risk we can take."

Rogue. Ice fills my veins. When a vampire doesn't feed, they go rogue. They basically turn into monsters, preying on anything alive, leaving a path of destruction in their wake. It doesn't happen very often, but when it does, the only way to stop them is a stake to the heart.

"So what do we do?" I ask, my throat burning. "We just let him die?" Tears are rolling down my cheeks now. There is a crack forming in my heart. It physically hurts. It hurts so fucking bad it steals my breath and makes me double over, clutching at my chest.

Cade looks defeated, his eyes swimming with unshed tears. "He won't die without being staked. He will stay like this, in a coma-like state," he says roughly. The pain etched across his face makes my heart break even more.

"We can't leave him like this," I cry. "We can't just do nothing. We have to try to help him!"

Sterling asks, looking back at me through the rearview mirror. "What can we do?" His usually shining blue eyes are dark and strain lines the corners of them.

I shake my head. What can we do? We can't take him to the hospital. Cade is right. It's way too dangerous. The wheels turn in my brain. We can't take him to the hospital, but what if we bring the hospital to him?

"Allie!" I turn to face Cade. "Allie is a nurse. Maybe she can do something." A flicker of hope takes up residence in my chest once again. An ember that I want so badly to fan into a wildfire.

Cade doesn't look hopeful, but I think he's as desperate as I am when he says, "Call her."

ELLIS

He hasn't moved.

I keep my hand on his chest just to make sure his heart is still beating. Logically, I know what Cade said is true. He won't die without being staked, but I can't shake the feeling that if I move my hand, his heart will stop. It doesn't help that he looks like a corpse and the black sheets of his bed only make the gray pallor of his skin more pronounced.

When Allie enters his room, I release a nervous breath. This is it. The next few moments are going to shape the rest of my life. I can't explain it, but there is an energy in the air, a heaviness that speaks of premonition, and I know something life changing is about to happen.

Allie looks nervous as she clutches her backpack straps and her wide eyes take everything in. From Sterling leaning against the far wall, to Cade looming behind her, to me sitting on the edge of a bed with a lifeless vampire. As soon as her gaze lands on me, she relaxes and rushes to my side, pulling me into a hug. I lean against her for a moment, soaking up her strength and letting it refill my empty reserves.

"I don't know anything about vampires, El," she cautions and looks fearfully over her shoulder to the other guys. "They are so different from humans. I'm not sure I can do anything." She tugs on her blond braid pulled over her shoulder.

"I just ... we have to try something," I whisper, sounding so lost. My voice is small and quiet.

Allie swallows and nods, shrugging her backpack off. "Okay. Tell me what you can."

Her no-nonsense, get-the-job-done attitude that makes her such a fantastic nurse, calms my nerves. If Allie is here, everything will be okay. It always is when she's around. Without her, I wouldn't have survived the past two years. My gaze returns to Malakai while Cade fills Allie in on everything. His lack of feeding, the injuries, the concern of him going rogue if Cade heals him.

Allie takes it all in stride, nodding and chewing on her lip as she thinks. "What if we get someone in here to feed him?" she asks. "Maybe that will kick start his healing?"

Cade looks at me, an unreadable expression blanking his face, and shakes his head. "It won't work."

"Why not?" I ask. "It makes sense. It's at least worth a shot, right?"

Cade kneels in front of me and takes my hands. "It won't work, Ellis. Just ... trust me on that," he says softly.

I search his gaze, filled with despair, fear, and exhaustion. And something I can't name. "You're not telling me everything."

His violet eyes are more serious than I have ever seen them. He releases a breath and stands, walking to the window before turning back around to face me. "Because it's not my place to tell you."

"But, if it's something that can help him, you have to tell me." I walk over to him and place my hands on either side of his face. Leaving Malakai is almost impossible, my very being rebels at the action, but I have to convince Cade to tell me what's going on. "Please, Cade. I don't know why, but every part of me is screaming that I can't lose him. I can't lose any of you. That pain would destroy me. I don't think I'd survive it." My words are nothing more than hushed whispers as I beg him for answers.

He closes his eyes and presses his forehead to mine. "He is going to kill me for telling you this." When he pulls away, he sits in the window seat and tugs me down next to him. He brushes a stray curl from my forehead before speaking. "Bringing in someone else won't work because his body will most likely reject the blood. It's the reason he hasn't fed in a month. He physically cannot feed from anyone right now. Except you."

Blink.

Blink.

I have to pry my tongue from the roof of my mouth. "Me? What do you mean?"

"Malakai told me this morning that he thinks you're his beloved."

The silence in the room is deafening. Everyone is staring at Cade with varying degrees of shock. I glance at Sterling, seeking some kind of clarification, but he is looking at Cade with so much pain it almost distracts me from my whirlwind thoughts.

"B ... beloved?" I stammer.

"A beloved is a vampire's form of soul mate," Cade explains gently. "Shifters have mates. Mages have soul bonds. Vampires have beloveds."

I know what a beloved is to a vampire, but I let him explain. At this point, I need all the explanations I can get. My hands grow clammy and I wipe them on my leggings. When I do, I notice the tremors making my fingers shake.

"Malakai believes you are his," Cade continues, either oblivious to or ignoring the chaos erupting inside of me. "There is no way for him to know with any certainty unless he tastes your blood. But whenever you were near him, he said his heart would race. A vampire's heart rate is usually slower than a human's. The first sign a vampire is near their beloved is a racing heart."

A million thoughts float through my mind, and I reach out and latch onto the first one I can. "Why didn't he ever bite me then? I wouldn't have stopped him." Just the thought of him sinking those fangs into my neck is enough to turn me on, despite the situation at hand.

Cade shakes his head. "Because it would have turned sexual immediately. The way a vampire ties their beloved to them is by biting them during sex. It would have bound you to him permanently."

I'm still failing to see the problem with that. Maybe I'm in shock and the answer is obvious, but I'm having a hard time finding a problem. Except ...

"He doesn't want me," I whisper brokenly. The world around me slows. My stomach lurches as dread overcomes me. I suddenly feel so very silly. Despite everything we've been through, and the connection I swear I have with them, I barely know these guys. They had lives before they were stuck with me. I probably threw a wrench in their plans. Of course, Malakai doesn't want me.

Cade grabs my cheeks in both of his hands and forces me to look at him. "Ellis, love, that is not true," he says firmly. "He wants you more than you can possibly know. He didn't bite you because he was protecting you. He's the Crown Prince of the vampires. His life is dangerous. Anyone associated with him has a target on their back. He didn't want that life for you."

Cade rubs his thumbs over my cheeks, wiping away tears I hadn't realized were falling. My heart beats sluggishly in my chest, like it's fighting to continue pumping blood despite the wound it has just taken.

"It's so much more complicated than you think," Cade continues. "As the crown prince, he has duties to his people. His dad has arranged a marriage for him. He would never accept a human for his son. None of that ever mattered to Kai, though. He only ever thought about your safety."

I rear back out of his grasp. "He's engaged?" I don't even recognize my voice. It's a weird combination of flat and shrill. Over the past two years, there have been plenty of times I have felt empty inside. But Cade's words hit harder than anything else I've experienced. Malakai is engaged, and he slept with me? "I need some air," I gasp.

Cade winces as I stand. I don't look at Malakai laying on the bed, or Sterling and Allie standing against the wall. I ignore Cade's attempts to stop me from leaving, and push through the door, making my way blindly to the library. Tears blur my vision, but I hold them at bay. Time moves strangely. My body is worn out and exhausted when I push through the door that leads to the patio, as if I've run for miles and miles. But at the same time, it's like it only took me seconds to reach the iron bench, where I collapse and bring my knees to my chest.

Engaged.

Beloved.

Human.

I'm a fool. Shame burns up my neck and into my cheeks. How could I ever think these guys cared for me? Just because we've slept together doesn't mean they care. I'm probably just another notch in their belt, as the saying goes. An easy target. Someone so desperate to *feel* they didn't have to put any effort into it. *I am such a fucking idiot.* I latched onto the first things that made me feel good and didn't think twice about the consequences.

The patio door opens and Allie steps out into the warm summer night. She sits next to me on the bench and wraps her arms around me. It's that familiar touch, her scent of roses, that finally breaks down my barriers. I cry. Soul wrenching sobs that shake my entire body. Allie holds me through it all, keeping me together when I just want to fall apart into a million tiny pieces. I cry, purging the wound that has opened inside of me. The one that pierces through my heart to my very soul, burning and gouging out any bit of peace I've experienced the past week.

When my body is too exhausted to continue, my tears finally slow, then stop. Weariness sits with me, driving into my bones. I just want to curl into a ball and never get up again. Allie rubs soothing circles on my back and says nothing while I try to piece myself back together. An impossible task.

"I am so stupid," I whisper, throat raw from my crying.

"You are not," she says. "Why would you ever say that?"

"He's engaged, Allie!" I pull away from her and wipe my cheeks. "I slept with him. I let myself fall for these guys when I mean nothing to them. How could they—powerful magicals—ever care about me? I'm just a worthless *human*."

"Okay, I'm going to ignore that last bit for now. We'll come back to it later." She tucks a stray curl behind my ear and stares me straight in the eyes. "As for those guys not caring for you ... are you blind? It's so obvious all three of them care about you. They have protected you and kept you safe through this entire thing when they could have just as easily handed you over. Standing in that room and watching the way Cade and Sterling look at you? I'm not going to lie, Ellis. It made me a little jealous. They look at you like you are the only person in the room."

"Even if that were true," I say, hiccuping, "Malakai is engaged."

"Cade said his dad arranged it," she says. "You, of all people, know what it's like to not have a say in who you are told to be with. If Malakai truly cared about his fiancé, do you think he would have signed up for this contest in the first place? If he truly cared about her, do you think he would have slept with you?" She wipes tears off my cheeks with her fingers. "*Beloved*, Ellis. That is so much more than an arranged marriage. No one in their right mind would ever walk away from that."

"But he was going to," I say sullenly.

Allie sighs and throws her hands up in exasperation. "He was doing what all guys do. They think they are doing what is right by protecting us and walking away. Don't you think you should get a say in this? You are half of the equation as well. What do *you* want, Ellis?"

Beloved. Essentially, a soul mate. What Allie says makes sense. But is that just because I'm grasping at straws? Am I just desperate to ease the ache in my chest? That tugging in my gut says no. It's like my soul knew what Malakai was to me this entire time. The safety and comfort I've felt around him makes sense now. Deep down, I knew he was so much more, so it was easy to let my guard down. Instinctually, I knew he wouldn't hurt me.

"Look, I've known you my whole life," Allie says. "It has been years, Ellis. Years since I last saw you smile for real. You haven't been yourself since your mom and sister's deaths. These guys have brought you back to life. You laugh when we talk on the phone. I missed that laugh. I miss the light in your eyes, and I can see a glimmer of that light again. Because of them."

She isn't wrong. I have been a shell of myself for years. Just going through the motions of everyday life. Surviving. That's all I've been doing. Even with all the shit of the contest, I've been *living* these past few weeks. Not surviving, but living.

I know what I need to do. Even if Malakai doesn't want me as his beloved, I can't let him die. Even if, at the end of this contest, they walk away from me, I will at least know Malakai is alive. A world without him is not a place I want to live, even if I'm living separate from him. At least I'll be living because of him.

———

I walk into Malakai's room and ignore Cade and Sterling softly talking by the window. Sitting on the edge of the bed, I smooth Malakai's hair back from his face. "It's going to be okay, I promise." I lean down and press a kiss to his clammy forehead.

Without giving the guys any time to stop me, I pull the scalpel from my pocket that Allie gave me and slice it across my wrist. The sting barely registers in the back of my mind. All I can focus on is getting my arm to Malakai's mouth before Cade or Sterling can stop me.

By the time they realize what I'm doing, it's too late. Blood wells ruby bright along the cut and I press my wrist to Malakai's lips, using my other hand to open them. I watch as drops of blood fall and land on his tongue.

"Ellis!" Cade rushes to my side, fear making his voice tremble. "What are you doing?"

"I won't let him die," I say with resolve echoing in my voice.

Just as Cade reaches out to grab my shoulders, Malakai's hand clamps down on my wrist. His mouth seals around the cut, and his tongue feathers over my skin. Shivers run down my spine as he sucks my blood into his mouth, the tugging sensation odd but not unwelcome. I watch his throat work as he swallows once, twice, three times. Each pull on my wrist sends lightning shooting through my veins, and it doesn't take long before I'm on fire.

On the fourth swallow, Malakai's eyes open. The gray is mostly swallowed by red, but I still see recognition flare in his gaze as it lands directly on me. Cade tenses, prepared to grab me if Malakai were to try to hurt me.

"Ellis," Malakai rasps against my skin. "What have you done?" He squeezes his eyes shut and his face screws up in pain. With tremendous effort, he releases my wrist and pushes it away. My blood stains his lips, and a drop slowly slides down his chin. "You need to leave. Now. I can't hold myself back much longer."

I watch as his muscles tense and shake. It's obvious he is fighting himself, holding himself back from launching at me. I grasp his face in both of my hands and lean down. I press a soft kiss to his lips, tasting the copper of my blood, and he groans in agony.

"Ellis, please," he begs against my lips. His entire body is shaking and sweat beads on his brow.

"I'm not leaving," I say firmly. "You don't get to make my choices for me. This involves me, too, and I get to have a say if I want it or not."

He opens his eyes. His chest heaves as he stares at me with gritted teeth, fangs digging into his lower lip.

"I want it. I want you, Kai." There is no fear, no uncertainty, as I speak those words. Only a sense of rightness. This is how it's supposed to be.

I press my lips harder to his. He's stiff at first, holding his body perfectly still. Until I pull away and angle my head to give him access to my neck, my gaze never leaving his almost entirely red-tinted eyes. His self-control snaps, and he moves faster than I can track. His arms band around me, knocking the breath from my lungs, and his mouth moves to my neck. A soft growl rumbles in his chest and sends shivers of anticipation down my spine. Heat is already building in my core when he slides his fangs along my skin.

"Ellis!" Cade's hand squeezes my shoulder like he's about to pull me away. "Do you have any idea what you're doing?"

"Yes," I breathe.

As if that gave him the permission he was looking for, Malakai's fangs sink into my neck. Fire erupts over my skin where he bit. It shoots through my veins and burns me from the inside out. I scream. It hurts so bad, but the pain only lasts for a second before it morphs, and my scream turns into a moan. It's like a light switch was flipped and I went from experiencing the most excruciating pain of my life to the most incredible pleasure.

Each tug from my vein is echoed in my core. It takes three pulls before I orgasm. It crashes through me so fast and harsh my body shakes and spasms uncontrollably, and light dances behind my eyelids. When it passes, I'm panting and sweating. My body is limp and heavy, like it's been wrung through the ringer. I distantly hear Cade and the others leave the room, but I spare no thought for them.

Malakai pulls away and I shudder as his fangs slide out of my neck. Blood dribbles down his chin snd his eyes, now mostly gray, are wide and shining. Complete and utter awe lines his features. "Ellis," he breathes. "You taste so fucking amazing. Like the finest wine—rich and dark, with a hint of fruity sweetness."

He licks his lips, my gaze tracking the movement, and his mouth curls into a seductive grin with his fangs on full display.

Fangs that were just buried in my neck. I clench my legs together, remembering what it was like to have them inside me. What would it be like to have his pierced cock inside me at the same time as his fangs? The pleasure from just his bite alone destroyed my world. What the hell would sex do to me at the same time?

Malakai's nostrils flare as he scents my arousal. "Ellis," he groans. "If we do this, you know what it means, right? There is no going back."

"Quit trying to talk me out of it." I swing my leg over his hips and straddle him. He's so hard under me, and *fuck,* I want him inside me. "I've made up my mind, Kai." I emphasize my point by tangling my hands in his hair and kissing him. The coppery flavor of my blood is still on his tongue, and I don't know what it says about me, but it turns me on even more.

Kai flips us so I'm laying on my back, and he hovers over me, resting his weight on his elbows. We stare at each other for a moment, drinking in the sight and committing everything to memory. The fluttering in my stomach makes me squirm. This man does things to me. The way he is looking at me like he never wants to stop makes my heart pound in my chest. Emotions build inside me, a rising tide I know I'll never be able to keep at bay. Knowing Kai will pick up on them, I force my focus elsewhere.

All the bruising and cuts have disappeared from his skin. He's completely healed from my blood. The thought that me, a human, can have that kind of effect on him, makes my heart stutter. Maybe I'm not so useless after all?

My hands slide under his torn t-shirt, skimming along his sides and drawing up the fabric. He shivers at the touch and reaches behind his neck with one hand to pull his shirt off. His beautifully sculpted body draws my attention, and I rake my gaze over him, drinking in the deep grooves of his muscles.

Kai makes quick work of removing the rest of our clothing. The first time we had sex, it was more frenzied. There was no time for enjoying the sight of each other. Now, he takes a moment to rake his gaze over my naked body and I return the favor. *Holy shit.* Kai is everything I could have ever dreamt up for myself. His beauty dries my mouth. I could stare at him all damn day.

"I want to take this slow," he mutters against my neck. "But I don't think I can."

Anticipation swirls deep in my gut as his fangs glide along my sensitive neck. "Then don't take it slow." I lift my hips and feel the cool metal of his piercings against my skin.

Kai curses, and he takes my head in his hands to tilt it to the side. His eyes are dark and bottomless, drawing me in and drowning me in desire. This time, when Kai bites me, I feel only a slight pinch before the euphoria of pleasure washes through me. My body is no longer mine to control. All I can do is ride the pleasure and do whatever feels good. My hips lift at the same time Kai grinds his cock against me. The pleasure is so intense my brain short-circuits. When Kai growls against my neck, the vibrations combined with the tugging on my vein almost send me over the edge.

Kai reaches between us to fist his cock and lines it up to my entrance. With his fangs still in my neck, he slides inside me. It's like nothing I have ever experienced before. The bliss roaring through my veins as he pulls more blood from me, combined with his cock and the piercings rubbing all the right places, the pleasure overwhelms me.

I rake my nails down Kai's back, feeling his muscle flex as he thrusts his hips. He wasn't lying when he said he couldn't take it slow. He pounds into me, fast and hard, and I take it all. Welcome it and beg for more. I never want this moment to end, this joining of more than just our bodies, but our souls. Kai's presence invades me in all the best ways. My vampire prince. My prince of darkness.

Tingles of pleasure start in my back and spread outward, roaring through me as my orgasm builds to a crescendo. My back arches and I scream out my pleasure with Kai's name on my lips. He growls against my neck and his cock thickens as he shudders over me, finding his release while my inner walls clench around him.

Gasping for breath, he pulls his fangs out of my neck and I whimper. It's so sensitive, echoes of pleasure rolling through me as he runs his tongue along the two puncture marks, licking up any blood and sealing the wounds. Tears prick my eyes unbidden when he pulls back to look at me. His gray eyes are shining brighter than I have ever seen, and he's looking at me with wonder and amazement.

Kai leans his forehead against mine. "Ellis. Baby girl. Why?" His question is a mixture of pain and hope.

I run my fingers through his hair, scraping my nails against his scalp. Nerves flutter in my belly as I contemplate what to say to him. "Because. I couldn't bear the thought of you dying. I don't think I would survive losing you." Swallowing thickly, I push his head away enough to look him in the eyes. "Before you, I didn't know who I was anymore. I was just floating through each day. But you—all of you—reminded me of who I am. I feel like myself after ten years of not knowing who I am. Finally, I'm where I'm supposed to be. I'm *who* I'm supposed to be."

My mouth snaps shut as I force myself to stop talking and hold my breath. I just laid it all out for him. I put my heart on the line and now I have to wait to see if he accepts it or crushes it.

Neither of us are breathing as he lowers his mouth to mine and kisses me gently. "I love you, Ellis," he whispers against my lips. "I can't describe it. The way my heart races when I'm near you and the pull in my gut tugging me closer to you. I knew as soon as I walked into your bedroom that night there was something about you. You called to me. In every way possible, you called to me. The only word I have to describe it is *complete*. Like I wasn't whole until that moment."

Those damn butterflies in my stomach have taken on a life of their own. Each one of his words is like a balm to my battered soul, healing me bit by bit. He grabs my hand and places it over his heart. It thumps against my palm, beating faster than it usually does. I place my other hand on my chest and my eyes widen. They beat at a matching rhythm. They even stutter together as realization hits me.

Kai smiles. "You are my beloved, Ellis." He brushes a sweaty curl from my forehead. "We are tied together now. Forever. Our hearts will beat as one, stop as one. You are the very reason I am alive."

He kisses me, deeper than before, and his fangs brush against my tongue. Instantly, I want them in my neck again. I replay his words in my head. *Forever. Beat as one. Stop as one.* It's like something out of a fairytale. Like one of the romance books I used to read, wishing my life would end up like that. My eyes widen as his words register, and I push his shoulders so I can look at him.

"Forever?" I screech. "If I die, you'll die?"

He nods, a small smile pulling the corner of his mouth up.

"But I'm going to die before you." Horror makes my voice crack. "I'm only human."

"You do realize that we are tied together, right?" He searches my face, brows drawn down. "In every way. You'll have the same lifespan as me. And fuck, stop saying that! You are not *only* human, baby girl." He cups my face with one palm and rubs his thumb over my cheek. "You are so much more than that. Strong, brave, and determined. You took what life dealt you and came through it even more amazing. Never once did you let your circumstances destroy you. You used it and made yourself stronger. I *never* want to hear you say that again."

This time, tears fill my eyes and spill over. I never realized how much I needed to hear someone say that. To validate me and my feelings. To let me know I am more than my failures. However, what he said before all that has snagged in my brain. "So, I won't die until you do?" I ask through my crying.

"Yes," he says simply. "Or vice versa. Basically, when one of us goes, the other does as well."

I stare at him. Blinking as the tears stall out. I'm having a hard time understanding what he just said. The same lifespan as him? "But ... But you're immortal," I whisper.

He chuckles. "Yeah, I am. So are you now." He laughs at my expression and rolls off of me, tucking me against him so my head is on his chest. "You didn't think to ask about the details before you gave me your blood?"

"I was a little distracted," I say faintly. "The fine print wasn't on my mind at the time." His heart under my hand beats in rhythm with mine, reinforcing the monumental moment that just happened between us.

Immortal. What did I just sign myself up for?

ELLIS

"I DIDN'T TELL YOU BECAUSE I WANTED TO KEEP YOU safe," Kai says as we lay in his bed, skin to skin. "Keeping you safe has been my top priority since I met you. Being tied to me, it's dangerous, Ellis."

"I still deserved to know," I murmur, tracing patterns on his chest and abs with my finger. "It's my life, my decision."

"I was scared. I *am* scared." His arms tighten around me. "How much do you know about my history?"

"Nothing, really," I shrug. "Only what I see on social media."

He takes a deep breath and releases it. "I was young when my mom died. A teenager, by vampire standards. She was an amazing woman. Beautiful, bright, loving. Everything a mother should be. I was too young to notice the difference in her before she died, but as I got older, I recognized it, and I began to question everything about her death."

He falls silent and idly twists one of my curls around his finger. I let him work through his thoughts, but a sinking feeling settles in my gut. This will not be a good story.

"I always thought my parents had a normal relationship. Looking back, I can see that I was wrong. They were civil to each other. I never saw them fight, but I also never saw them show any affection toward each other. They were more like roommates sharing a house. All of my mom's time was devoted to me, and she rarely interacted with my dad."

"Why did they marry?" I ask, propping my chin on his chest so I could look at him.

"It was arranged. Her family is one of the wealthiest vampire families. It was the perfect alliance. My dad got more money, and her family got the status." He shrugs, eyes clouded with painful memories. "Arranged marriages are commonplace in the vampire world. We're still old school in our thinking. Something I've always hated."

"Not just the vampire world," I say bitterly, tucking my head back against his chest, snuggling closer. "What happened?"

He kisses the top of my head before continuing. "She stopped spending as much time with me. At the time, I thought it was because I was a teenager and didn't need her around as much. I thought she was giving me space to grow into my own person. I was wrong, and looking back, I can see the signs now." Sadness laces each word he speaks, and a heaviness settles in the air around us. "She was a wonderful person, but always slightly reserved. I think she resented her life and being forced into a loveless marriage. She would smile at me, but never anyone else. During that time, though, she'd started smiling more. There was a light in her eyes I didn't recognize at the time. It was like she was glowing from the inside out."

He pauses again, his words catching in his throat. I ache for him. I know all too well what it's like losing such an amazing person who meant so much to you. I lost two of them. Pressing a kiss to his chest, right over his heart beating along with mine, I give him the only support I know how.

"She had met her beloved," he whispers. "She kept it hidden, obviously. Divorce is not something vampires believe in. Eventually, my dad found out. He was livid, but he told her as long as she stayed married to him, she could have her secret relationship with her beloved." He pauses, and I can tell he's gearing himself up for something painful. "A couple of months later, they were both found dead. The reports all say they were ambushed while out on a date, victims of a robbery gone wrong. I believed it for the longest time. But now I wonder. I question if my dad didn't have something to do with it."

"Kai," I breathe. My heart breaks for him. Even though I understand his pain all too well, I'm positive my dad had nothing to do with mom and sister's death. While he wasn't happy with my sister and I being human, he loved my mom tremendously. One of his only redeeming qualities.

"As much as I want to shout from the rooftop that you are my beloved," he says, "I think it's safest to keep it quiet. Not only will my dad not handle it well, but it will put a target on your back. I can't let anything happen to you."

"I understand," I say quietly.

It hasn't fully registered what all of this means. Beloved. Immortal. Those are big words a human like me isn't used to hearing. Everything is kind of numb, but in a good way. It's like when you have a good dream. You know it isn't real, but damn, it sure as hell seems like it is, and you want nothing more than to wake up and find out it wasn't a dream at all. That's what I keep thinking. That I'm going to wake up and realize none of this happened, because it's too amazing to be real.

I push up on my elbow to look at him, with his tousled hair and hooded eyes. "This is so surreal to me," I whisper, tracing his features with my gaze.

Kai grins, and the tips of his fangs glint in the lamplight. "You and me both, baby girl."

I want to soak in this moment forever. The lazy touches and soft conversation heal parts of me I thought were broken for good. But, nothing can last, and I'm terrified my next question will make it all crash down around us. But I have to know. "Kai?"

"Hmm?" he asks lazily.

"What about Cade?" I ask so quietly my voice is barely audible.

He doesn't tense under me like I expected him to. Instead, he huffs a small laugh. "What about him?"

"Well ... I think ... maybe ... I kind of like him too?" The words rush out of me, tripping and stumbling over each other.

This time, his laugh rumbles his entire chest. "Really? I never would have guessed."

I slap his stomach and sit up so I can look at him. The adoration shining in his eyes warms my heart, despite my irritation. "Kai ..."

He pulls me back down and tightens his arms around me. "Relax, baby girl. You're my beloved, and that means the world to me. But it doesn't mean I can't share you. If you want to be with Cade as well, I would never stop you. Whatever you want, you'll get. I promise."

———

Kai and I finally get out of bed. That time with him, laying in his arms, listening to our hearts beat together, was divine. But, there are two other guys who also hold a piece of my heart. I'm hopeful that maybe things will work out in the end for all of us, now that I know Kai and I are tied together forever, and he doesn't seem to mind sharing.

Immortal.

I shudder as I push open the door to the library, not sure I'll ever be able to wrap my human mind around that concept. Before I make it five steps into the library, Allie barrels into me, almost knocking me to the ground. She hugs me tightly and breathes a huge sigh of relief.

"I told her you would be fine," Cade says drily from his spot on the couch. "A vampire would sooner stake themselves than hurt their beloved. But she didn't believe me."

"I had to see you with my own eyes," she says as she pulls away, scanning me for injury.

"I'm fine," I reassure her. "More than fine."

I glance at Cade, my heart rate doubling as I take in his handsome features. While he's attempting to look relaxed on the couch, I can already read his signs. His shoulders are tense and his fingers tap restlessly on the armrest. Those violet eyes I love so much bounce between Kai and me, guarded and a little sad. I can practically see the wall he's building around himself. That won't do.

Shaking my head, I walk to him. He watches me approach, tracking my every movement like a hawk, but doesn't reach out to grab me like he would have before. I don't need Kai's empath abilities to know exactly what he is thinking, and he couldn't be more wrong. The room is quiet, almost oppressive, as everyone watches the scene unfold before them. Wrapping my arms around his neck, I plop down in his lap, straddling his waist. He hesitates before his hands settle on my hips, fingers contracting and digging in, like he's scared and doesn't want to lose me.

I stare into those violet eyes, ensuring he understands exactly what I'm saying. "Just because Kai is my beloved doesn't mean there's no room for you in my heart," I say. "If I can't have all of you, I don't want any of you."

Cade relaxes under me, but concern still pulls his brows down. "Does *he* know that?" he asks, nodding his head toward Kai.

We both look at the vampire in question, who is leaning against the door with his arms crossed over his chest, watching with amusement. He snorts and walks forward. Fisting my hair in his grasp, he tugs my head back and leans down. I expect him to kiss me, to lay his claim, but instead, his mouth lands on Cade's. His surprise is evident in the way his body jerks under mine, his fingers tightening on my hips. And when he kisses Kai back, molten heat pools in my core.

"You are both mine," Kai growls against Cade's mouth.

Holy. Shit. Pretty sure I just came in my panties.

"Oookay, well." Allie coughs and clears her throat. "I'm just gonna ... go ..."

I laugh and shake my hair out as Kai releases me. "Don't go." I slide off Cade's lap and walk to my bestie. "I miss you."

"I miss you, too, but I have no desire to be part of your orgy." She smirks at me and waggles her eyebrows suggestively.

"But they're so hot," I mock whisper. "How could you turn them down?"

Allie rolls her eyes and my chest squeezes. That interaction was so normal. Something most people have with their friends without thinking about it. When was the last time Allie and I really joked with each other? I grab her hands and pull her to a chair.

"No orgies, I promise." I push her into the chair, then turn to sit on the couch between Cade and Kai.

Kai wraps his arm around my shoulders, and Cade sets his hand on my thigh. A girl sure could get used to this. I take a moment to revel in the fact I have no fear of being touched by either guy. Instead, I know with absolute certainty I couldn't be more safe. It warms my chest, spreading happy tingles over my body to my hands and feet.

"Where is Sterling?" I ask, looking around the library.

Cade gives me a knowing look. "He went for a run. I think his wolf is riding him harder than normal."

I push thoughts of Sterling aside. For the first time in a very long time, I'm happy. A weight has been lifted from my shoulders, and I'm lighter than I have been in years. There is no fear hanging over my head. No anxiety or uncertainty of what will happen in the next minute or hour. I have two amazing guys on either side of me and my bestie sitting across from me. I'm not going to waste this moment with what-ifs and worry over the future.

"Do you guys have a deck of cards?" I ask, looking at Cade.

Allie squeals from her chair and bounces on the cushion. "Up and down the river?"

"Yes!" I screech, just as enthusiastically as Allie.

Cade chuckles as he stands. "Up and down the river? What's that?" He grabs a deck of cards from the console holding the video games and tosses it to me.

I grin and clear off the coffee table. This is exactly what I need.

———

After hours of playing cards, drinking, talking, and laughing, Kai opens his bedroom door and ushers Cade and me inside. My stomach hurts from all the laughing. It's crazy to think that a few hours ago, Kai was laying in his bed, dying. A few hours ago, I was unsure about my future or where I stood in this world. A few weeks ago, I was in an abusive relationship. I was tired, scared, and sad all the time.

Things have really changed. It seems like a dream. One I'm scared to wake up from.

"Is this real?" I whisper to no one in particular, stopping just inside the room.

Cade wraps his arms around me from behind and leans down to whisper in my ear. "Remember what you told me earlier? When we were in the shower?"

My cheeks heat because I do remember what I said. Cade chuckles, low and sexy, and my toes curl against the marble floor.

"I thought you would remember." He licks up the side of my throat to my ear and bites my earlobe, sending heat coursing through me.

"What exactly did she tell you?" Kai asks in a low voice as he approaches. His gait is prowling and dangerous, and it lights me up inside.

"She wants me to fuck her while you fuck me." Cade's breath fans across my neck, and his words rumble in his chest pressed against my back.

I squeeze my legs together, already turned on by Cade's dirty talk and his body against mine. Fire erupts in my veins when he rocks his hips and his very noticeable erection makes its presence known. These two have the ability to utterly destroy me, and while it's not easy to give them the power to do so, there is a thrill in letting it happen. Knowing they would never harm me helps to put me in the correct mindset to just let it all go.

A slow grin spreads across Kai's face, revealing his lengthening fangs. "I think we can make that happen," he says, gray eyes darkening as his pupils expand.

He places his hands on either side of my face and kisses me. It's deep and all-consuming. My heart rate picks up and I press my hands to his chest, still surprised to find his heart thumping to the same rhythm as mine.

Behind me, Cade places open mouth kisses on my jaw and down my neck. He slides his hands under my tank top and runs his fingers up to the bottom of my bra. I arch my back, silently asking him with my motions to keep going, but he doesn't. Instead, he moves his hands back down my belly. He pauses with his fingers just under the waistband of my leggings. Frustration grips me. I'm already primed for them and I need someone to give me what I want.

I pull away from Kai long enough to growl at Cade, "Touch me already."

Apparently, that was the wrong thing to say. Both guys step away from me and I whimper at the loss of heat against my front and back.

Kai looks over my shoulder at Cade. "I think we need to teach someone a lesson." His gray eyes return to me and I get wetter just from that dark and dangerous look. "You are ours, baby girl. We own your pleasure. You can beg us all you want, but you don't get to make demands."

A thrill runs through me at his words. Cade grabs my wrists and pulls them behind my back, holding them in a firm grip. A shadow of fear trickles through my system, but I forget about it as

Kai slowly and methodically removes my leggings and panties, throwing them to the corner of his room. Kneeling on the ground, Kai looks up at me with his hands wrapped around the back of my knees. Such adoration and affection shine in the depths of his gray eyes, and it makes my breath catch in my throat.

Cade lets go of my wrists long enough for Kai to slip off my tank top and bra, then he recaptures my hands behind my back. The fear doesn't have a chance to grow, as Kai distracts me with his thumbs rubbing my nipples until they harden. I arch my back on instinct as the pleasure zips down my spine and settles in my core.

Cade walks me forward, then sits on the edge of Kai's bed, dragging me down so I'm laying on my belly across his thighs. With my hands still in his grip behind my back, it's almost impossible to move and I tense. The fear rises, making it difficult to breathe and fine sweat breaks out on my skin. I don't like being restrained. It drags forth memories better left buried.

"Trust me, love," Cade says, running a gentle hand down my back. "I'm not going to hurt you." He pauses with his hand on my ass, before whispering, "Much."

I raise my head to look at Kai, my beloved, reminding myself he wouldn't let anyone hurt me. And by his hooded eyes and hard cock tenting his pants, this scene is playing out exactly how he wants it. I swallow and lick my lips, forcing my body to relax and trust him. Kai's gaze tracks the movement of my tongue and he slowly takes off his shirt and pants. When he's standing in front of me with his dick in his hand, pumping up and down, I eagerly watch the bead of precum form on the tip. If only he were standing closer so I could lick it.

Cade squeezes my ass. "I'm going to enjoy teaching you this lesson," he growls.

That is the only warning I get before Cade brings his hand back down on my ass. I gasp as pain flares, spreading like fire over my backside. Tears build on my lashes instantly, and I struggle to get my hands free, but he tightens his grip on my wrists. His cock hardens under me the more I squirm, and he groans low in his throat. The sick bastard is turned on by this.

I barely have time to draw in a breath before his hand connects with my ass again, just inches from his first hit. This time I cry out as the stinging pain spreads over my skin. Cade rubs over the two spots, like he's admiring his work. I open my mouth to scream, or cry, or rip him a new one, when he slaps me again. Heat blooms over my other cheek, only this time it spreads to my core. I clench around nothing as Cade rubs my ass, soothing the ache. Okay, maybe I'm a sick bitch too, because that kind of turned me on.

When he spanks me a fourth time, I can't keep from moaning as the pleasure pain rolls through me. Heat creeps up my neck and into my cheeks. How could I find this arousing? Cade is hitting me and my thighs are slick from the desire raging in me.

"Enjoying yourself, baby girl?" Kai asks roughly, stepping into my vision.

He grabs my hair and yanks my head back. The sting in my scalp completes with the burn on my ass, and I squirm against Cade's grasp, desperately wanting to ease the ache growing between my legs. He grunts as my movements make me rub against his erection, and he slaps my ass again, three times in quick succession. My mouth opens, my breath leaving me in a whoosh, and I close my eyes. If Kai weren't holding my head up, it would probably fall forward on weakened muscles.

"Such a pretty shade of pink," Cade mumbles as he rubs away the ache.

Kai slips his cock in my mouth and I close my lips around him without thought, running my tongue along his piercings and up to the slit, finally tasting the salty precum beading there.

"Have you learned your lesson, baby girl?" Kai asks as he tightens his fist in my hair.

I shake my head with his cock still in my mouth, causing the roots of my hair to pull painfully against his grip. The pleasure building in me is leading to something amazing, I just know it. I want more. I want them to draw me further to the precipice. The fall will destroy me.

"Bad girl," Cade says. This time he slaps me hard, hard enough to make me cry out. The scream turns to a moan, and he runs his hand further down my ass and slides a finger through my wetness. "Fuck, you're soaking wet."

I'm about to beg Cade to touch me more. I'm aching and empty, desperate to feel full. Before I can, he brings his finger to Kai's mouth. It's glistening from my juices and watching Kai lick me off of Cade's finger is the most arousing thing I've seen.

"I think she's learned her lesson, haven't you, baby girl?" Kai asks, pulling his hips back and freeing my mouth.

"Yes. Please," I beg. "I've learned my lesson. Please, touch me." My words are husky and breathy as I try to get enough air into my lungs.

Kai's eyes glitter as he releases my hair. "Good girl," he says darkly.

Pride at his words brings a smile to my lips, as Cade lifts me off his lap and lays me on the bed. Watching him remove his clothes, seeing each newly exposed inch of his muscular body, makes me ache even more. I move my hand down my abdomen, slowly sliding lower, desperate for some kind of touch.

Cade smiles at me and shakes his head. "Don't even think about it, love. That's our job."

I bite my lip in frustration but say nothing, not willing to do anything that would make them stop. As much as I loved that punishment, I really just want one of them to stick their dick in me and fuck me senseless.

Cade, now completely naked, climbs into the bed and crawls over me. He kisses me while one of his hands trails down my neck, brushing against the bite Kai left earlier. Pleasure spreads from the mark, shocks of arousal shooting straight to my core.

"Please, Cade," I gasp, chest heaving. "Please. I need you."

His eyes shine as he smiles at me. "Well, how can I deny that?"

He grasps his cock, running it through my folds and teasing me even more. When he lines it up with my entrance, I lift my hips, begging for him to slide in, practically crying from need. This is torture. The burning need to be touched, to aleve the ache, is not something I'm used to.

So slowly, Cade slides in. My head falls back against the pillows and I close my eyes, feeling each inch that stretches and fills me. It's so fucking good. We both moan in pleasure as he stills and waits for me to adjust.

"You have no idea how hot it is to see you two together," Kai says breathlessly from the foot of the bed.

I snap my eyes open and glance at him. The piercings lining his length glint in the low light as he pumps his fist up and down, gaze locked on me and Cade. All three of us groan as Cade shifts his hips. He slides out slowly and thrust back in, but it's still just teasing me. I need so much more.

"Don't stop," I pant. "Please, don't stop." I wrap my legs around his waist and pull him in tighter. Lifting my hips changes the angle and the next time he slides in he hits just the right spot. "Oh fuck, keep going."

Instead of listening, he stills. "It's not fair that we're the only ones having fun." He looks over his shoulder at Kai who grins.

Kai grabs a bottle of lube from the mini bar and quickly preps himself. I bite my lip, wishing I could see more as Kai runs his hand down Cade's back. Cade tenses inside me, his breath stuttering in his chest before he hangs his head and groans, low and deep. The ache is still there between my legs. Even with Cade filling me, I'm desperate to feel him move again.

I squeeze my inner walls around him and he obliges me with a few short thrusts before he stills once more. This time, I watch Kai fist his cock and roll his hips forward. His face is strained, but not in a bad way. It's like he's trying to control himself and he's struggling. Cade exhales against my skin and his dick twitches inside me. Bliss makes his face slack, and for a moment, he closes his eyes and breathes deeply.

"You good?" Kai asks Cade, his fangs biting into his lower lip.

Cade groans, "Fuck, yes."

That's all Kai needed to hear. He moves behind Cade, causing Cade to move inside me. Before long, Cade is rocking back and forth, thrusting into me, then rocking back to thrust Kai's cock into him.

It's the hottest fucking thing I have ever done. Both guys are grunting and groaning. Their expressions of pleasure only fuel my own. Sweat is dripping down my neck and between my breasts, and I can't get a full breath of air as Cade pistons his hips harder and faster. I'm so close to tipping over the edge.

"Shit," Cade groans. His pace falters before picking back up again. "I can't hold out much longer."

Kai meets my gaze over Cade's shoulder and he runs his fangs over his lower lip. The tug in my gut I get for each one of these guys, is pulled so taut, like it's trying to pull me into their bodies. I stare into Kai's eyes, the connection between us growing stronger as the pleasure builds even higher. I clench around Cade, who groans at the sensation.

"Come for us, baby girl," Kai growls at the same time Cade reaches between us and presses hard on my clit.

I scream as I come. A rainbow of color explodes behind my closed eyelids and I'm pretty sure I black out for a second. Cade keeps moving, even as his body jerks above mine, drawing out my orgasm until I'm nothing more than a puddle on Kai's bed. When I open my eyes, both guys are sweating and breathing heavily. I was so lost in my own release, I missed theirs.

Cade collapses next to me and tugs me into his arms. Aftershocks of pleasure work through my body as I try to piece myself back together. I float in a haze of contentment, oblivious to anything around me except Cade's arms and Kai walking to his bathroom, his steps uneven. He returns with a wet washcloth, and gently cleans us up, before laying down behind me. Wrapped in both of their arms, I know I'm safe and protected. Cared for, for the first time in so many years.

Kai kisses his mark on my neck and brushes a curl from my sweaty face. "You are so amazing, baby girl."

Cade hums his agreement and pulls me tighter to his chest. It isn't long before I hear their breathing even out and feel their bodies relax. I smile to myself and close my eyes.

STERLING

I don't know why I'm trying to read. The book has been open to the same page for the last thirty minutes. For some reason, I thought reading would help clear my head of the woman who has invaded it. But in reality, all it's done is given me time in a quiet space to think about only her. She's become an obsession that gets harder and harder to ignore as the days go on. Even though I avoid her as much as I can, her scent is everywhere, I can't escape it, and it's making my wolf absolutely feral.

The library door opens and I know who it is before I look. Vanilla and lavender hit me, and my wolf perks up. Ellis walks in and pauses when she notices me. My wolf is panting as I run my gaze over her. Wearing nothing but a t-shirt and her hair in a messy bun, she's sexy as fuck with all that tan skin on display. A smile tugs at her lips, and it's like the entire room brightens. When her gaze lands on the stuffed wolf I have tucked under my arm, I grimace.

"Ellis." I sigh, mentally preparing myself for fighting my wolf and keeping my emotions in check.

She gestures to the stuffed animal, fighting a grin by biting her lower lip. "What's his name?"

"Fluffy," I say reluctantly. I can only imagine how she'll react.

Her eyes glimmer and she hums in her throat. Cocking her head to the side, she asks, "Does your wolf have a name?"

"No. He's just ... I don't know how to describe it." I shrug. "He's just part of me, so no name."

"We should name him." She walks to the couch and I move my legs off the cushions so she can sit. When she looks at me, her eyes shine mischievously. "He deserves to have a name."

I shake my head, already knowing what she's going to say. "No," I say firmly.

"But he *is* fluffy. And so soft." Her fists clench like she's remembering the time she ran her hands through his fur.

The smile on her face is like a kick to the groin. It sucks the breath from my lungs, and I want nothing more than to see her do it again. "You're not naming my wolf Fluffy." I try to sound stern, but my voice lacks the heat.

"You can't stop me," she teases. "I like Fluffy. It's fitting. And I think he'll like it, too,"

In response, my wolf growls deep in my chest, a rumbling sound that travels through the room.

Her eyes widen. "What did that mean? Does he like it?" she asks.

"No." I'll never tell her he really loves it. He'd let her call him anything. Whatever makes her happy makes him happy.

"Hmm," she narrows her eyes at me like she doesn't quite believe me. "What are you reading?" she asks, changing the subject.

I show her the cover of the post-apocalyptic book. It's strange how I can want her to leave so badly, yet need her to stay at the same time. It tears me up inside. Sometimes I think I should just leave. She's clearly happy with Cade and Kai. They can keep her safe and take care of her. She doesn't need me. Not really. But I'm not sure if I can physically walk away from her.

"Any good?" she asks.

"It's okay. A little slow." It's clear she won't let me keep reading, even though I wasn't really reading to begin with, so I set the novel on the coffee table.

She leans back on the armrest of the couch and stretches her legs out, setting her feet in my lap. It's such a casual move, something a normal couple would do without thought. And the mental picture her actions conjure is dangerous. Us, happy together, as a couple. Easy glances and comfortable touches.

"How did you, Kai, and Cade meet?" she asks curiously.

I sigh, pushing my dreams aside. "Kai and I have been friends since we were kids. I guess you could say we ran in the same circles. We're both sons of influential and powerful leaders of our races, so we got stuck attending all the same parties and events. When Cade started working for your dad, he also attended the same events."

She wiggles her foot on my lap, and I don't even realize when I grab it in my hands and dig my thumbs into her arch.

"Those events were awful," I continue, reminiscing about those stuffy parties. "Surrounded by people who couldn't care less about anyone except themselves. It was disgusting. Kai, being able to read emotions, picked up pretty quickly on Cade's stance on everything. We sought him out, and it didn't take long for us to bond over our shared trauma and hate for society. We've been friends ever since."

She gives me a small smile and wiggles her other foot. "How old are you?"

Again, without thinking, I switch feet. "I'm 163 years old. Kai is 150, and Cade is the baby. He's only 109."

Her eyes pop open wide. "163?" she asks faintly.

I grin. "You know the magical races age slower." She has to know that. Her parents are mages. "We live for hundreds of years, besides Kai who is immortal."

"I know. I guess I never paid attention to your ages," she shrugs. "It's just weird thinking you guys are so old. Makes a girl feel young and inexperienced. If Cade is a baby, I'm a freaking infant at twenty six years old."

"We're all essentially the same age," I explain. "In terms of how we age. We're all young adults."

She's quiet for a moment, lips pursed as she thinks. "What kinds of trouble did you guys get into growing up?" she asks, changing the subject. "I can only imagine the hell you raised."

I chuckle. She has no idea. "The usual kinds, and no, I won't go into details. What kind of friend would I be if I shared all of my brother's dirty secrets?"

I punctuate my statement by digging my thumbs harder into her foot. A moan slips from her mouth and she lets her head fall back, exposing her throat. The sound travels straight to my cock, and I let my gaze roam over her body. She's wearing only a black t-shirt—Kai's by the smell. The hem rides up her thighs, displaying so much of that tan skin I want to lick and nibble. I take a breath through my nose to clear my head and instantly regret it. Kai and Cade's scents are all over, and irrational jealousy sweeps through me.

"Why are you awake?" I ask gruffly, trying to distract myself.

"I can't sleep. I'm not used to sleeping during the day." She shrugs and the neck of the t-shirt slips down one shoulder.

I clear my throat and force my gaze away from her. "Yeah, I've never been able to sleep during the day. Luckily, being a shifter gives me extra stamina, so I don't have to sleep as much."

She stares at me, her amber eyes trying to pierce my soul. When she pulls her feet from my lap and moves to sit on her knees next to me, my wolf rises to the surface. He won't stop riding me about claiming her. It's a battle waged within me every second she's near us. I clench my jaw and my neck and shoulders tense. It's getting harder and harder to keep from grabbing her and claiming her as ours.

Tentatively, she lifts her hand and runs her fingers through my loose hair. I don't know how I keep myself from grabbing her. Vanilla and lavender swirl around me, and my wolf pushes against my barriers as he catches her scent. With more strength than I thought I possessed, I grab her wrist and push it away.

"Don't," I say quietly, but firmly. "You need to stop, Ellis. I don't want ..." the words get stuck, but I force them out. "I don't want you like that."

Her entire body jerks like I've slapped her. And from her pain-filled expression—wide eyes rapidly filling with tears, trembling lips, neck and cheeks turning crimson—I may as well have. She won't look me in the eye as she turns away.

"I'm sorry," she whispers. "I didn't mean ... I won't ..." she stutters and stands from the couch. Shoulders curving inward as she wraps her arms around her middle, she takes a step toward the door. "I'm sorry."

Before she can take another step, I jump from the couch and grab her wrist, turning her to face me. I track the tear that slides down her cheek and I know I've lost the battle. My wolf howls inside me, desperate to make sure she isn't hurting.

"Fuck," I growl, clenching my free hand. "That's not true, gods dammit. I want you Ellis. I want you so fucking bad it hurts. You're all I can think about. My wolf is desperate to claim you. But none of that matters, because this"—I gesture back and forth between us—"can't happen."

Tears no longer fall from her eyes, but they still cling to her lashes as she steps closer to me. "Why not? Why do you keep pushing me away?" She places her hands on my chest and presses her body against mine. "Please, Sterling," she whispers. The yearning in her voice tugs at my heart, and my wolf whines.

Her lips tremble slightly, those perfect lips I've been dying to taste. She's a temptation I'm not able to fight anymore. Her body pressed against mine is a drug I need more of. Before I know what I'm doing, I slide my hand into her hair, gripping the strands and tugging her head backward. She gasps, eyes widening, and a delectable blush creeping over her cheeks.

I lower my mouth to hers, not breathing until our lips meet. In my chest, my heart pounds erratically and my wolf paces, ready to pounce. Ellis exhales softly, her breath fanning across my lips, and I use that moment to sweep my tongue inside, claiming her.

It's not gentle, and there is no way I could make it gentle. I've been denying myself for too long.

Something slimy worms through me, causing me to pause. Pulling away, I look into her eyes. "I shouldn't do this." I say, my voice rough and filled with need. "We need to stop."

"Please don't." She shakes her head and grabs my shirt in her fists. "Stop pushing me away. I know you want this as much as I do." She emphasizes her point by rocking her hips against my erection.

I groan, and she does it again. This is wrong. If we don't stop now, it will be impossible to stop later, and she will regret it if we take it any further.

"Sterling," she breathes as she slides her hand down my chest and cups my dick through my sweats. "Please." She bites her lip, pleading in her eyes.

I'm powerless against her. Fighting this is getting too hard, and I snap. I pick her up and carry her to the couch, settling her on my lap with her legs straddling either side of my hips. It's a frenzy as our mouths crash together again, tongues tangling, teeth scraping. We've both been wanting this for so long, it's impossible to control ourselves.

The shirt she's wearing smells like Kai, and my wolf growls possessively. I pull away long enough to slide my hands up her sides and tug the shirt over her head. My gaze lands on her breasts and I cup them in my palms, teasing her nipples with my thumbs. The little sound she makes as she arches her back goes straight to my cock.

"Ellis," I murmur as I suck one of her nipples into my mouth.

"Shh," she says, rocking her hips. "Don't think about it, just do it."

Her hands slide into my hair and she holds my head to her chest while I lick and bite her nipple. It's almost surreal as my hands run all over her skin, taking in her naked body under my fingers. For so long I've dreamt of this moment, and now that it's happening I could kick myself for fighting it. But then I remember why I've been pushing her away.

I force her hips to still and wait for her to look at me. When she does, I almost forget what I want to say. She looks beautifully erotic, flushed with her pupils blown from desire, hair tangled from my fingers.

"Ellis, stop," I breathe. "You don't want to do this."

"No, I do. I want you, Sterling. It's not complete in here without you." She places her hand on her chest. "I need all three of you. I know I do. Every fiber of my being screams with the need for you. Please, Sterling. Please." Her amber eyes are so wide as she stares at me, begging me to hear her.

On an instinctual level, she knows. She just doesn't understand it. I can't resist her anymore. With her skin under my fingers, and her heat surrounding me even through my pants, she's a siren and I'm not strong enough to fight.

"Fuck," I moan, giving in.

She lifts herself off of me enough for me to slide my sweatpants down my hips. Since shifting ruins clothes, I always go commando, and Ellis moans as she sits back on my lap and rubs her pussy over my cock, spreading her juices that are already coating her thighs.

"Oh, fuck, kitten. You feel so good." I bury my nose in her neck and inhale her scent. My wolf goes wild. We can't wait any longer.

Wrapping my hands around her waist, I lift her up, and she wraps her fingers around my length to guide it to her entrance. Slowly, I lower her back down, inch by inch her wet warmth swallowing me. Holy. Shit. This is divine. I fit inside her like a puzzle piece settling into place. I'm not even moving, but my chest is heaving. All I can do is stare at her and the utter bliss lining her features.

"Yes," she breathes. "Oh gods, yes."

Her thighs work and she lifts herself up and down as she braces her hands on my shoulders, nails digging in. They elicit the most delicious pain, sharp pin pricks that spread over my skin. My hands around her waist help to lift her and I watch as my dick disappears inside of her, only to slide back out, glistening with her arousal. The sight of her, head thrown back in ecstasy, wild and flushed with desire, makes my wolf growl in my chest.

"Harder, Sterling," she pants. "Fuck me harder."

Lifting her off me, I lay her on the couch. Her legs fall open and I'm momentarily distracted by the sight of her pussy, wet and waiting for me. "So perfect," I growl.

I thrust inside her, hard enough to drive her backward on the couch. The sound of her screaming my name drives me harder, until our flesh slapping together drowns out our moans and heavy breathing. Her nails rake down my back hard enough to draw blood and it lights a fire in my veins. The idea that she's marked me sends me into overdrive and I bite her neck, right over Kai's puncture marks. I don't break the skin, but I hold her there with my teeth and run my tongue along the mark. It drives her wild, just like I knew it would. Those marks are sensitive, and I'm not above using it to my advantage.

Her hips buck against mine, meeting each of my thrusts with equal force. This woman is everything I could have ever imagined. Perfect for me in every way. No one will ever compare to her. As her pussy clenches around my cock and she screams her release, I know I will never be able to walk away from her. With her inner walls milking me, I follow her over the edge, shooting my seed deep inside her.

We're both gasping for air as reality settles around us again. Sweat drips down my neck and back, making my hair stick to me uncomfortably. I pull back to look at her face and she takes my breath away. Her hair has come undone from its bun and falls around her shoulders in wild curls. Strands stick to her forehead and I brush them away with trembling fingers. Her amber eyes are heavy, and her perfect lips are puffy from my kisses and tilted in a satisfied smile. I lean down and kiss her.

"Thank you," she whispers against my mouth.

Shaking my head, I roll us so she is laying on top of me. If wolves could purr, mine would sound like an engine rumbling as she snuggles against me. Goosebumps rise on our skin as the sweat cools, so I grab a blanket from the back of the couch and pull it over our bodies. She relaxes and her breath across my chest evens out. My post-orgasm euphoria slowly fades as I realize what I just let happen. Guilt churns in my gut. I'll never forgive myself for letting it go that far. She'll never forgive me.

"I'm so sorry, Ellis," I whisper to the top of her head.

I'm such a fucking idiot.

CADE

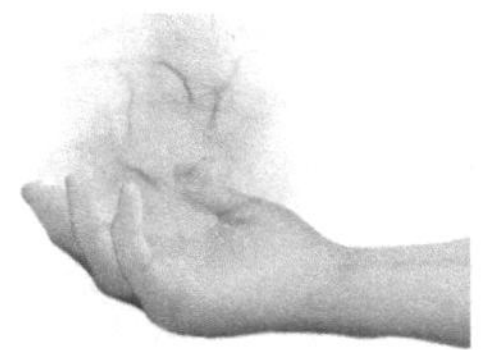

WAKING WITH KAI SPRAWLED OVER MY BODY IS definitely something I could get used to. The only thing missing is Ellis. I look for her, but she isn't here. As comfortable as I am, there is a weird sensation in my gut. It's like a warning that's making my insides twist and turn. Maybe I'm just paranoid. Last night was amazing. With Ellis and Kai bonded together, I assume that means she won't be leaving any time soon. But the joy that thought brings is tempered by the nagging sensation that it can't last.

Kai grunts as I shove him off of me. "What the fuck, man." He grumbles and sits up, looking around for Ellis. "Where is she?"

I take a moment to stare at him with his messy hair and sleep filled eyes, but I ignore the emotions that try to distract me. "No idea, I just woke up," I say, climbing over him.

We quickly dress and head for the library, the most likely place for her to be. As we push through the door, I smile. Ellis is sprawled across Sterling's chest, both completely naked under the blanket that has fallen to her waist. Looks like she got what she's been wanting. I'm not sure why Sterling has been holding out, but I knew there was no way he could keep saying no to her.

Sterling glances at us as we walk through the door. The look of regret and guilt in his eyes makes me miss a step. What's that all about? His hand rubs gentle circles on her bare back and my palm itches to replace his hand with mine.

Kai plops on the chair across from them and grins. "You assholes are lucky I'm willing to share my beloved."

Sterling stiffens and closes his eyes tightly. I study him with narrowed eyes. There is something going on with him. And I'm worried whatever it is has to do with Ellis.

"I got an email yesterday," Kai says quietly, holding his phone up. "About the next challenge. Ellis's dad will call me tonight at nine. The email said he has a message for Ellis before he gives out the details."

We all fall silent as we think about what message her dad could have for her. Whatever it is, I'm sure it won't be good. The uneasiness in my gut intensifies. Could this be the cause of my concern? Does my subconscious somehow know something bad is going to happen? There's only one hour until nine and it will be the longest hour of my life.

Ellis stirs against Sterling's chest, and his arms tighten around her briefly before he helps her sit. Swiping her hair from her eyes, she stares at us. "What's happened? You all look so serious." Her voice is husky with sleep and it shoots straight to my cock.

I shift in my seat and adjust myself, noticing Kai doing the same thing in his chair.

"Your dad is going to call in about an hour," Kai says. "He says he has a message for you."

Ellis swallows and looks to her lap. "I should probably get dressed then." Standing, she wraps the blanket around her.

I almost forgot what she looks like when she feels small and human. Her shoulders curl forward and she keeps her head down. The brightness of her eyes that I have come to love, is missing. The past week, she's slowly come out of that darkness that haunts her, and I want so badly to keep the shadows at bay.

"Do you want someone to come with you while you get ready?" I ask, studying her closely.

She shakes her head. "No. I think I want to be alone. To prepare myself."

I nod and watch her leave, itching to follow her and make sure she's okay.

"Nothing good will come of this," Kai says after the door closes behind her.

"Think we could skip the call?" I ask, glancing at him.

"Probably not a good idea," Kai answers. "We need to play by the rules if we want to win. Kennedy will do everything in his power to make sure we lose. If we step out of line one time, it's over for us."

"What if we tell him she's your beloved? I mean, that bond trumps everything." I'm grasping at straws, but I'm desperate to keep the smile on Ellis's face. "Maybe he would call the whole thing off when he realizes this is bigger than him."

Kai snorts. "Not likely. My gut tells me he wouldn't take it seriously, especially since Ellis isn't magical." He shakes his head and a muscle feathers in his jaw. "Besides, just look at how my dad handled a similar situation—he had both my mom and her beloved killed. I wouldn't put it past Kennedy to do the same thing."

I glance at Sterling, who hasn't said a word since we walked in. "What's up with you?" I ask. "This mopey bitch act is getting old."

He shrugs his shoulders before he stands and pulls his sweats on. "I just have a bad feeling about all of this."

I narrow my eyes on him. Sterling has always been the subdued one of the group, so this isn't too far out of the ordinary, but it's gotten worse since we brought Ellis into the mix. We're going to have to sit him down to talk about whatever this is.

When Ellis returns a couple minutes before nine, her face is drawn and pale. It's like she took that time to hide the part of her we've worked so hard to bring back to life. There's a negative energy swirling around her, a pessimistic aura that threatens to swallow every bit of light she owns. It makes my heart ache to see this side of her again.

Kai reaches out and pulls her onto his lap. He gently pulls her lip from between her teeth with his thumb. "Try not to worry, baby girl. We're all here for you. Nothing your dad says will change that."

She jumps when Kai's phone rings, her skin paling even more. As she watches Kai's thumb slide across the phone screen, she swallows.

"Malakai Thorne," Thomas Kennedy says on the other end.

"Kennedy," Kai says in his most unfriendly voice.

Ellis's dad grins as his gaze travels over the group huddling around Kai's chair, before landing on his daughter. "Ellis, darling," he drawls. "How are these men treating you? Good, I hope."

I scowl at the false concern in his voice. What a load of shit. This man let his daughter get raped and beaten repeatedly under his roof and did nothing to stop it. Ellis swallows again like she's drawing on a cloak of resolve, and straightens her shoulders. She says nothing but stares her dad down through the phone.

"What do you have to say?" Kai asks through clenched teeth.

"I would like to speak with my daughter in private."

"Fuck that," I mumble.

Ellis takes the phone from Kai in a shaky hand and walks around the coffee table to sit on the couch. When Kai attempts to follow her, she gives him a look, so we sit across from her and watch like a hawk. The first sign of distress and one of us will step in.

"This is as good as you'll get," she says. Only a slight tremor is noticeable in her voice.

There is a pause before her dad says, "Fine. Look, Ellis. I have recently learned of something that greatly disturbs me, and I'm afraid it will affect you as well." He pauses dramatically, and I roll my eyes. "I'm concerned about your safety, Ellis. I wish you would come home."

Ellis barks out a humorless laugh. "You think I'm safe at home? With you?" Incredulity paints her words, and she shakes her head. "You knew what was happening to me. You knew I was being raped and beaten, but you did nothing to stop it. This stupid challenge *you* insisted on starting has turned out to be the best thing that has ever happened to me."

"But do you even know who those guys are?" he counters. "How do you know you're safe with them?"

"I know enough," she says firmly.

"Do you, though?" The slimy smile on his face is evident in his voice.

What is he getting at? The three of us stiffen, ready to jump in and rescue her.

"If you have something to say, spit it out already," Ellis snaps.

Her dad sighs. "I don't want to be the one to say this, as it seems like you trust those boys. But one of them is hiding something from you. I just learned of it, or I would have stopped Malakai from competing."

"What are you talking about?" Ellis asks, exasperated.

"The night your mother and sister were killed ..." Kennedy trails off.

In the silence following his statement, no one breathes. Ellis is shaking already, her fingers clutching Kai's phone so tightly it would break if she had any supernatural abilities. I hesitate. Should I stop this? Is what her dad is about to say the truth? Or is it a ploy to get her away from us? I look at Kai and see the same indecision on his face. Glancing to my other side, my brows draw down. Sterling is sweating. His face is drained of all color and his icy blue eyes are wide with fear. What the hell? Ellis's dad continues, but I keep my gaze trained on Sterling.

"The authorities never found out who killed them. They never found any evidence. But just the other day, I received a letter in the mail. I don't know who it was from, but inside there were pictures. Images from the security cameras before they were wiped. Ellis, Sterling Harrison was there that night. He was part of the group that killed your mother and sister."

I whip my gaze from Sterling, who has gone completely still, to Ellis, who is shaking uncontrollably. Before the phone hits the floor, Kai shoots forward, impossibly fast with his reflexes, and snags it from her fingers. I'm right behind him, grabbing Ellis's shoulders to keep her upright.

Kai growls into the phone, "This conversation is over. Next time you want to slander one of my brothers, you do it without involving Ellis." He hangs up and drops his phone on the coffee table before Kennedy can say anything else.

Ellis stares at Sterling with wide, disbelieving eyes. "Is it true?" she gasps through hard, fast pants. Tears fill her eyes, but she holds them back. She doesn't acknowledge Kai or me sitting on either side of her.

"It's true," Sterling rasps, shifting on his feet.

I snap my head in his direction. What the fuck? Did I hear that right? Devastation lines his features, but I really don't care about how he's feeling right now. Especially as Ellis gasps and places a hand on her belly. The tears spill over and track down her cheeks, each one like a knife to my heart.

"It's a complicated story, but yes," he confirms again. "I was there when your mom and sister were murdered." His gaze drops to the ground in front of him, like he can't bear to watch her fall apart.

"You better start explaining yourself," Kai says in a deathly quiet voice.

The small hairs on my arms stand to attention at his tone. That is the voice of a predator who is hellbent on protecting his beloved.

"I guess to fully understand, I have to start back when my dad died." Sterling sighs and sits in a chair across from us, still not looking at Ellis. "My dad was the alpha of the Iron Shadows pack. He died of a rare cancer that only affects wolves. I was too young to assume the title of alpha, though had I been older, I would have. Instead, Noah Martin stepped into the role. He'd been thirsting after the title for as long as anyone could remember. He forced my mother into marriage, threatened her children's lives if she didn't comply. He was abusive, not too dissimilar from Sam, actually." He glances at Ellis before looking back at the floor. "When I was old enough to take part in pack missions, he used my mom and little brother as leverage to get me to comply with his orders. Orders I never approved of, but had no choice but to follow. For my family's sake."

Out of all of our histories, Sterling's always hit me the hardest. It's horrible what happened to Kai's mom, but at least she isn't suffering under some asshole's thumb like Sterling's mom still is. Like mine is.

"One night, he came to me and told me we had business to attend to. He didn't tell me what was happening until we arrived at your house. I knew who lived there, but I shut myself down from feeling anything, just like I did with every other mission. The orders were simple. Kill everyone." He pauses and takes a deep breath. When he continues, his voice is filled with emotion. "As soon as I stepped foot in the house, I knew. Your scent hit me hard enough to rock me back a step. Somewhere in that house was my mate, and I'd been ordered to kill her and her family."

Mate?

Ellis isn't breathing. She looks absolutely devastated. Unfathomable sadness shines in her tear filled eyes, a mix of betrayal, hurt, and disbelief. Her lips tremble and she presses them together to hide it. I watch her breathing closely. Each one comes faster and shallower than the one before. She's on the verge of a panic attack.

"I searched you out immediately," Sterling continues. "Your scent led me to the kitchen and the pantry where you were hiding. I debated then and there, grabbing you and running. Taking you as far from this place as I could. But I knew you would fight me. Instead, I decided to make sure you lived through the night and then I would walk away. It was safest for you that way. If Noah knew you were my mate, he would kill you without question.

"I pretended like I searched the kitchen but didn't find you. When the other's search turned up empty-handed, Noah gave up. We were running out of time, and we had to get out and wipe the footage from the security cameras before your dad got home." Sterling swallows hard and closes his eyes. As he exhales, his entire body deflates, head hanging down and shoulders slumped forward—defeated.

"Walking away from you that night was the hardest thing I had ever done in my life." His voice cracks, but he pushes on. "I knew I would never have the chance to be with you, but I swore that night that I would protect you anyway I could. I've kept tabs on you all these years. I've made sure Noah never got it in his head to go after you again." He raises his head and looks at Ellis. Tears shimmer in his winter eyes. "I know it doesn't mean anything, but I'm sorry. I'm sorry I was part of it at all. I'm sorry I never told you. I just ... I couldn't bear the thought of you looking at me like you are right now."

Ellis is quiet for a moment. The only sound in the room, her rapid breathing. "You slept with me," she whispers brokenly. "You slept with me but never told me you were there the night my family was taken from me. All this time you could have told me, but you didn't." She doesn't yell. Her voice remains quiet, broken. It hits harder than any screaming ever could. She stands and snatches Kai's phone from the coffee table before she dashes for the door to the patio.

"Ellis ..." Kai starts.

"No," she gasps through her tears. "I need to be alone."

The door slams behind her, and I don't know what to do. Every instinct in my body is telling me to go to her, to make sure she's okay. But I know she doesn't want my comfort right now. Instead, I stare at Sterling. All these years and he never told us. He never told us he has a mate. Never told us about that night.

Looking back, I can see the changes in him. Sterling has

always been the serious one of the group, but never quite so distant. After that night, he changed. He was more reserved. He didn't smile as much. He would disappear without a word and reappear the same. Now, I know he was keeping tabs on Ellis.

Holy shit. Mate.

I glance at Kai, who is staring at Sterling like he wants to tear his throat out, and I don't blame him. But at the same time, I wonder how it's possible Ellis is Kai's beloved *and* Sterling's mate. What are the chances a human girl could be bound to not one, but two magicals? A slimy bit of jealousy spreads through me, but I stomp on it. Hard. I won't be that kind of person. My brothers are incredibly lucky, and I'm happy for them. I won't let envy ruin what we have.

Faint growling rumbles through the room, and I glance at Kai. His body is tight as a bowstring, vibrating with barely restrained fury. Red creeps into the gray of his eyes, and his fangs have lengthened threateningly.

"Kai, come on." I grab his shoulder and push him to the door. "You need to calm down, and we need to give them time to talk once Ellis has processed everything."

He snarls at me and snaps his teeth in my direction. Great. Now I have an almost feral vampire to deal with.

"I know," I placate. "I want to hurt him, too, but we can't. Let's go get ourselves under control before we do something we'll regret."

CADE

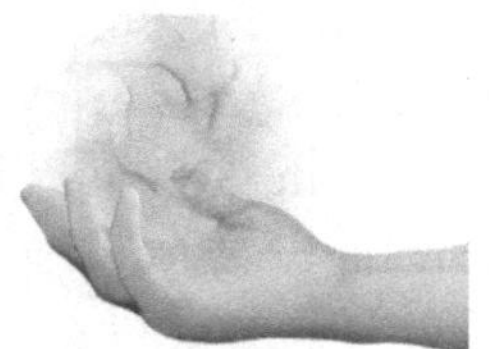

TWO HOURS OF KAI PACING BACK AND FORTH HAS SET me on edge. My skin is crawling and I swear one wrong word from anyone, and I'll snap. Kai's had enough blood bourbon that his steps are uneven, and I'm not far behind him, to be honest. I tip back my glass of regular bourbon, reveling in the burn as it slides down my throat. It's better than the anxious nausea that has settled in my stomach since Sterling's confession.

Mate. Beloved. The wheels are turning, but the connection I'm looking for keeps eluding me. There is something bigger going on—bigger than the contest, bigger than our feelings for her. The pieces of the puzzle are floating around in my brain, but I can't make any of them connect to show me the full picture.

Kai's mumbling draws me out of my thoughts. I only catch a bit, but it's enough to make me laugh, despite the severity of the situation. "You can't put a bark collar on him, Kai," I say, setting my glass down. "That's not nearly painful enough, anyway."

"You're right," he growls. "I'll pull his teeth out one by one, followed by his fingernails, then his toenails. I'll slice open his veins so he slowly bleeds out—"

"Okay," I sigh, cutting him off. "I get it, Kai. I'm just as pissed as you are, but we need to let them work it out. This is between her and Sterling. As much as we want to intervene, as much as we want to rush to her side and care for her, you know we can't. She won't appreciate us handling this for her."

Kai pinches the bridge of his nose and closes his eyes. "Yeah, I know. It's just hard ignoring my instincts to protect her. I want to eliminate any threat, and right now, Sterling is a threat." He paces a few more times before he stops again. "I can't believe he didn't say anything to her."

I snort. "Like you have room to talk. You were going to keep the fact she was your beloved from her for the exact same reasons. To keep her safe."

"But this is different. I didn't have anything to do with her mom and sister's murders."

"That's true," I concede.

We fall silent again, and Kai takes up his pacing once more. My thoughts drift back to the puzzle I can't solve. I don't know how long we wait in Kai's room—at least a couple more hours— before Sterling crashes through the door.

"Is she in here?" Sterling asks with his chest heaving.

"No ..." I say slowly, standing from the window seat, unease growing at the wild look on Sterling's face. "She's not in the library?"

"She's gone," Sterling whispers.

My heart stops in my chest.

"What the fuck do you mean, she's gone?" Kai's voice rumbles across the room. Once again, a predator on the verge of losing control.

"I was giving her time. I didn't want to push her into talking to me, so I went for a run behind the estate. When I came back, she wasn't there. I looked outside and your phone was lying on the table, but she was gone."

With shaking hands, I pull my phone out of my pocket and call the number of the burner phone I gave her. Fear floods my system when I hear it ring from the bathroom. She doesn't have her phone on her. I quickly pull up the security cameras around the estate and watch in horror as the video shows Ellis standing from the table on the patio and walking away.

The floor beneath my feet wobbles. "She left," I say in a daze, looking at Kai and seeing my terror reflected in his eyes.

This was her dad's plan all along. He wanted to drive a wedge between us so she would leave. He wanted her alone, without our protection, so he could steal her back. My magic rushes to the surface. It tingles in my fingers and spreads through my veins like fire. Purple sparks erupt over my skin as I lose control. They stutter and hiss, not the full-blown force I usually have running through my system. I glance at my hands in confusion. It's like my magic has pulled away from me, like the tide receding in the ocean. The further it goes, the harder it is to grasp.

Kai closes his eyes, and when he opens them again, they are fully red. No hint of gray to be seen. His muscles tense, the only warning we get, before he launches himself at Sterling. When my phone rings, he pulls up short, fangs inches from Sterling's neck.

Allie's name flashes across the screen, and I swipe my thumb to answer. "Allie? Is she with you?" I ask.

"He took her." Her voice is so shaky it distorts her words. "She was here, Cade. We were sitting on the couch and he broke in. She didn't even have time to fight him. He just grabbed her and left. I don't know what to do. He has her again." By the end, she's openly crying, gasping sobs that make it difficult to understand her.

But I hear enough. My world stops. My magic, already drawing away from me, turns into mist in my veins. I'm left empty and reeling, cold and utterly terrified. "Who has her?" I rasp, already knowing the answer.

Kai and Sterling still, like predators on the hunt just before pouncing on their prey.

"Sam," Allie sobs. "Please, Cade. You have to save her. He ... he ..." she breaks off with another sob, unable to finish her sentence.

"We're on our way." I hang up and look at Kai and Sterling. "She went to Allie's. Sam broke in and took her."

Kai points a finger at Sterling and growls, "I swear to all the gods, if something happens to her, I will destroy you."

"Enough!" I snap, stepping between them and holding my hands out to either side. "We need to get to Allie's. Now."

The entire drive to her apartment, my magic is wild inside me. Either I can't grasp it to save my life, or it sparks into existence without me even trying. This is my worst nightmare. It's like a band has wrapped around my chest and I can't seem to draw in a breath deep enough to calm my nerves. And my magic responding in ways I've never experienced is only making this situation worse. The one thing I've always been able to rely on, is completely unreliable when I need it most.

There is only one reason for my magic to be reacting this way. I shake my head at the thought, because there is no way that can be true.

When Sterling parks the car on the street, we all climb out. I know I'm the only one who is halfway in their right mind at the moment, so I take a second to scan our surroundings for anything that doesn't seem right. There is no sign of Ellis or anything out of place. Sterling inhales, scenting the air, but shakes his head at my questioning look. Nothing.

Inside the building, we skip the elevator and dash up the stairs to the fourth floor. I'm thankful I picked up Allie when Kai was hurt, so we know where to go. Before we reach the apartment, I take a deep breath, steeling myself for what's to come. The door is busted, hanging off the hinges at an unnatural angle, and I slowly slip inside.

"Allie?" I call out.

"Oh, Cade. Thank the gods you're here." She crashes into me, burying her face in my chest, shoulders shaking with the force of her crying. "I didn't know what to do or who to call. I'm so scared, Cade."

"You did the right thing. We are going to get her back. I

promise." It's a promise I can't afford to break. I lead Allie to the couch and sit her down. "Now, tell me everything."

With her eyes red and mascara smeared down her cheeks, Allie looks wrecked. Her blond hair is a tangled mess, and she tugs on the strands, making it worse. Sniffling and wiping tears with the back of her hand, she visibly collects herself. "We were sitting here, talking, and Sam busted down my door. He had her wrapped in his magic before either of us could react. He threw her over his shoulder and left." She takes a shuddering breath and tears fill her eyes once again. "She looked so scared," she whispers.

A knife to the heart would hurt less. Thinking of Ellis, scared and alone, captured by the man who has done nothing but brutalize her, is enough to bring me to my knees. Fear makes my stomach clench, and anger makes my blood boil. I fist my hands, knuckles turning white, as I try to control my shaking.

Kai growls and slams Sterling against the wall before the shifter can defend himself. Bracing his forearm across Sterling's neck, he bares his fangs. "I am seconds away from ripping out your throat. It's your fault my beloved is missing. Whatever pain she suffers, I will make sure you suffer ten times over."

Sterling's fingers elongate into claws and he rakes them over Kai's chest as he pushes the vampire away. "She is my mate, asshole. I am just as worried as you are. Do you think I'm happy we're in this situation? Do you think I want my mate in the hands of that bastard?" His words are barely decipherable over the growl rumbling up his chest from his wolf.

Kai swings and catches Sterling in the jaw. The shifter's head snaps to the side, but he doesn't stagger. Instead, he grabs Kai by the throat and lifts him effortlessly off the ground.

"What the fuck!" I yell, jumping from the couch. "Ellis is out there somewhere, scared and in danger, and you two are acting like fucking children. Grow the fuck up and calm down. You are doing nothing but hurting her by fighting like this."

My magic shoots out of my hands and barrels into the Kai and Sterling. They slam into the wall, rattling the picture frames hanging in a neat row. I press my magic against them, holding them in place as I stalk forward. They glare at me with their chests heaving, fangs and teeth on display.

"Now," I say firmly, "You guys can stay here and fight each other wasting precious time, but my soul bonded is out there, and I'm not letting another second go by where I stand around and do nothing to save her."

The tension in the room falls away. Kai and Sterling stare at me in shock and I realize what I just said. Fuck. I didn't mean to blurt that out.

"Soul bonded?" Kai asks.

I close my eyes and take a deep breath. "Yeah. I'm positive."

Soul bonded. Basically, the same thing as a mate or beloved. Soulmate. For mages, soul bonded goes so much deeper than a beloved or mate. As soon as I acknowledged what she was to me, my magic was tied to her. It's why it's been acting so erratic since I found out she was gone. Without her, my magic doesn't know what to do. She is the tether to it, and I need to get her back. For so many reasons.

"Are you two going to cool it long enough to save Ellis?" I ask. "Because if not, I have no problem leaving your asses here and doing it on my own."

Kai and Sterling look at each other before nodding. I let them go, relieved because holding them there was harder than it should have been. Already, I can feel the difference in my magic. That simple task of pinning them to the wall is something I should be able to do for days without breaking a sweat. But I'm not sure I could have held them for another two minutes.

"Where do we even begin?" Sterling asks, shaking himself off.

I roll my shoulders, unsettled and unmoored, not liking the way my magic is acting so strangely. "I'm going to hack into the street cams. Hopefully, I'll be able to find her."

Thankfully, no one asks what happens if I can't find her, because I don't have an answer to that possibility. I pull my phone out and sit next to Allie on the couch while Kai paces the living room, and Sterling leans against the wall and broods.

"What time did he break in?" I ask Allie.

"Around 12:30," she replies dully.

"So she's been missing for about 45-minutes," I mutter. Mentally, I think of all the possible directions Sam could have gone when he left the apartment. There are so many, it seems impossible I'll be able to find them. "Do you have any idea where he may have taken her or what direction they could have gone?"

She shakes her head, eyes welling with tears again. I take a deep breath before getting to work on my phone. This is going to be like finding a needle in a haystack.

"Isn't there any way to track her with your ... bonds?" Allie asks. "I mean, you are all tied together, right? Beloved, mate, soul bonded. That has to come with some kind of tracking device."

All three of us shake our heads.

"If we were close enough to her, we'd be able to narrow it down," Kai says. "But she must be too far away for us to do that."

My fingers fly over my phone screen as I hack into the street cams. I pick a direction and go with it, praying it's the right one. I've been at it for over an hour, my eyes dry and gritty, when Sterling cracks.

"Fuck this!" Sterling shouts and pushes off the wall. "It's taking too long."

"She wouldn't be in this situation if you hadn't fucked up so badly!" Kai shouts back.

"Guys," I interject, breaking off their staring contest. "Calm the fuck down. Fighting with each other will not help get her back. Besides, I think I got something."

Ellis

Panic has completely taken over. Even if Sam's magic wasn't binding my arms and legs, I wouldn't be able to get away. All the self-defense lessons have flown right out the window. My mind is eerily blank. It's like a snowglobe up in there, with swirling white flakes and nothing else. Sam's hands on my body paralyze me. My skin crawls and nausea churns in my stomach as every fear-filled and painful memory is brought to the forefront of my mind, and I'm helpless to escape them.

Thrown over his shoulder with green bands of magic sizzling painfully over my skin, I do my best to keep track of where we're going. Cataloging my surroundings is the only thing keeping me from spiraling into a full-blown panic attack. As it is, Sam's shoulder digging into my abdomen only increases my difficulty breathing.

The sidewalk blurs by as he drags me through the city. It's early enough that people are still out enjoying the vices of Altair, but everyone looks the other way. It's how things go around here. No one wants to step in where they aren't wanted. Besides, most of them are doing things that are equally illegal.

The buildings on the street he turns onto look familiar, and I think I know where he's taking me. My suspicion is confirmed as he climbs the steps to the Kennedy building. Inside, he takes the elevator to the top floor where his office is, the same floor my dad's is located. Is my dad in on this? I don't know whether that would make this better or worse.

Sam doesn't speak until he drops me into his office chair. "You made that entirely too easy." He smirks at me. His brown eyes swirl green with his magic as he binds me to the chair.

It burns. Fire branding my wrists and ankles, seeping into my skin to the bone. It's just like the times he's raped me. My heart accelerates to the point where my vision starts to go dark, and I'm scared I may pass out. I close my eyes and take a deep breath, trying to stop my thoughts from their downward spiral. Allie knows I was taken, and she's probably already called the guys. I'm sure they are searching for me at this very moment. I can't imagine what they're thinking, how furious they'll be with me for just walking away. Sam's right. I made it way too easy for him.

When I open my eyes, some of the panic has receded. It still sits just below the surface, waiting to bubble up again, but I'm able to think a little more clearly. I do my best to keep my expression neutral, not wanting to give Sam anything to use against me.

I've been in his office before. It's sparsely furnished, with just the usual office furniture—desk, chair, shelves, filing cabinet. Books sit on the shelves, books I'm sure he's never opened in his life. A picture of us mocks me in its shiny silver frame. Taken before I knew who he was and the lie he was keeping from me. I look content, smiling with his arm around my shoulders. We look like the perfect, happy couple. I want to smash the picture into a million tiny pieces and shove the sharpest glass shards into his eyes.

Sam sighs and sits down on the edge of his desk, too close to me for comfort. "Do you know how much you hurt me, Ellis? And I'm not talking about when you stabbed me, although that did hurt. I'm talking about you not wanting to marry me." His brows furrow and a frown pulls the corners of his mouth down.

"I only want to keep you safe. Why won't you let me do that? Why won't you let me provide for you and give you everything you need?"

He's such a good fucking actor. If I didn't know him, that sorrow-filled speech would have swayed me. His voice rings with hurt and his eyes shine, like he's holding back tears. I know better, though. Instead, I grind my teeth together to keep myself from saying anything. There is no point in trying to talk to him. He knows exactly what he's done to me, and he doesn't care. Nothing he says will ever make me think he cares for me. I'm hoping the more I keep him talking, the more time it will give the guys to find me, and the less likely Sam will be to touch me. I just can't make him angry.

He hums in his throat. "Playing that game, are we? That's fine." That quickly he turns off the act. He flips the switch, and the monster comes out to play. "You don't need to talk, just listen."

He pulls me closer to him and I can't prevent myself from stiffening. Tremors make my entire body shake as he reaches out and tucks a curl behind my ear. The gesture is soft and sweet. At least, it would be, if it came from anyone else but him.

"Ellis, you ar—"

The door to his office opens, and my heart jumps in my chest. Is it them? Have my guys found me already? But no, it's another mage who pops his head in. He barely spares me a glance, and my heart drops as the hope I had goes up in smoke.

"Sorry to interrupt, sir, but there's been an incident at the warehouse. They've requested your assistance."

Sam sighs and pinches the bridge of his nose. "I'll be there shortly. I have to take care of something first."

The other mage leaves, and Sam turns his gaze back to me. He studies me like he wishes he could peel my skin back and examine my insides. His eyes heat and he lifts his hand to rub his thumb along my lower lip. Bile climbs up my throat, burning as much as Sam's magic does. I don't think I can survive more of his abuse. I thought I'd escaped, that I was free. My breath catches, and I can't force it out. Tears build on my lashes unbidden. They only fuel his fire.

Sam brushes his fingers over my cheek and down my neck. The movement causes my hair to shift, exposing the bruising on my neck. Sam's gaze lands on the two overlapping bite marks, Kai's and Sterling's, and his expression shifts. It's terrifying how fast he goes from calm to enraged, making my blood turn to ice in my veins.

"What the fuck is this?" He leans forward and runs his finger over the mark. "You let that fucking blood sucker bite you?" His eyes flash and his words are low and harsh. "You spread your legs and let him fuck you while he sucked your blood?"

I've never seen him so angry before, and that's saying something. I can't even remember all the times Sam has yelled at me and degraded me. A vein throbs in his forehead and his face is steadily turning a darker shade of red. I keep myself still and clamp my lips shut. Making him angrier will only end in more pain for me. He trails his finger over the bruise again and the sensation causes goosebumps to break out over my skin.

That mark is so sensitive. I feel it all the way to my core. Against my wishes, my pussy throbs and I whimper. It's so wrong to have Sam touch that mark, to be the one drawing forth these sensations. He rubs it again and I squirm in the seat as much as the bindings allow, desperate to relieve the ache that has formed.

Sam's lips curl in disgust, but he pulls his hand back. "That may come in handy. What would it be like to fuck you without needing lube?"

His eyes glitter with need, and I swallow. I say nothing, but inside I'm begging him. *Please, no. Don't use that mark against me. It's one of the few bright spots in my life. Don't ruin it.*

Sam leans back and crosses his arms over his chest. "You know, there is one question I have asked myself over and over since I first met you." He pauses dramatically, but I don't give him what he wants. He'll tell me when he's ready. His gaze travels over my face and down my neck, expression tightening as he looks over my mark. He rakes his eyes over my body before returning to my face. "What is so special about you? How did you, a human, gain the interest of Noah Martin?"

I snap my gaze to him. Noah Martin? That's the alpha of Sterling's old pack. Sam notices my recognition and his eyes light with curiosity.

"You know the name. Interesting," he muses. "I assume your dad told you about the night your mom and sister were killed?" He doesn't wait for an answer. "The Iron Shadows pack carried out the orders. Everyone always assumed Noah was hired to remove your family from the picture. He wasn't. He was the one who wanted you and your family dead."

Wait, what? But why? I don't know this man. I've done nothing to him to warrant that kind of attention. Did my mom do something? My dad? I try to think of anything that could have happened to make someone want to hurt my family, but I'm too overwhelmed. Too much is going on.

"But why? Why did he want to kill you?" Sam continues lazily, echoing my own questions. "What is so special about you that he was determined to end your life, as well as your mom and sister's?" A cruel smile spreads across Sam's face. "I have asked that question countless times. I think after all these years, I may have finally found the answer. Of course, as is the way of things, the answer only leads to more questions."

In my head, I'm shouting at him to just say it already. What is the answer? What has he found out? On the outside, I'm calm and uncaring. I don't understand why he's telling me this. My first guess is that he's trying to throw me off balance, and I'd be lying if I said it wasn't working.

Sam tilts his head to the side and squints at me. "I can see it now. You so strongly resemble your mom. I never would have noticed it without finding that document in Noah's desk."

The world tilts around me, and I gape openly at Sam. He can't be saying what I think he's saying. Everyone always says I look just like my mom did when she was my age. And in pictures, the only way to tell me apart from my sister was the height difference. All three of us were clearly related. I'd heard whispers around the house from staff that they thought we weren't really my dad's children. We look nothing like him. Not one single feature.

I look at Sam and I cave. "What are you saying?" I whisper hoarsely.

"It makes sense," he replies. "Your mom was almost more powerful than your dad. How could they ever produce two human children?" He laughs. "They didn't. You know what happens when two different species procreate?"

Of course I do, and holy shit. Why hasn't that ever crossed my mind? Two different magical species cannot procreate. Their offspring will have no power. They will be, essentially, human. Like me. Like my sister was. In my 26 years of living, that thought has never occurred to me.

Sam's smile turns wicked. "Thomas Kennedy isn't your dad, Ellis. Noah Martin is."

———

Sam left the room not too long after he dropped that life-changing bomb on me. He got a call, and although I couldn't hear the person talking on the other end, whatever was going on pissed him off. He muttered something about the warehouse and stormed out of the room, slamming the door behind him.

I sit in a daze, trying to process everything I just learned. Thomas Kennedy isn't my dad. That changes so much. He can't force me to marry anyone. However, if what Sam revealed is true, that makes Noah Martin my father. And apparently, he wants me dead. Not sure that's much of an improvement.

My mom had an affair. And not just once, but twice. My guess is, Noah found out my sister and I were his, and he took care of the issue by trying to remove all three of us. But why? And why he's let me live all these years, I have no idea. Maybe Sterling really had done something to change his mind.

As soon as my thoughts turn to Sterling, I force them away. I can't handle thinking about him right now. The pain is too fresh, the betrayal burrowing deep in my soul. I rub at my chest to relieve the ache. *I rub my chest.* Looking down, I realize my hands are free. The green bands of magic are gone. I was so lost in thought, I didn't even notice.

Jumping to my feet, I rush to the door but stop before I grab the handle. There is no way Sam would just leave and let his bindings disappear. I drop to my belly and peer under the door. In the little sliver between the doorframe and the floor, I can just make out a pair of boots. So, he let his bindings go, but left a guard. If I'm going to escape, I need a weapon.

Returning to the desk, I open the top drawer and paw through the contents. My adrenaline spikes when I find a letter opener fashioned after a dagger. This will work perfectly. I take a few deep breaths to calm my body and clear my mind. The tremors will only hinder me, and I need my focus to be on my surroundings. All the lessons I learned at the gym and with the guys come flooding back. I know what I need to do, and I need to move fast. The element of surprise will be the one thing to save me. I have no doubt the guard is a mage, and I can't go up against a magical without powers of my own.

Slowly and silently, I turn the doorknob. Taking one last breath, I fling the door open and step out into the hallway. The guard turns to me with a lazy grin. No doubt underestimating me, a human girl. Faster than I've ever moved, I jump forward and jam the letter opener into his neck.

His eyes go wide, and I don't give him any time to recover. I drag my weapon back and forth, ignoring the way it catches on muscle and tendons, ensuring there is no way his magical blood can heal him. His life force bubbles out of the gash and coats my hand, warm and sticky. It's similar to the time I stabbed Sam. The mage uselessly attempts to stop the flow of blood, but it's too late.

He drops to the floor and the letter opener slips from my numb fingers.

"I'm sorry," I whisper.

On shaky legs, I run to the elevator. It's not until I'm inside and on my way to the ground floor that what I've done finally registers. *Oh, fuck.* I killed someone. I stare at my blood covered hand, fingers trembling with adrenaline and fear. Bile climbs up my throat, but I swallow it down. There is no time to think about what just happened. I have to get out of this building.

I hold my breath as the elevator doors slide open, praying there's no one there. I dart from the elevator, as silently as possible, and make it through the lobby to the front doors before someone sees me.

"Hey!" a man yells.

Heart in my throat, I dash through the doors and out into the warm night. I risk a glance behind me as I run down the front steps. Two mages race through the lobby, straight for me. I push myself faster. If I remain in their line of sight, there is no way they won't catch me. I rush across the street and in between two buildings, hoping to get to the next block so I can round the corner and put the buildings between us.

A blast of blue light hits the wall next to me, spraying brick in all directions, slicing into my exposed skin. I gasp. These guys aren't playing. That would have killed me if it hit me. I put on another burst of speed and round the corner, already thinking of my next move. There's an alley to my left and I dart inside. My legs are burning, my lungs protesting the lack of oxygen. How will I ever outrun them?

"This way!" one mage yells. "And don't kill her!"

Their boots pounding on the ground behind me are like a noose slowly tightening around my neck. At least one of them remembers Sam wants me alive. Pushing myself even harder, I whimper. I'm not going to make it. There is no way I'll outrun them, and with their magic to aid them? I can't go back. Tears blur my vision, but I blink them away.

Not now. I won't cry now. I need all my energy to keep running.

Keep running. Keep running. Keep running.

My mantra plays over and over in my head as I run through downtown Altair. Always staying just out of reach of their magic. Blasts hit the corners as I turn each one. Just a little slower, and they'll have me.

A cramp in my side makes it even harder to breathe. I'm gasping, trembling, and my legs can't go any faster. Something catches the toe of my shoe and I stumble as I turn the next corner. This is it. I can't go any farther. I can't outrun them. I've pushed my body to the limits, and I can't push it any more.

The intersection ahead of me seems like it's miles away. I'll never reach it. The mages round the corner behind me, and I know this is it. Just as I'm about to give up, three figures appear from around the corner in front of me. Even in the darkness, I know who they are. The tugging in my middle pulls me to them. I sob, almost falling to my knees right there.

The sight of them gives me the strength to push on another fifty feet. Sterling dashes past me in his wolf form, with Cade on his heels. I spare them no mind as I crash into Malakai, and all my strength leaves me.

He wraps me in his arms, holding on tightly. "Ellis," he breathes onto my neck.

I sob against his chest, so thankful to have his arms around me again. With them here, I know everything will be okay. It will always be okay as long as they are with me.

He pushes me away to run his gaze over my body. "Are you hurt?" His nostrils flare as he grabs my blood covered hand. "It's not yours," he says to himself.

I shake my head, unable to form words through my crying, and he tugs me against him again, his hand tangling in my hair as he presses my head against his chest. Under my ear, his heart beats the same rapid rhythm as mine. I could stay like this forever, but Sterling growling behind me draws my attention away from Kai.

I turn around to see Cade picking himself up from the ground, favoring his right arm. Sterling's jaws are wrapped around one mage's throat. The guy's screams are brutally cut off when the wolf shakes his head, tearing through flesh and muscle. My heart stutters to a stop in my chest, and I watch the remaining mage level his hand at Sterling. The world slows down, as blue light blasts into Sterling, sending him rolling down the street, to land in a heap of fur against a building.

Between one blink and the next, Sterling shifts back into his human form, his body lifeless and unmoving. A blindingly bright light erupts from Cade as he roars and launches himself at the mage. I stare unseeing at Sterling's body, until a choked sob escapes me and I dash to him. Dropping to my knees, my hands shake as I hover them over his naked body. He really isn't moving. His chest isn't rising and falling. I scream. It rips from my throat, echoing off the brick buildings. That connection between us, the one I now know is the mate bond, is thin and wavering. My body shudders with the force of my crying and I collapse on top of him, burying my face in his chest.

It can't end like this. There was so much between us. He can't die before we figure it out.

"Please," I beg though my choking breaths. "Please, Sterling. Don't leave me."

I raise my head, tears streaming down my face, and look at him. His eyes are closed and his silver hair is splayed out around his head. There is no injury that I can see. He looks peaceful, like he's sleeping. But he's not just sleeping. He's gone.

Sterling is gone.

"Cade!" I scream, voice hoarse.

He kneels next to me, his purple eyes solemn and shining with emotion.

"Help him," I beg. "Please, save him."

"I don't think I can," he says shakily, looking lost as he turns to face me. "It's too late, Ellis."

"No! You have to try!" I grab the front of Cade's shirt and

cling to him. "Please. Try. Cade, you have to try. I can still feel it. It's there. The bond is still there, Cade. Don't let him ..." The flood of words trail off. Is it still there? Was that it? The little flutter in my chest, was that the bond? Or was that my imagination?

Kai approaches from behind and gently pries my hands off Cade. He wraps his arms around me and holds me close as more tears fall from my eyes. Cade turns to Sterling and his shoulders raise as he takes a bracing breath. Violet light erupts from his hands as he places them on Sterling's chest, enveloping his body like a second skin.

Cade closes his eyes and his brow furrows. "It can't be ..." he mutters. Something resembling hope lights in my chest when Cade cocks his head to the side and his breath hitches.

The light intensifies as Cade sends more of his magic into Sterling. It's so bright now I have to squint to see through it. I'm not sure I'm breathing, and from how tight Kai is holding me, I'm not sure he is, either.

Cade grunts and wobbles on his knees. With his inhuman reflexes, Kai jumps in and wraps his arm around Cade's waist, preventing him from falling. All of a sudden, Cade's magic disappears, sucking back inside of him like it was never there. I don't spare Cade any notice, I know he'll be okay. Instead, my focus is on Sterling.

I hold my breath and close my eyes as I press my hand to his chest. His skin is warm under my fingertips, and a faint thump pulses against my palm. Gasping, my eyes fly open as hope sends my own heart into overdrive. I search his face for any sign of life. Under my hand, another thump, this one harder. It's followed by another, then another. Before I know it, a steady rhythm is beating against my palm. Sterling's eyes move under his eyelids and I brush a silver strand of hair from his forehead.

"Sterling," I whisper. "Wake up. Please, wake up."

At the sound of my voice, his eyes flutter open, and I'm staring into those icy blue orbs.

"Don't cry," he whispers. He lifts a hand and cups my cheek, brushing away the tears that are falling again. "I hate seeing you cry."

It only makes me cry harder. Collapsing on top of him, I bury my face in his neck. I don't know what to think or feel. The bond growing weaker inside me was terrifying. The thought of losing that forever, makes my skin cold and clammy. I don't know how to reconcile that with the pain of his betrayal.

His arms come around me. "Ellis," he breathes. "I am so sorry. Please believe me, I never wanted to hurt you. I fucked up, and I will do anything to make it up to you. Just ... give me a chance. Please."

I nod my head, not trusting my voice. Of course I'll give him a chance. It might take me a while to trust him again, to open myself up to him again, but at least we have the time to figure it out.

Kai puts his hand on my back, and I sit up, looking over my shoulder. He's supporting Cade, who looks like he's one breath away from falling over. Dark circles line the underside of his eyes, and his breathing is wet and labored. Healing Sterling took a lot out of him.

"We need to get out of here before anyone else shows up," Kai says, pulling me to my feet.

As soon as I'm steady, he helps Sterling stand while I wrap an arm around Cade's waist. We follow Kai and Sterling through the city. It's quiet now. Most people having gone home or passed out somewhere. Sterling's land rover is parked in front of Allie's apartment and we pile in, with Kai at the wheel.

As Kai pulls away, I take my first deep breath since being captured. I made it out. My guys saved me, and we all survived. I close my eyes and lean my head against the headrest. Adrenaline leaves my body in a flood, and I'm pulled into unconsciousness.

MALAKAI

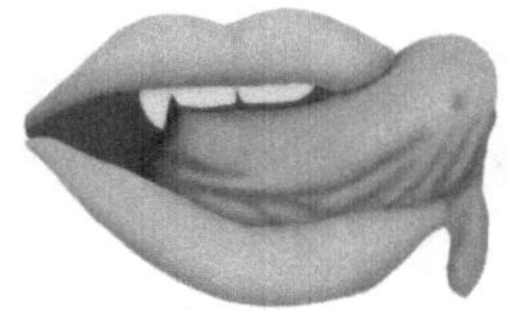

I can't believe we got her back.

I sit against the headboard of my bed as she sleeps next to me, snuggled in Cade's arms, wearing nothing but one of my shirts. Unable to keep myself from touching her, I smooth her hair down her back, over and over. Those few hours were the scariest moments of my very long life. I don't think I took a full breath until she was crying in my arms in that alley.

When we got back to my place, Ellis barely managed to shower without falling over from fatigue. Sterling and Cade weren't much better off, so I quickly helped her wash and pulled one of my shirts over her head before I tucked her into bed.

Sterling is slouched in a chair across the room, eyes glued to Ellis. It takes all my self control to not lay into him. I still can't believe he lied to her like that. There had been plenty of opportunities for him to say something, but he was a coward, and in the end, he hurt her. How the fuck he can live with himself now, knowing he hurt his mate and almost lost her because of it, I'll never know. The only thing that's keeping me from tearing into him is the self-loathing rubbing against my barriers. He hates himself for what happened, and I'm content to let him stew in that vitriol he feels toward himself.

Cade is laying on the other side of Ellis, fingers trailing up and down her arm laying across his chest. Both Cade and Sterling should be sleeping, but they're fighting it. I know they're just as desperate as I am to watch over Ellis, to know that she's safe. We're also all dying to know what happened to her. As much as I dread learning, and as much as I hate for her to relive it, we need to know.

"It's still not over," Cade mumbles. He yawns so wide his jaw pops and tears spring to his eyes. "This won't be over until Sam is taken care of."

I fight my own yawn as I twirl one of Ellis's curls around my finger. "We could just leave. I doubt they would bother trying to find us."

"We don't know that for certain. Besides, would you really give up your title?" Cade asks.

A grunt is my only response. Honestly, I haven't thought about it. I was raised to eventually take my dad's place as king of the vampires. I've always known I wanted to change the way things were done, but I also know I can't do it alone. It's not just the vamps who are corrupt. Sterling and Cade's stories are perfect examples of how the other magical races are just as fucked up. Hell, Ellis's story is the textbook definition of how corrupt mages and shifters are.

"I would do anything for her," I muse aloud. "Even if it meant giving up my title and my dreams of changing things." I look at my beloved and my heart speeds up, as it always does in her presence. "She is my reason for living now."

Both Sterling and Cade hum their agreement. It's crazy to think just a month ago we were living our lives and enjoying the fruits single life had to offer. Now, all three of us are tied to this woman, and none of us would change a damn thing.

"I want him dead," Sterling says quietly from his chair, his eyes like chips of ice. "Sam. I want him to suffer for everything he's done to her."

"Her dad, too," Cade says.

"Thomas Kennedy isn't my dad," Ellis says sleepily.

Cade and Sterling's brows furrow as their focus lands on Ellis. She struggles to sit up and I help her lean against the headboard next to me. She rubs her eyes and yawns before looking at me with sleep-filled eyes.

I smile. She looks so fucking adorable when she first wakes up. "Are you hungry? Thirsty?" I ask.

"A little." She exhales heavily and lays her head on my shoulder. "Actually, I could really use some coffee."

"Coffee it is," Cade says as he jumps up with more energy than I thought he had.

As the door shuts behind him, I wrap my arm around her waist, needing to touch her. My tension melts away with her skin touching mine and her scent calming my nerves. My girl is back where she belongs.

Ellis shifts her head so she's looking at Sterling. "Are you okay?" she asks.

"I'll be fine. Just tired." The shifter hesitates before looking at her.

"We probably need to talk," she says to Sterling. "I have a lot of questions."

"We will," he agrees. "But there is a lot we have to discuss first regarding what just happened."

"I'm sorry," she whispers, drawing in on herself. "Are you mad?"

Unease and regret roll off of her. I gently grasp her chin and make sure she's looking at me. "We're not mad. Scared, yes, but not mad."

She swallows and tears build along her lashes.

I wipe away one that escapes. "You scared us, baby girl. Realizing you were gone, then finding out Sam took you." I shake my head, pushing down the fear that rises with the memory. "It was horrible. My entire world came to a crashing halt."

Her lips tremble, and she attempts to calm herself by taking a deep breath. But more tears slide down her cheeks as she squeezes her eyes shut.

I wipe away each one. "We don't want to keep you locked up, Ellis. But it's not safe for you right now," I say quietly. "Until we can take Sam out of the picture, you need to stay with one of us. You can't go off by yourself. Your safety is our top priority. If you get hurt or ..." I trail off, unable to finish that thought.

She nods her head. "It won't happen again. I promise. I'm so sorry. I didn't mean for any of that to happen."

"We know." I kiss her forehead and rub circles on her back until her tears dry.

When Cade returns carrying a tray laden with coffee and an assortment of breakfast foods, he sets it on Ellis's lap, and takes his spot next to her again. Steam rises from a mug and she picks it up, bringing it to her face. As she inhales, I swear I see some of the anxiety lift from her shoulders.

"Thank you," she says between sips. She looks around the room at all of us and her brow furrows. Setting the mug down, she says, "You all look exhausted. Maybe you should rest before we talk."

I shake my head. "We might as well get it over with. Besides, the sooner we know what's going on, the sooner we can make plans on how to keep you safe."

She shifts on the bed and takes a bite of bacon. "Okay. Where do I start?"

"You said Thomas Kennedy wasn't your dad. What did you mean?" Cade asks as he snags a piece of bacon off her plate.

"Sam told me." She looks at Sterling for a moment before taking another sip of coffee. "He said Noah Martin wasn't ordered to kill me. He was the one who ordered it."

Sterling sits up straight in his chair, his icy blue eyes pinned on Ellis. "What do you mean?"

"Sam found a document in Noah's desk," she answers. "I don't know what kind, but basically, it said I was Noah's child. Along with my sister."

Silence meets her statement as we all let it settle. Holy. Shit. That would explain why Ellis and her sister weren't mages.

"Does Thomas know?" Cade asks.

Ellis shrugs. "I have no idea. It would make sense if he does. I mean, what kind of father would treat their daughter the way he's treated me?"

She sounds so bitter, and I absolutely hate it. It's not just Sam who has hurt her. Thomas Kennedy needs to pay as well.

"Why would Noah want to kill Ellis, and her mom and sister?" Cade asks Sterling.

"Ellis and her sister would be a threat to his rule." Sterling says, looking at Ellis intently. "They could challenge him and take his position as alpha. Not to mention my mom could use that knowledge of his affair to get a divorce, which would give me the opportunity to step in without the threat of him hurting her or my brother."

"Ellis could be a threat even if she has no magic?" Cade asks, brows furrowed.

"It's not common, but it has happened in turbulent times. And, currently, the pack is struggling under his rule." Sterling sighs, a heavy weight settling on his shoulders. "He's not a good leader. Many of the older pack members see how corrupt he is and what he's doing to the pack. They don't agree, but there isn't much they can do. He's too powerful for any of them to challenge." Sterling rubs his jaw as he thinks. "Ellis would be able to challenge him, and he knows that. Despite her not having magic, there is always a chance she would win. Any threat to his rule, he eliminates." He gives us a bitter smile.

Sterling was a threat to his rule, and Noah made sure he wouldn't be a problem by kicking him out of the pack.

"So he decided to kill us," Ellis says quietly.

Sterling's eyes dim as he stares at her. I know him being a part of that night will haunt him for the rest of his life. As will his choice to not tell her.

"Are we sure we trust this?" I ask. "Sam could have said it to throw you off, Ellis."

"I thought about that, but it makes sense." She looks at me, hope lighting her eyes. "Everyone always said my sister and I look nothing like our dad. I don't have any magic, neither did she. Maybe he lied about Noah being my dad, but I feel pretty confident saying Thomas Kennedy is not."

"Sterling, how much danger is she in if Noah is her dad?" I ask. "I can't imagine he forgot about her. Why hasn't he come for her since that night?"

"I convinced him she wouldn't be a problem. I told him I would keep my eye on her, and if I ever thought she was a threat, I'd deal with it." He looks at Ellis apologetically. "I never would have actually done anything, but this way I could keep my eye on you and make sure he kept his word."

"Do you think he will attempt to remove her from the picture again?" Cade asks.

"If he ever finds out we're mates, he will do whatever he can to remove us both from the picture." Sterling's words are quiet, but sure.

Something doesn't add up for me. I'm about to question why Noah would let it go and why he would trust Sterling's word, but Ellis distracts me.

She sucks in a sharp breath. "Why?"

"Many of the older pack members remember when my dad was alpha," Sterling says. "The pack flourished under him. He was a natural born leader, and he was taking us places. I take after my dad in a lot of ways. If I were to return, and with a mate? The added strength I would gain from that bond would make me unstoppable, Ellis. We could take back control of the pack and have the support of many of the members. Obviously, Noah will want to stop that from happening."

Ellis's emotions assault me. I turn to look at her, and the panic is evident in her wide eyes. She has a death grip on the edge of the tray on her lap, and if she had any magical strength, I'm sure she'd break it in her grasp.

"Breathe, Ellis," I murmur in her ear.

Her chest expands as she takes a deep breath and shakes her head. "Okay," she says slowly. "So we just don't tell anyone."

"That would probably be for the best. For now." Sterling says.

I can tell she gets caught up on the 'for now,' so I quickly ask another question. "Is there anything else you learned?"

She blinks a couple of times before answering. "Um, while I was there, Sam kept getting calls or notifications about something happening at a warehouse. He would get super pissed about it. I have no clue what the warehouse is, but it seemed important." She shrugs one shoulder and bites her bottom lip. "I just thought maybe someone should know about it."

I glance over Ellis's head to Cade. "Do you know anything about a warehouse?"

He shakes his head. "Never heard of it. I can do some digging, though. Probably best to make sure it's not a threat to her."

I nod my head in agreement. "Anything else?" I ask her gently.

She shakes her head. "I don't think so." Her brow furrows before she turns to look at me. "Do you think all this shit with my dad, I mean ... Thomas, can just be over? Do we have to continue this stupid contest? He's not my dad. I don't have to do what he says, right?"

The hope shining in her eyes almost breaks my heart. This woman has been beaten down her entire life, literally and figuratively. I want nothing more than to take her away from this gods forsaken city and start a new life with her. To show her what it is to be loved and cared for. To make her happy and never see her cry again.

"I think if we can prove he isn't your dad, we can walk away from it all." I say. "But we'd need that proof first. And we'd need to keep it as quiet as possible. If Noah finds out that you know, he'll do anything to keep it from getting out to the public. I have no doubt he'd come after you to make sure this information doesn't get leaked."

Tears well in her eyes, and she buries her face in my shoulder. Cade moves the tray from her lap and rubs gentle circles on her back while I smooth her hair away from her face. I meet Cade's gaze over her head and nod. They need to talk about being soul bonded. It's tempting to tell him to wait, she's had so much thrown at her recently, but that wouldn't be right. If I didn't know how strong she was, I'd be worried it would be too much.

"Hey, love?" Cade says, still rubbing her back. "I need to talk to you about something. I know it's probably not the best time, but I think it should happen now."

Ellis sits up and wipes her eyes, looking between him and me. This conversation needs to be private, but it's hard to leave her side. I just got her back, and for some reason, I have this irrational fear that if I leave, she'll disappear again.

Before I walk away from the bed, I bend down and kiss her gently. "Don't go anywhere. This is where you belong."

I don't leave the room until I see her recognize the truth in my words.

CADE

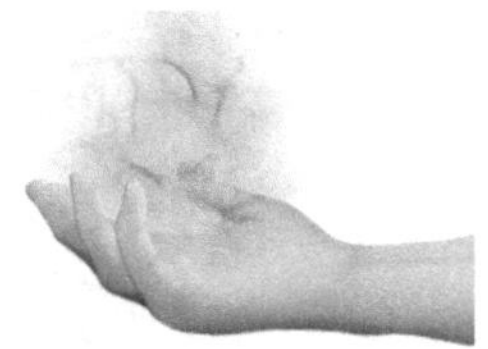

Nerves flutter in my belly so hard it's making me nauseous. It's weird. I can't remember the last time I was actually nervous about something. Sweat slicks my palms, and I wipe them on my sweats. *Dude, get it together.* I don't know why the thought of telling Ellis we're soul bonded is so terrifying. It's not that I'm not thrilled to be soul bonded to her, it's just that she has been through so much since we met, and I'm worried this will be what breaks her. And the last time she found out she was fated to be with one of us, she took off and got kidnapped. Granted, there were extenuating circumstances, but still.

Ellis sits up straighter and places her hand on my thigh. "What's wrong?" She scans my face with her amber eyes and frowns. "You're worrying me, Cade."

"Don't be worried." I give her a shaky smile, and she settles back against the headboard. "I'm sorry. I'm not trying to freak you out, I'm just … nervous." I take one of her hands in mine, hoping she doesn't notice how sweaty I am, and thread our fingers together. "I'm not sure where to start, so I'll just start at the beginning." I take a deep breath and look into her eyes. "The first night we met, when I lowered you to the ground from your window, my magic reacted differently than it ever has. Usually, it's just like an extension of me. Like a habit, a natural reaction, something I don't even think about doing."

I turn my free hand up on my knee and let my magic swirl around in my palm. Ellis twirls her fingers through the purple light, a smile playing at the corners of her lips. Goosebumps raise on my arms.

"As soon as my magic touched you, I knew something was different," I continue. "It's like it sang to me. It echoed inside me in a way I've never experienced. It's never felt sentient, but at that moment, it did. I had to force it away after I got you on the ground. It didn't want to leave you. Any time my magic touches you, it's like that."

Her eyes are wide as I tell my story. She's stopped twirling her fingers in the purple glow, distracted by my words, but she hasn't removed her hand from the light. It pulses gently and she gasps.

"I didn't do that," I say wryly. "It did it all on its own."

"What does that mean?" she breathes.

My pulse races, and my hand shakes, causing the violet light to waver. "We're soul bonded, Ellis. Fated to be together, the same as you are with Kai and Sterling."

Her face goes slack, mouth hanging open. "Soul bonded?"

I nod. "I'm assuming you know what that means." Being raised by mage parents, surrounded by other mages, she is bound to know what it means.

"I do. But ..." Her words trail off, like she can't find the right ones to speak

"How is it possible?" I ask for her. "How are you fated to be with all three of us?"

She nods, her eyes so wide in her pale face.

"I have no idea, but it has to mean something, right?" Shrugging, I squeeze her hand gently. "I mean, a mage, a vampire, and a shifter all fated to be with a human? It seems too strange to be a coincidence."

Her gaze falls to her lap, and she pulls her hands away from mine. "Do you want it? Do you want to be soul bonded to me?"

Her voice is so small in the quiet of Kai's room. The fact she feels the need to ask that question is like a knife in my chest. When will she understand how amazing she is? What will it take to show her she is worth so much more than what she has been shown?

I take her face in my hands and force her to look at me. "There is nothing I want more."

She presses her lips together, but it doesn't hide their trembling. Tears well in her eyes and spill over, running down her cheeks. I wipe them away with my thumbs and gently press a kiss to her lips before tucking her against my chest. She feels so good in my arms, so right. The fear I felt while she was missing disappears like smoke drifting away on a breeze.

"I'm sorry," she says as she wipes her face with her hands, making little hiccup noises that make me smile. "So much has happened, and I haven't really had time to think about it. I'm like a balloon about to pop. I'm so full of emotions and feelings."

"Don't apologize. It's a lot to take in. You're doing great handling it all." I kiss her forehead and her eyes flutter shut.

When she opens them again, a spark has been lit in their depths. It's tiny, but it's there. She leans forward slightly and whispers. "Kiss me. Show me what it means to be soul bonded."

"Are you sure? You've been through so much, I don't want you to think—"

Reaching for me, she cuts me off, wrapping her arms around my neck. Her mouth meets mine hungrily and I'm lost, helpless to not give her everything she wants. I push her backward on the bed and hover over her until she wraps her legs around my waist and pulls me on top of her. The move makes me pause for just a second. Not too long ago she never would have done that. Ellis has blossomed since we abducted her from her room. We gave her a place to grow. A place where she feels safe and cared for. And damn, she's taken what we gave her and ran with it.

An intense joy settles in my chest knowing I was able to help her overcome her nightmares. Being the one she can turn to, someone she can trust, makes me grateful. My lips coax hers open and our tongues clash in a dance. She lifts her hips, rubbing herself against my rapidly hardening cock, and I moan into her mouth.

I break the kiss, only to nibble my way down her neck. Kai's mark will be extra sensitive, so I run my tongue along it, and her reaction doesn't disappoint. The noise she makes, the way her body flushes, and her hips seeking more contact, makes my dick ache.

I chuckle darkly and do it again. "A little sensitive there, love?"

"Fuck, Cade," she moans. "I need you, now."

Her fingers grip the back of my shirt, nails gently scraping through the fabric. The shirt has to go. Now. I need her skin against mine. We break apart long enough for me to rip the tee over my head and throw it to the floor. As soon as my mouth is back on hers, she runs her fingers down my back and I shiver. Nothing could beat the sensation of her skin against mine.

Slowly, I draw Kai's shirt up her body, tracing the exposed skin with my tongue as I go. By the time the tee joins mine on the floor, she's breathing fast, her chest rising and falling rapidly. Goosebumps rise in the wake of my fingers as I skim them along her skin.

"You are so fucking beautiful," I whisper as my gaze travels over her body.

She isn't wearing a bra, so there is nothing to impede my view of her breasts, her nipples hard from desire. I wrap my lips around one peak and flick my tongue over it, smiling against her skin when she digs her fingers into my hair to hold me in place. Lavishing her nipple with my tongue, I pinch the other one between my thumb and finger and pull.

"Oh gods, Cade," she gasps as her back arches off the bed.

"What do you want, love?"

"You," she pants. "I want you."

"I'm going to need more than that, Ellis." I push my thumb between her lips and she swirls her tongue along the pad. "Do you want me here?" Pulling my thumb out, I trail my hand down her neck and over her breast. I pinch her nipple again, and ask, "What about here?"

She whimpers and squeezes her legs together like she's trying to relieve an ache.

"Or is it here that you want me?" I whisper in her ear and run my fingers gently down her belly and just barely through her folds.

Even with that slight touch, I can sense how drenched she is, and my cock throbs in my sweatpants, dying to be let loose. Ellis gasps and raises her hips in a silent plea for more.

I chuckle darkly. "Words, Ellis. Tell me with your words where you want me."

Her cheeks flood red in embarrassment, but her eyes are pure fire when she looks at me. "I want your mouth, your tongue, in my pussy."

I grin at her as I slide down her body and push her thighs apart. "I will happily drown in you, love."

That first lick draws a groan from both of us. Her hands fist in my hair and tug the strands almost painfully, and I love it. I nibble, and lick, and suck until she's writhing under me, but I don't give her enough to send her over the edge. I savor her taste, the sounds of her pleasure, drawing out her desire until she begs me for release. Only then do I look up and let our gazes meet. I suck her clit into my mouth and thrust two fingers inside her, stroking that most sensitive spot, over and over. She screams my name as I lap up her release and bring her through the waves of ecstasy wracking her body.

Pushing up on my hands, I wipe my mouth and chin on my shoulder with a grin. "Fucking delicious," I growl as I climb up her body.

Looking into her eyes, I'm blown away. There is so much emotion shining there, and it's vastly different from when I first met her. The shadows are gone, replaced by happiness and joy. She looks at me with such adoration it causes my heart to falter.

That she trusts me enough to be vulnerable, is not something I will ever take lightly.

Impatiently, she grabs at my shoulders and pulls me up, and it's then that I realize I'm still wearing my sweats. I quickly tug them off and settle over Ellis with my cock nudging her entrance. When she wraps her legs around my waist and attempts to pull me closer, I resist. A soft growl climbs up her throat and I chuckle. It's adorable she thinks she can control what I do to her in bed.

However, I want it as badly as she does. Relenting, I slowly slide in. Each inch of her wet warmth around my hard length is like coming home. My eyes fall closed and I focus solely on the sensation of sliding in to the hilt. Ellis makes little mewling noises that tug my lips into a smile, and I open my eyes to watch her's roll back in her head in ecstasy.

I pull out and gently thrust back in, repeating that motion over and over. Not a punishing pace, but slow and deep. "Never forget this, Ellis," I breathe as I make her writhe underneath me. "You are more precious, more important, than anything in my life. In all of our lives." I punctuate each sentence with a thrust of my hips.

Her eyes open and she stares at me. They shine so brightly. Emotion swirls as my words hit home and she realizes them for the truth they are.

"This is where you belong. Here, with me. With the three of us." With each statement, I thrust harder and harder. "Our soul bonded. Our mate. Our beloved."

She's gasping now, hanging on to every word that falls from my lips. It's like she can't get near enough to me. Her legs wrap around my waist and she pulls me closer.

"You are safe," I whisper against her lips. "Protected. Cared for."

Reaching between us, I rub her clit with my thumb. She moans as her release barrels through her and makes her shake from the force of it. I bring her through it, and only once her breathing has calmed, do I kiss her gently.

"You are loved, Ellis."

———

I wake up in a tangle of limbs. Too many to just be mine and Ellis's. I pry my eyes open and find Kai sprawled across the bed with Ellis tucked safely between us. Looking around the room, I find Sterling passed out in a chair, his neck bent at an angle I'm sure he'll regret when he wakes.

It didn't take long for Ellis to fall asleep after we had sex last night. Her eyes shone with tears at my words, but they didn't fall. Holding her, tucked tight against my chest, brought me a sense of peace I'll remember for the rest of my life. My soul bonded, safe in my arms, loved and cared for. I only hope I can be what she needs and not let her down.

I grab my phone from the floor next to the bed and check the time. Damn. We slept for almost an entire day. It doesn't surprise me, though. Even before Ellis was captured, we hadn't really been getting a lot of sleep with the challenge and everything. And considering I used more of my magic in a record amount of time than I ever have in my life, it's a miracle I was able to stay awake at all.

Now, I stretch out and glance at Kai over Ellis's sleeping form. My movements wake him, and he gives me a bleary smile as he stretches, too. I'm hit with this quivering in my chest. A sensation of free falling when I look at him. This bloody and vicious vampire who cares so deeply for his friends and his beloved. This creature who has somehow wormed his way into my heart, settling next to the spot Ellis has claimed as her own.

It started as just a way to help him burn off his emotions. Being an empath has always been hard for him. He struggles with separating his emotions from those he pulls from people around him. There are times he gets so wound up, the only way to bring him back down is to fuck him. And at first, that's all it ever was. A rough fuck. Something to take the edge off. Somewhere along the way, it's morphed. At least for me. And, from the things he's said, and the things he's done, I'm almost certain it has for him, too.

His gray eyes shine as he watches me. No hint of red this morning. A slow smile pulls up the corners of his mouth. A shiver travels down my back at the glint of fang peeking out from under his top lip. I have always wondered what it would feel like to have him bite me.

His smile grows, and I just know he is reading me right now. And fuck it. I don't care. I let him read all my emotions, the same ones I feel for Ellis. The ones that have slowly grown over time from friend to something ... more. I let him know just how much he has burrowed his way into my heart—and now shares a piece of it with the woman lying between us.

Kai leans up on his elbow and reaches across Ellis to palm the back of my head. He draws me in and surprises me with a gentle kiss, unlike any we have ever shared. Usually, it's a battle for dominance. A clash of tongue and teeth. Bruising kisses that leave our lips puffy and chests heaving.

This kiss throws me. It's slow and drugging. It steals my breath and makes my head spin. It's dangerous. Addicting. Emotions erupt inside me, and I don't repress them. I let them flow through me, let them float out into the universe so Kai can read them. The kiss deepens, and as his tongue brushes against mine, I moan deep in my throat.

A soft, sleepy chuckle breaks us apart. "I think I could wake up to that sight for the rest of my life," Ellis says, smiling at us as she blinks sleep from her eyes.

Kai laughs and leans down to kiss her, just as soft as he kissed me. Ellis's hands tangle in his hair and she heaves a sigh as he pulls away.

"It's a good thing you have eternity to do so," Kai says as he slips out of bed.

My thoughts try to linger on his words, on the fact that Ellis has eternity with Kai as his beloved, but I'm distracted by Kai's naked body. He stretches his arms overhead and I know by her stillness, Ellis is just as invested in what she is seeing as I am. Kai has never never been bulky like Sterling. He is all long, lean muscles covered in tats and piercings. As discreetly as I can, I adjust myself under the covers as Kai pulls on sweats and shoves his erection into them.

"You're both drooling," Kai says drily. "And I'd appreciate it if you didn't drool all over my sheets." He winks as he saunters into the bathroom and closes the door.

Ellis settles against my side and closes her eyes with a smile. "Yeah. I can definitely get used to that."

I laugh and place a kiss on her forehead. "How are you feeling?"

"Better." Her eyes open, but I catch a few shadows still lingering. "I'm happy to be back."

I run my fingers through her curls. "But ..."

She sighs. "I just have so many questions. Is Noah really my dad? Why am I bonded to all three of you? What is this warehouse Sam kept mentioning?" She sits up and shrugs her shoulders. "I don't know. I just feel like something is hanging over my head and whatever it is, it's about to drop, and it's not going to be pleasant."

"I hate to agree with you, Ellis, but I think you're right." Sterling grumbles as he wakes up and stretches his neck with a wince. "Holy fuck. That was a bad idea sleeping in the chair."

Ellis looks at Sterling and bites her lip like she is debating saying or doing something. But in the end, she just looks down at her hands. I squeeze her shoulder as I climb out of bed and walk to Sterling. Purple light flares around my hands and I place them on his neck, letting my magic heal his aches. Sterling groans and rolls his head from side to side as I step away.

"Thanks, man."

"Sure thing," I say and pat him on the back.

I let the magic linger in my hands, marveling at how easy it was to call forth. In all my 109 years of living, I always thought it was second nature. But since accepting Ellis as my soul bonded, it's easier than breathing. I blink and there it is. No thought required. It blows my mind.

Ellis gasps, and my head shoots up, the grasp on my magic failing. "What the hell was that?" she asks, voice trembling, as she stares at her hands with wide eyes.

I rush forward to kneel on the floor next to her. "What was what? Ellis, what happened?" I sense Sterling standing behind me, and I turn to look at him, but he shrugs and shakes his head.

"There were ... sparks ... purple sparks in my hands," she breathes. Her face is drained of color and her lips are pressed tightly together.

I hop up onto the bed and grab her hands, looking at them closely. "Purple sparks? Like my magic?" Possibilities swirl through my mind, but none of them make sense.

She nods her head, eyes still wide. The bathroom door opens, and Kai emerges from a cloud of steam wearing only a pair of jeans. He frowns at us and climbs onto the bed.

"What's going on?" His gaze bounces between us before settling on me.

"Ellis said she saw purple sparks in her hands." When I look back at her, I'm not sure she's breathing.

"It was like when you use your magic on me," she says quietly.

"What do you mean?" Sterling asks. "Usually, when being healed, it's like you're being squeezed to death."

She shakes her head. "No. Cade's magic is always warm and light. I don't know how to explain it."

I pull my bottom lip between my teeth as my mind digs into everything I know of mages and soul bonded. I have never heard of anything like this happening. "Hold out your hands," I direct her.

She does as I ask and I place mine in front of hers, palms up. My magic surges to the surface without me even thinking, like it knows what I want it to do without asking. Violet light glows in my palms and I coax it brighter, letting it twine up my forearms.

We all gasp when purple sparks light up in Ellis's palms. They don't last long before they flicker and die out. I urge my magic farther, up to my shoulders, and more sparks flicker to life in her palms. When these flicker out, I direct my magic to surround me, a purple glow that covers my whole body.

This time, there are no sparks. Instead, Ellis's hands are wreathed in the same light that surrounds me. I look up at her face in wonder, only to see violet light dancing in her amber eyes.

"Cade," she breathes.

"What the fuck ..." Kai and Sterling mutter at the same time.

I let my magic settle back within me, the purple glow fading from around my body. The light in Ellis's hands lingers a second longer before also disappearing.

I grin at Ellis. "Nothing can ever be simple with you, can it?"

She looks at me before a wide smile stretches across her face. "Apparently not."

MALAKAI

"I CAN'T READ ONE MORE FUCKING PAGE," I COMPLAIN and rub my eyes.

We've been sitting in the library for the past three hours pouring through any book that looks like it might mention something about soul bonded sharing power, or a non-magical being bonded to three magicals. So far, we have found absolutely nothing.

Ellis, her head resting in my lap, lowers her book and looks at me. "Just a little longer and I'll give you a reward," she purrs.

I narrow my eyes at her. "What kind of reward?"

"You shouldn't need any kind of reward," Sterling says and throws a coaster at me, which, of course, I bat away. "You should do this because you want to help her."

I snort. The bastard is going to be insufferable as he attempts to suck up to her.

"Fuuuck me," Cade grumbles from his chair with his laptop perched on his knees.

"No luck?" Ellis asks and turns her head to look at him.

"I have hacked into just about every real estate company database in Altair," he responds as he runs his hands through his hair, mussing up the brown strands. "I found a sale listed in one of their databases that has no information for seller, buyer, or even location. The price is listed, and it's around the price I would assume a warehouse to be, but I can find no other information. It's infuriating."

For Cade, who is a master at all things tech, it's probably more than infuriating. I close the book I'd been looking through rather uselessly, and contemplate the warehouse situation.

"What if it isn't a true warehouse?" I ask. "Maybe that's just what they call it."

"That's an idea," Cade muses as he bends over the laptop again, reinvigorated.

I roll my eyes and toss my book on the coffee table. Plucking Ellis's book from her hands, I add it to mine. She looks up at me with narrowed eyes and I give her my best smile, the one I know she melts for.

"That won't work, Kai." She reaches up and places her hand on my cheek before giving it a not-so-gentle pat.

A tap on the patio door stops me from saying something I'd probably regret, and Ellis pops up so fast I almost think she used supernatural powers to do so. Before she can get to the door, though, Sterling is there and peeking out into the darkness. His shoulders relax and he pushes the door wide to allow Allie to step inside.

The girls look at each other and emit such a high-pitched squeal I'm certain they hit a frequency that causes dogs in all of Altair to go deaf. I chuckle when I see Sterling rubbing his ear with a grimace. Ellis and Allie rush at each other and collide with a force that knocks them to the ground. They sit like that on the floor, hugging, laughing, and rocking back and forth, exchanging whispers I can't hear even with my supernatural hearing.

Cade looks up from his laptop and watches the display with amusement. Our eyes meet and my heart thumps harder when I remember what happened earlier. The emotions I picked up from him are ones I have been pushing down for a while now. What do

I do with it, though? Dragging my gaze away from his is harder than it should be.

"Cade called me," Allie says, as Sterling helps her to her feet. "He told me to come over and see you. I was so worried about you, Ellis."

Ellis glances at Cade with gratitude shining in her eyes. "I'm sorry I worried you," she says, tugging Allie to the couch. "I'm okay, though. But shit, so much has happened in such a short amount of time."

Ellis launches into the tale of her finding out about her dad, and us discovering her sharing Cade's power. They demonstrate, and I still can't believe it when I see the purple light wreathing Ellis's arms. The violet that sparkles in her amber eyes is breathtaking. Typically, when a mage uses their magic, their eyes will take on the color of whatever magic they possess. Cade has always been different, with his violet eyes always the color of his magic

Allie's expression mirrors my own. Awe, confusion, wonder. She stares until Cade lets his magic disappear, the glow fading from Ellis as well. "How is that possible?" Allie breathes. "How is any of this possible? Ellis, there has to be something bigger going on here than just Thomas Kennedy and Sam wanting you for their sick purposes."

"I agree," Cade says as he shuts his laptop with a *snick*. "It's unheard of for someone to be bonded to three different people, let alone three different races. And to top it all off, you have no magic of your own. Now, you're suddenly able to use my magic at the same time I'm using it?" He rubs his chin, beard scruff scratching in the quiet. "I'm really wondering if Kennedy and Sam know something they're keeping hidden."

"How could we ever figure it out?" Ellis asks quietly.

"I wonder ..." Allie says before trailing off.

We all look at her as she intently stares at Ellis with a furrowed brow until Ellis squirms uncomfortably.

"Sorry," Allie says. "I just ... I wonder if my aunt may be able to help?"

Ellis jerks at the suggestion. "Your great aunt? Crazy Aunt Madge?"

Allie shrugs and gives us a small grimace. "She is a little crazy, but I'm pretty sure she's crazy because she is part witch. Or maybe elf? I'm not sure. Either way, she has predicted the future a time or two, and has an uncanny ability to read people."

"I knew it," Ellis says, sitting back against the couch cushion. "I always assumed you had a distant relative with some kind of magical blood. You were always spot on when something happened and would call to check in on me."

"I always just got a feeling. I would get anxious and jittery. Something would tell me I needed to call you."

"I don't think I've ever told you how much I appreciated those phone calls," Ellis says quietly, looking at her hands in her lap. "Or any of your attempts to get me out of that situation, no matter how much I resisted."

Allie leans over and hugs Ellis tightly. I'm eternally thankful Ellis had a friend to support her in her darkest times. I glance at my two friends, my brothers, if not by blood. We've had each other's backs countless times. And to know we now can add Ellis to our family, to protect her and care for her? Damn, that's a powerful feeling.

"So," Cade says thoughtfully. "It sounds like a visit to Aunt Madge is in order."

———

"Well this isn't creepy or anything," I mutter under my breath.

We are standing at the base of some seriously rotted stairs that are attached to an equally rotted porch. One pillar has fallen over, now just a pile of wood that is no longer holding up the saggy roof over the porch. The other three pillars look like a gentle breeze is all it will take for them to join their fallen brethren.

Vines cover every inch of the facade, hiding the color of the house behind a wall of dark green. In the dying light of the sun, the shadows between the vines are impenetrable. A screen door hanging by one hinge swings in the wind, emitting a screech that sends shivers over my skin. No light pours forth from the windows, and when I look closer, I realize it's because they are completely boarded up.

Who the fuck knows what's hiding inside that house.

"Nope, not doing this." I grab Ellis's hand and tug her backward. "That house is haunted. It's infested with ghosts, I guarantee it."

Ellis rolls her eyes. "Is my big, bad vampire afraid of ghosts?"

"Uh, ghosts who live in that house? Yeah. Yeah, I am." I shudder dramatically.

"It's not so bad once you're inside," Allie assures us. "She gets a little paranoid and doesn't like leaving the house. I tried keeping up with the outside, but it was too much for me."

Allie walks up the steps like she isn't worried they will fall out from under her. When Ellis follows, I tense, ready to jump in and save her if needed. Luckily, the stairs only creak alarmingly under her feet. With a grin, Cade makes his way up the steps and I swallow down my anxiety. I'm sure I look ridiculous as I try to step lightly, like I can keep my full weight from landing on the stairs.

"Fuck me," Sterling mutters as he eyes the steps. The heaviest of the three of us, he's the one most likely to fall through.

To my surprise, it's not Sterling who falls through the rotted wood. It's Cade. As soon as his foot lands on the porch, the board under him gives way, and he tumbles gracelessly into a pile of broken wood, dirt, and spiderwebs. He rolls over with a curse and stares up at us through a cloud of dust.

We're all shocked when Ellis giggles. Then the giggle turns into full-blown laughter, and she snorts, slapping a hand over her mouth. She laughs until she has to bend over and gasp for air. Sterling and I stare at her while Cade stares at her from his position on the ground. We've never heard her laugh that hard, and it's such a beautiful sound.

Ellis wipes her eyes with the backs of her hands. "Are you okay, Cade?" she asks between little chortling noises.

"Yeah," he says, staring at her in a slight daze. "I'll gladly fall through porches if I get to hear that laughter again."

As I reach down to give him a hand up, an enormous spider crawls across his chest.

"Oh, fuck that!" he yells and jumps up, brushing himself off and dancing around to dislodge any other hitchhikers. "I fucking hate spiders."

I grin at him and pluck a spider web from his hair. He shivers dramatically and rubs his hands over his head, making sure there are no living critters there. When he looks back at me, the brown strands are all out of order, sticking out at random angles. I quickly smooth them back into place as Allie knocks on the door.

"If I find a spider on me later, I'm going to freak the fuck out," Cade mutters while we wait for Allie's aunt to answer the door.

"Spiders and ghosts," Ellis muses. "What are you scared of, Sterling?"

He gives her a mysterious smile. "I'm not about to share that weakness with you. Who knows how you'll use it against me?"

"Clowns," I whisper loud enough for everyone to hear me.

Sterling's icy stare pierces me through the growing darkness, but I'm saved from his retort by screeching hinges as the front door opens.

Aunt Madge glares at us from the doorframe. With long black hair down to her waist, I would never have assumed her to be Allie's great aunt. Only a few silver strands are hidden among the black. She's holding a cane made of a gnarled piece of polished wood, although I don't think she's leaning on it. Her thin frame is hidden by a bulky black dress that almost swallows her. Despite her frail appearance, her back is straight and her blue eyes are almost as piercing as Sterling's.

Her glare moves through the group until she sees Allie. Then her thin lips pull into a smile and her angry brows relax over her eyes. "Niece," she says warmly in a scratchy voice.

"Aunt Madge," Allie says, stepping close and giving the woman a hug. "It's good to see you."

"It's been three weeks," Aunt Madge snaps. "Where have you been?"

So much for smiles. The glare is back in full force.

"I'm sorry, Aunt Madge. It's been a crazy three weeks." Allie pulls a small box from her pocket and waves it in front of her aunt. "I brought you something, though."

"Bribes? Trying to make me forget you've neglected to visit your old aunt?"

"Never. Just a token to show how much I love you." Allie gestures to us standing around her. "Now, do you think we could come in before Cade adds more holes to your porch?"

The old lady harrumphs, but turns and disappears into the house, cane thumping rhythmically. Allie smiles at us before following, tugging Ellis along with her.

"Watch out for ghosts," Sterling whispers in my ear as he walks past and into the hallway.

I follow him, and say, "She probably has clown dolls in every room. Super creepy clown dolls."

He flips me off over his shoulder, but I see him shudder as he peers into the gloomy darkness.

The inside is not as neglected as the outside. The lighting is dim though, and it definitely gives me the creeps. The walls are brown paneled wood, worn dull with age. The same color wood creaks underfoot, decorated with red and gold tassel rugs. Cobwebs gather in the corners of the ceilings and layers of dust coat shelves full of odd nicknacks and ancient-looking books. The air is musty and old, with an undercurrent of something green, like leaves or grass.

Aunt Madge leads us into the small living room, and she and Allie settle into a pair of Victorian-style chairs, complete with a large red and pink flower pattern. Sterling takes up residence behind a matching couch, eyes scanning every nook and cranny. I can almost picture his wolf's ears perked and twitching at every little sound. Cade and I sit on the couch with Ellis in between us.

"Aunt Madge," Allie begins, "we need your help."

The old lady huffs. "I figured as much. It's not everyday Altair's infamous bachelors drop by for a visit."

"Ellis, do you want to tell her what's going on?" Allie asks.

Taking a deep breath, Ellis squares her shoulders and dives into her story. "I guess it's easiest to start at the beginning." She glances at me, and I give her an encouraging nod while Cade squeezes her thigh gently. "I'm sure you've heard of the contest my ... Thomas Kennedy started to find me a husband. Well, during this contest, I found out I am bonded to all three of these guys." She gestures toward us with her hand. "Kai is my beloved, Cade is soul bonded to me, and I'm Sterling's mate. I'm also only human, as you know."

Aunt Madge's eyes narrow on Ellis as she tells the story. "Your mom and dad were both mages, correct?"

"Well, my mom was," Ellis answers. "It turns out she had an affair. We think it was with Noah Martin, the alpha of the Iron Shadows pack. It would explain why my sister and I were born with no magical ability."

"How salacious of her," Aunt Madge murmurs, but her blue eyes spark with interest.

Ellis ignores that comment, and continues her explanation. "Well, now, after bonding with the guys, I seem to be sharing Cade's magic somehow."

"Explain."

"When Cade uses his magic, I'm able to, as well."

She looks at Cade and his magic flares to life in his palms. As she raises her hands, a purple glow pulses to life, twining between her fingers. Cade lets his magic dissipate and the light fades from both of them.

"Well, isn't that interesting?" Aunt Madge says with a curious look at Ellis. "Are you experiencing any other magical gifts? Speed? Strength? Any of Malakai's empath abilities?"

Ellis shakes her head, and I frown. I never even thought about her gaining abilities from Sterling or me. Aunt Madge continues to stare at Ellis—or rather, it's as if she is staring *into* Ellis. She hums and nods her head, holding a silent conversation with someone or something we can't hear. The hairs on my arms stand on end and Ellis shifts uncomfortably in her seat.

"There are a few things we can do to get you the answers you seek." Aunt Madge groans as she stands from the chair and walks off to the kitchen.

We wait in a tense silence, the sounds of cupboards opening and closing and pots banging echo from the direction Aunt Madge went. Ellis looks at Cade, then me, questions burning in her amber eyes.

Aunt Madge returns, holding a tray laden with a steaming pot, a teacup, and various herbs. Cade jumps up to help the old woman, but she scowls at him until he sits back down with a quiet curse. With the tray sitting on the coffee table between the couch and chairs, I notice a wicked-looking knife resting on the tray, glinting in the dim light.

What the fuck is that for? My unease grows, and so does Cade's and Sterling's. A heaviness fills the air—all of our emotions intensify and swirl together, causing my stomach to twist into knots.

Aunt Madge dumps the herbs into the pot of steaming water, swishing them around to mix it together. Once she deems it ready, she pours the brew into the lone teacup and hands it to Ellis. The liquid sloshes, a few drops spilling over the edge, as Ellis takes it with shaky hands. Steam curls from the liquid, and Ellis brings it to her face, inhaling. She pulls the cup away, lip curling in disgust, and nose crinkling at the scent.

"It will taste like shit," Aunt Madge says bluntly, "But it will help me get a read on you."

"What's in it?" Ellis asks as she stares into the murky liquid suspiciously.

"Oh, this and that." Madge waves her hand side to side. "Nothing harmful, if that's what you're asking."

Ellis takes a deep breath before squeezing her eyes shut and downing the tea. She coughs and splutters, but she gets it all down. Shuddering, she sets the teacup on the tray and sits back, leaning closer to me than she was before. I open myself to her and feel her uncertainty growing. Nerves, fear, dread. It's like a storm building on the horizon, slowly growing in strength. I wrap my arm around her and pull her close, lending her my strength.

Aunt Madge bends back to the tray and snatches up the knife. Immediately, the tension in the air thickens, and I know Cade and Sterling have gone on high alert. I shift on the couch, angling myself to better shield Ellis.

"Oh, do settle down," Aunt Madge says as she waves the knife around in the air. "I just need a little blood. A drop or two."

She steps in front of Ellis, brandishing the knife. Shimmering on the edge of the knife catches my attention. It's almost invisible, but a faint pearlescent sheen coats the blade. I grab Aunt Madge's wrist and stare at her, baring my fangs.

She rolls her eyes. "It's not poison. You boys are too overbearing." Exasperation fills her voice, and she shakes her arm, trying to dislodge my hand. "It will help me decipher the properties in her blood. Hopefully to give me an idea of why she can bond with three separate races and use their magic."

I glance at Cade, and we share a silent conversation, debating whether or not we allow this to happen. Biting his lip, Cade nods once, and I let Aunt Madge's wrist go. Ellis looks at me, eyes wide in her pale face.

I give her an encouraging smile. "We need answers, right? This is our only lead. If she hurts you in any way, she'll have to deal with all three of us." I turn my glare to the old woman.

She rolls her eyes again and huffs. Muttering under her breath about overbearing assholes, Aunt Madge grabs Ellis's wrist and turns her hand palm up. Quick as an adder, she slices the blade down Ellis's palm. Ellis hisses through her teeth and clenches her free hand.

I watch her blood well along the cut. It's strangely bright in the dim lighting. All it takes is one inhale for the scent of her blood to hit me like a ton of bricks. Spice, fruit, rich red wine. My gums sting as my fangs descend. Luckily, I don't need to feed, so the urge to sink my fangs into Ellis's neck is easily managed.

Aunt Madge brings Ellis's palm to her lips, and my stomach clenches. It doesn't seem right to let anyone else have my beloved's blood. Her tongue darts out, licking the wound, tasting the blood pooling in Ellis's hand. Distantly, I'm aware of Cade healing the cut and speaking quietly to Ellis, but all my attention is on the old lady, whose face has gone unnaturally pale. Her blue eyes grow wider and wider and her breathing accelerates. From the moment Ellis's blood touched her tongue, her intense gaze hasn't wavered an inch.

Uneasiness settles along my bones. My skin prickles as a charged energy fills the room, the sensation reminding me of the moment before a lightning strike. Whatever Aunt Madge is about to tell us will be life altering.

The old woman trembles in her chair. She opens her mouth and breathes one word into the silence.

"Harpy."

End.
For now.

Acknowledgments

This book originally started as a fun, simple book to write in between working on Of Flames and Curses. It quickly morphed into something more. It was so fun to write, and I hope you enjoy reading it as much as I enjoyed writing it.

As always, a huge thank you to my hubby (my Cade). If it weren't for him, this book would never see the light of day. Even though he never reads a single word I write, he supports me and gives me all the time I need to get my writing done.

Also, my sister, Ashley. Even though she hasn't read this one yet, her constant support and cheerleading is always appreciated!

To my Midnight Tide family, you guys are the best. My writing has grown tremendously since joining, and I appreciate and love each and every one of you!

Finally, thank you to ... you! Without your support and love of reading, I wouldn't be here! Happy reading!

ABOUT THE AUTHOR

Whitney L. Spradling is a full time Occupational Therapist and autism mama, who has had a dream to write and publish a novel since she was a little girl. She lives outside of Cincinnati with her husband, son, and two cats. When she is not writing she can be found in her craft room making custom tumblers, or curled up with a good book and a cup of coffee (or glass of wine).

unlikely of places.

Born with horns that set him apart, Prince Ander is an outcast in his own mother's court. Unwilling to stay and suffer it any longer, Ander leaves to try to make his way in the mortal realm. However, even amongst the humans, tragedy follows the half-muse.

Orphaned before she was given a name, Mab Duchan has never known a real family outside of those paid to care for her. Just when she thinks she's found one, the arrogance and jealousy of a hateful noble nearly destroys her. When all hope seems lost, the most unlikely of heroes arises.

Now it's Ander and Mab against the world, but the stronger their bond as a family, the more life seeks to break them apart. Can they hold on to the ties that bind, or will love be the one thing that finally tears them apart?

www.ingramcontent.com/pod-product-compliance
Lightning Source LLC
Chambersburg PA
CBHW061524210726

48287CB00006B/1818